MR GANDY'S

GRAND
TOUR

ALAN TITCHMARSH

MR GANDY'S GRAND TOUR

HODDER &
STOUGHTON

First published in Great Britain in 2016 by Hodder & Stoughton
An Hachette UK company

1

Text acknowledgements

Page 1. P.G. Wodehouse, *The Adventures of Sally*. (London: Random House, 1920). Page
43 and 196. E.M. Forster, *Howard's End* (London: Edward Arnold Publishers Ltd, 1920)
and *A Room With A View* (London: Edward Arnold Publishers Ltd, 1908). Reprinted by
kind permission of the Provost and Scholars of King's College, Cambridge and The
Society of Authors as the E.M. Forster Estate. Page 73. Extract from Conversation Piece
copyright © NC Aventales AG 1933 by permission of Alan Brodie Representation Ltd
www.alanbrodie.com. Page 122. W. Somerset Maugham, *Strictly Personal*. (London:
Doubleday, 1941) Copyright by the Royal Literary Fund. Page 116 and 148. Ron Goodwin,
Monte Carlo or Bust!, 1969. Reprinted by kind permission of Sony/ ATV Music
Publishing, EMI Music Publishing. Page 158. Peter Shaffer, *Equus*. (London: Penguin,
1973). Page 216. Phyllis McGinley, *What Every Woman Knows*. (London: Penguin, 1960)

Every reasonable effort has been made to contact the copyright holders, but if there are
any errors or omissions, Hodder & Stoughton will be pleased to insert the appropriate
acknowledgement in any subsequent printing of this publication.

A CIP catalogue record for this title is available from the British Library

Hardback ISBN 978 0 340 95307 5
Trade paperback ISBN 978 0 340 95308 2
Ebook ISBN 978 1 444 70807 3

Typeset in Sabon by Palimpsest Book Production Ltd, Falkirk, Stirlingshire

Printed and bound by CPI Group (UK) Ltd, Croydon, CR0 4YY

Hodder & Stoughton policy is to use papers that are natural, renewable and
recyclable products and made from wood grown in sustainable forests. The logging
and manufacturing processes are expected to conform to the environmental
regulations of the country of origin.

Hodder & Stoughton Ltd
Carmelite House
50 Victoria Embankment
London EC4Y 0DZ

www.hodder.co.uk

For Bessie
with much love

1

CHICHESTER

SEPTEMBER

'Chumps always make the best husbands . . . All the
unhappy marriages come from the husbands having
brains.'

P.G. Wodehouse, *The Adventures of Sally*, 1920

'In every marriage there are moments when one partner comes
to the fore and takes charge. It is the natural state of things
and plays to the respective strengths of either party. Traditionally,
on the domestic front, men remove mice and spiders and women
know how to load the dishwasher properly. It is seldom wise
to express such a view for it can give rise to criticism, especially
when articulated by the male of the species, but, nevertheless,
it is a situation which prevails in most households. On weightier
matters, of course, the decision making is best arrived at by
means of give and take. Happy the couple whose sense of values
is so aligned that these more important issues can be arrived
at by free and frank discussion and then acted upon in unison.
That is the ideal. Alas, in many circumstances, the balance of

power may shift with the years until one party is regarded as the decision maker and the other as the passive partner. Should the male dominate then he is regarded as a tyrant. Should the female take charge, then the husband is described as being henpecked. For the male of the species marriage is a battlefield where the best he can hope for is a truce.'

Timothy Gandy closed the book and looked again at the title on the excessively lurid dust jacket: *Marriage: An Insider's Guide*. His facial expression gave little away. He looked at the author's name: Dr Randy Finkelstein. His eyebrows rose a little. An American; a resident of the land of the free. This was not the sort of sentiment loudly expressed on this side of the pond – not by anyone keen to avoid the wrath of female society anyway.

The book was not his. Neither did it belong to his wife. It sat on the kitchen table on top of a teetering pile of paperbacks collected by Isobel Gandy for the bookstall at the local Lib Dem Coffee Morning where she regularly did her bit to redress the balance of power. It was a wonder she had not binned it. Perhaps she had not really noticed it was there, or not registered the title. She had most certainly not opened it and absorbed its sentiments, otherwise she would have had a lot to say about Mr Finkelstein's attitude to marriage and the book would have been found a comfortable home in the recycling bin outside the back door.

Timothy smiled – well, half smile, half wince – and slipped the book underneath the topmost volume, *The Diary of a Dog*, and mused on the appropriateness of that as a title for his own life. Silly really. Then he shivered involuntarily and walked to the kitchen to make himself a cup of coffee. He was not ordinarily so introspective, so downcast, so . . . morose even. But today was no ordinary day. The electric kettle began its slow hiss – the hiss that would, in a moment or two, turn into a bubbling hum that signified boiling point – a feeling which, inside himself, he had not felt for a long time now.

This unwonted introspection was the result of one thing – a complex state of affairs summed up in two deceptively simple words, 'early retirement'. This would be his last day at work. He was fifty-five, had hoped to go on working until he dropped – working at something at any rate. Granted, he expected to be pensioned off when he reached sixty-five (or was it seventy, now that the government explained that we would all have to work longer?). The prospect of delaying the evil moment suited him fine. But then it had all come to a head. The small but successful company for whom he had worked – Novio Graphics – was taken over by a larger conglomerate. Timothy's job was safe, they said, but there would be some reorganisation; a re-allocation of duties; a realignment. It was the sort of management-speak that made his spirits sink.

When push finally came to shove the choice lay between a role that would fail to satisfy one fluid ounce of his creative juices, or voluntary redundancy. He lay awake night after night – while Isobel slept soundly beside him – weighing up the pros and cons. He finally came to the conclusion that it would be better to leave a job that he had so far enjoyed and attempt to find another – even at fifty-five – than to labour on soullessly for another ten or fifteen years in some managerial role akin to that of social worker and diplomat rolled into one. The decision was made and communicated to the powers that be. And to Isobel, too – the other power that was. He had asked for her input, of course. Would have valued it. But she said it was entirely up to him. What did *he* want to do? It was his life, after all. Funny how it didn't feel like that.

Should you have pressed him, he would not have described his marriage as an unhappy one. Not really. Though to outsiders it might have seemed a little . . . ordinary. It was, in common parlance, comfortable for the most part; a situation arrived at by virtue of kindness, familiarity, pragmatism and Timothy's ability to make the best of whatever life threw at him. From childhood he had been possessed of the ability to be happy in his own company. He was not antisocial, indeed he was capable of quite sparkling conversation when the occasion demanded, and when those listening could discern, underneath the calm carapace that others might have considered to be insularity, a ready wit and an engaging smile. His was a quiet humour, not in the least ostentatious, but well developed nevertheless. It was just that in certain circumstances it was not always obvious. Loud and raucous gatherings would cause it to be submerged beneath a veil of reserve; a veil that would allow the wearer to observe, to understand and to marvel at the variety of temperaments displayed by his fellow beings. There was within him not a trace of smugness nor an ounce of animosity, though when circumstances dictated – perceived injustice, rudeness or cruelty – he would feel anger rising within him and an uncontrollable urge to intervene and put matters right. It was something his fellow students at university had come to be wary of and also to secretly admire.

He had met Isobel there, all those years ago – he studying art, she politics. They had married within a month of leaving. Timothy would have happily cohabited for a year or two, just to see how things went, to see if they were really suited, but Isobel was adamant that she would not live with him – or enter into any kind of physical relationship – until they were wed. He acceded to her wishes; it would be the first of many occasions when he would do so. Sometimes he wondered if he should have been more assertive, but the willingness to make her happy had seemed to override other considerations.

Both families were dubious of the alliance. Isobel's were

strict Methodists who at least waived their objection to alcohol for the day of the nuptials. (Timothy suspected that judging by the way they took to the sherbet on that rainy July day in 1980 they had had more than a little practice.) His own parents were lapsed Anglicans devoted to a 6pm gin and tonic followed by a bottle of wine. At the end of the wedding breakfast both sets of parents exhibited an air of unsteadiness and facial expressions that betokened the drowning of sorrows rather than the celebration of a happy union. They never met each other again.

After honeymooning in Bournemouth in the attic of Isobel's auntie (a complete lack of funds precluded anything more luxurious), the happy couple settled along the coast in Chichester. Like so many things in his life it seemed to have happened by chance – fate taking a hand while he was still thinking about what to do next. There was no conscious decision on his part to find work and set up home there, but Isobel had spotted an advertisement in the Bournemouth paper and pushed it under his nose. It seemed churlish to spurn her apparent enthusiasm, and at least it was a start – a foot on the commercial ladder. The owner of the graphic design firm – Ted Henderson – was pleasant and encouraging. He offered Timothy the job and asked if he could start the following week. Timothy was surprised and relieved in equal measure. The job gave him the opportunity to be creative – albeit in a small firm and on a small scale. Yes, he did wonder if he should have been more daring; gone it alone, perhaps, and worked for himself. But that would mean touting himself around; making contacts, and he was never very good at selling himself. And this was the definite offer of a job, an income, and he had a wife to support now.

At first they lived in a flat overlooking the harbour in the coastal town of Emsworth. Small and rather shabby, the flat was another property owned by Isobel's aunt – a savvy lady, Timothy discovered, whose idea of a balanced investment portfolio was a fiver each way on the horses and a string of rather dilapidated apartments in houses along the south coast. As the small firm grew, due in no small measure to Timothy's talents and his capacity for work, his income expanded, albeit slightly. He and Isobel took out a mortgage on a modest town house in Chichester – it would be closer to Timothy's work. He could walk there now, as Isobel pointed out, and she could use the car. The first of their three children arrived two years after the wedding.

Always a challenging child, Oliver lost none of his intractability with the passing years. His general demeanour – ebullience coupled with a stubborn streak – along with the slightly arrogant expression he wore even in repose, perfectly suited him to his subsequent role as a barrister. He was now a junior advocate in chambers in Gray's Inn; not exactly at the top of his game, having succeeded in irritating most of the senior partners in the practice. He battled on, convinced that one day he would take silk and rise to the top of the judicial tree. He was married to Vita, a fair-haired stalwart of the local NSPCC tennis championship and rivalling her mother-in-law when it came to organising ability. The epitome of a head girl, Vita had a voice that was not so much cut glass as capable of shattering it. There were, as yet, no children of the union. In moments when thoughts that he considered were unworthy rose to the surface, Timothy reasoned that it was probably just as well. He could not imagine what sort of offspring these two strident powerhouses would produce. Whenever such thoughts occurred he chastised himself for his lack of generosity of spirit. He tried hard to feel some kind of empathy with Oliver, but it was, he frequently admitted to himself, an uphill struggle.

Alice, the second child, was the exact opposite of her brother.

Sickly and rather fey from birth she remained a single woman whose outlook was never of the sunniest and who seemed to make her way through life managing never to quite enjoy herself. After displaying a surprising degree of academic ability at school, she had settled into the quietude of librarianship at an Oxford college. The obligatory silence seemed to suit her introspection. Holidays, when they came, were reviled, and she frequently took to her bed with some imagined ailment until the beginning of term put her on her feet once more and she could resume her duties and greet favoured students with a weak smile and a habitual sniff.

Having produced two children who were less than companionable, Timothy would happily have called it a day, baffled as to his own input in creating two such disparate charges who seemed to owe nothing to their easy-going father in terms of genetics or general demeanour.

Then along came Rosie. The choice of name was his – it seemed to suit the sunny disposition and the general pinkness she displayed as a baby and, as luck would have it, her outlook on life altered little with age. She was twenty-seven now; the only fair-haired child of the three and the only one of his children to show any interest in having children of her own which was, as far as her mother was concerned, unfortunate, since she was unmarried and now with child, courtesy of Ace, a conservation officer with the local naturalists trust. (On first hearing of his existence, Isobel had assumed that he had a fondness for nudist beaches, but Rosie swiftly explained the difference between a naturist and a naturalist. Isobel thought the distinction a narrow one).

Relations between mother and daughter became strained. Timothy, while surprised by the speed at which his daughter's relationship seemed to be progressing (and the responsibility about to be thrust upon her in terms of an imminent family) could not bring himself to dislike her chosen partner. There was a freshness, a warmth of personality and an openness about Ace that Timothy found both engaging and infectious. His name was an acronym of his initials; Ace thought Alexander Charles Elliott sounded far too upper crust for comfort. His parents had not been nearly so aristocratic as his names suggested – the father a council worker, the mother a shop assistant.

Ace and Rosie might have little going for them as far as Isobel was concerned (conservation officers were paid a pittance, the pair had only a rented flat and little in the way of prospects with Rosie soon to relinquish her job as a primary school teacher) but as far as Timothy was concerned they were in possession of the greatest thing in life – an adoration of one another and shared values that would, he hoped, see them through thick and thin. In that at least he had to agree with Dr Randy Finkelstein. He hoped and prayed their mutual affection would last.

The kettle was almost boiling now and he reached into the kitchen cupboard for the favoured Colombian roast. That was one of the first things he would do: buy one of those espresso coffee-making machines. Isobel would be grateful – she hated the messy coffee grounds he kept depositing in the sink. As the thought occurred to him, he carefully laid down the spoon and stared out of the window across the damp autumnal garden scattered with dew-laden leaves.

He knew in his heart that re-employment was unlikely and, if he were honest with himself, his appetite for job interviews was non-existent. He would need to look elsewhere now for a sense of purpose. Money would not really be a problem. Oh, they would not exactly be living in the lap of luxury, but his assiduous nature had ensured that a modest pension fund was fully paid up and would allow a comfortable . . . retirement. That word again. He turned his gaze from the damp garden to the small kitchen. Was this house and garden to be the manifestation of his ambitions now? Was this what it had all been leading up to: a new coffee machine? No; there must be more to life than that; his release from work must be regarded as a new-found freedom. He must shed the self-analysis and the sense of foreboding, and treat what lay ahead as a new and exciting chapter in his life; a chapter with its own delights. He must alter the obvious mindset and find a sense of purpose that had been sadly lacking of late.

Here he was, on the brink of his own precarious future, with three grown-up children and a grandchild on the way, wondering what tomorrow held and with the uneasy feeling that he had totally squandered the life that lay so promisingly before him thirty-five years ago. Surely his aspirations must exceed the acquisition of a state-of-the-art coffee maker? He knew, in his heart of hearts, that it would take more than that to turn him into George Clooney.

The sky showed some promise of breaking from an even shade of grey. There were small patches of blue perforating the otherwise all-enveloping blanket of cloud, and the wind, whipping off the sea, although keen, still possessed a vestige of late summer warmth. Timothy was walking along the beach at West Wittering, the better to shake himself out of the gloom that threatened to overwhelm him.

Wavelets broke on the sand with a faint sigh and he walked a yard or so back from them, feeling his heels sink into the firm but slightly yielding sand. The marram grass of the dunes imitated the rippling serpentine motions of the sea itself – both grey-green in the watery light. A salty tang gave the air a welcome astringency.

That, coupled with the stiff breeze, helped to clear his head and gradually he found his spirits rising. The words of old man

Henderson's son, uttered the previous evening at his farewell drinks party, echoed in his head. There was talk of 'gratitude' for how he had taken the firm to new heights. 'Regret' that they had finally come to a parting of the ways after more than thirty years. And 'good wishes' for the future, whatever it held. All the customary platitudes rehearsed once more. Today they would have moved on. Someone else would be doing the job he did. He was no more significant than . . . a grain of sand on West Wittering beach.

And yet somehow, with the sea lapping at his feet, the wind ruffling his grizzled hair – mercifully still present in quantity, though now greying at the temples – and the sun trying its best to break through and promise future brightness, his thoughts became more positive. Never one for pointless soul searching he breathed deeply and mused on the possibility of future plans, whatever they might be. His foot caught a shell. He bent down and picked it up, rubbing the sand from it on his jacket and running his finger over the hollow side to reveal a rainbow light that glistened upon the mother-of-pearl surface. The convex side was rough and blackened; a row of neat holes ran along its rim. An ormer: rare in this part of the world. Not something you would have expected to find much further north than the Channel Islands. Perhaps the current had washed it here after it had perished or been discarded by a diver once the tender contents had been eaten. He turned it over in his hand and remembered eating ormers on Guernsey during childhood holi-days. He would watch the fisherman flip them out of their shells with a knife, flatten them with a wooden mallet, coat them in flour and fry them with onions and bacon. His mouth watered at the memory. He slipped the ormer shell into his pocket and looked up, to see a figure walking along the tideline towards him. At first he was unsure, but then the camouflage jacket and the sturdy boots, the binoculars and the loping gait confirmed his suspicions. It was Ace.

''Ello, guv'nor! What you doin' 'ere?'

Timothy put his hand out to greet his putative son-in-law, who ignored it and, instead, enveloped him in a bear hug.

The older man half laughed at the friendliness of the greeting and, when they had parted, said, 'Just blowing the cobwebs away.'

Ace glanced at the chronometer on his wrist. It was one of those 'outward-bound' type instruments with assorted dials and a rugged plastic strap. 'Shouldn't you be at work?'

Timothy regarded him apologetically.

Ace realised his mistake. 'Oh, God yes! Today's the day isn't it? I mean . . . the last one.'

'That was yesterday. This is the first.'

'Well, yes. Of the rest of your life . . . and all that. How was it? I mean, did they give you a gold watch.'

'No.'

'But they gave you something?'

'Yes. They gave me a coffee-making machine.'

Ace's look, at first incredulous, turned into one of amusement. 'You've worked there for thirty-odd years and they gave you a coffee maker?'

'It's a very good one,' offered Timothy. 'And I do need one.'

Ace shook his head. 'I don't know, guv'nor. You'd find a kind word to say about Genghis Khan, you would.'

'Well, he wasn't all bad. Apparently he did allow people to worship the God of their choice, you know. And he abolished torture.'

'Was that before or after he slaughtered them?'

'But it's true.'

Ace slapped Timothy on the back. 'So what now?'

'Oh, I was just having a walk to clear my head. To leave it all behind I suppose.'

'Anything planned for the rest of the day?'

Timothy looked out to sea and murmured softly. 'Not sure. Think I might walk a bit longer.'

Ace thought he detected the merest note of fear in his girl-friend's father's tone. 'I'm just about to have a bite if you fancy a spot of lunch.' He pointed to the dunes. 'I've got the Land Rover over there. We can nip to the pub.' And then, seeing Timothy's hesitation, 'Just a quick one. I've a fence to put up this afternoon.'

Capitulating, the older man smiled. 'Yes. Yes; that would be nice. Sea air gives you an appetite.'

'An appetite for the future, that's what you need, guv.'

Over thick soup, jaw-fatiguing 'artisan' rolls and a pint of local bitter in a quiet corner of the quayside pub, they talked about Rosie and the imminent arrival; a welcome break from the self-absorption that had dogged Timothy over the last few days.

'They asked again if we wanted to know what sex it was,' confided Ace.

'What did you say?'

'No. We don't. It's not natural. It's against nature. We'll take what we're given and be thankful.' Getting into his stride Ace explained how he and Rosie planned to manage once the child was born. Through all of this there played upon his mind the fact that Ace could, temperamentally, so easily have been his own son. The shared values, the love of the outdoors, the enquiring mind, the belief in a positive outlook so lacking in himself recently but, hopefully, soon to re-emerge as the old life was left behind and the new one began to materialise more clearly in his mind.

He remembered the ormer shell and pulled it from his pocket.

'I found this on the beach. Not seen one here before.' He passed it to Ace who turned it over in his hand.

'*Haliotis tuberculata*.'

'I thought it was an ormer,' offered Timothy.

'It is but . . .' Ace saw the smile on the older man's face. 'Yes. Not a very attractive Latin name is it.'

'But an attractive shell. A wonderful example of natural design. Look at the arrangement of the holes around the edge.'

Ace held the ormer so that the inner surface caught the sunlight now streaming in through the window of the pub. 'Fancy finding it here. And so late in the year. It must have been washed up from Jersey.'

'Or Guernsey. I ate them there as a boy. On holiday.'

'In a stew?'

'No, fried with onions and bacon. I've never forgotten the flavour.'

'They can only dive for them between January and April you know. And only when there's a new or a full moon – and two days after. To conserve them.'

'It sounds wonderfully mysterious.'

'But practical.' Ace saw that Timothy was withdrawing into himself once more. 'A bit like you, guv'nor.'

'Mmm?' murmured Timothy absently.

'Mysterious but practical.'

'Well, I'm grateful for the former compliment, but I'm not yet sure if the latter still applies.'

'Uncertain of what to do?'

'Yes. I've a few ideas but . . . I can't get my head round it really. I'd like to travel, but Isobel . . . well, she's got so many commitments – charity work, that sort of stuff. I can't see us finding the time.'

'What about doing it on your own?'

Timothy lurched backwards, laying down his soup spoon. 'I couldn't really do that. It'd be a bit selfish, gadding off and leaving Isobel behind.'

Ace wanted to say 'Do you think she'd notice' but he thought better of it. Instead he said: 'You could go for a week or two, surely.'

'Maybe. But I think Isobel has a few jobs lined up for me.'

'Jobs?'

'About the house. Well, not just ours. Oliver and Vita's. They need a wardrobe fixed in their bedroom, and some shelves in the spare. Oliver wants to use it as an office.'

Now it was Ace's turn to sit back. On his face was a look of incredulity. 'You can't settle for that, guv'nor.'

'What do you mean?'

'Well, becoming an odd-job man. It's a waste.'

'But I'm good with my hands and Oliver . . .'

'Isn't.'

'No.'

'Is that what you want to do.'

'Well, I don't mind helping out . . .'

'And you'll put all your other ambitions on hold?'

Timothy looked uncomfortable. 'Well, just for now. I mean, it's not that I *have* any other ambitions. Not serious ones anyway. I haven't the appetite to start looking for a new job. I've a small pension that should see us through.' He shook his head, then said softly, 'A pension at fifty-five. It seems weird.'

'It *is* weird. You're in your prime. It's a set-back that's all, guv'nor. Don't settle for second best. You've years ahead of you; there must be something you want to do?'

'Just this silly thing about seeing a bit of the world.'

Ace shook his head and his sandy curls spun about him like a rustic halo. 'That's not silly. It's what you want to do. It's what you deserve. You've worked all your life so it's high time you had a bit of – what do they call it – me time.'

'I've always hated that phrase. It sounds so selfish.'

'Well, I reckon you've been unselfish for long enough. You've helped us out – financially and spiritually . . .'

Timothy made to protest.

'No . . . you have. And it's been appreciated. I don't see how anyone could begrudge you a bit of self-indulgence.'

'But that's what it would be wouldn't it? It doesn't really take into account what Isobel wants.'

The younger man said nothing immediately, but there was upon his face a look that spoke volumes.

'What?' asked Timothy. 'Why are you looking like that?'

'You know, anyone listening into this conversation would think you were a downtrodden apology for a man who was scared to death of his wife and afraid to stand up to her and be himself.'

'That's a bit harsh.'

'Well, it might *sound* a bit harsh, but from where I'm sitting that's exactly what's coming across. Put it to Isobel. Tell her that you want to take yourself off for a bit. She might be taken aback but the chances are that she'll be so busy with the Lib Dems and the reading circle, the bridge club and heaven knows what else that she'll soon hardly notice you're not there.'

Timothy found it hard to find a response. Instead he took another spoonful of his soup.

'It's true, isn't it?' asked Ace.

The older man pushed away the roll whose seed-studded carapace had defeated all his attempts to break into it and leaned back in his chair before murmuring softly. 'Yes. I don't know how it happened but sometimes I think I really am.'

'Think you really are what?'

'The invisible man.'

2

GUILDFORD

OCTOBER

'I wear the trousers. And I wash and iron them, too.'

Denis Thatcher (attributed), 2003

Oliver and Vita's detached house stood on the outskirts of the city, commanding a view of distant Aldershot. It was not something of which they boasted – at least, they boasted of the view, but declined to be specific about the town whose high-rise buildings perforated the distant horizon.

Unlike Rosie and Ace, whose priorities were focused almost entirely on providing a warm and friendly environment in which to bring up their impending offspring, Oliver and Vita's outlook was more materialistic: nice house, nice garden, nice friends and nice meals in expensive restaurants. Unfortunately, due to the infrequency of profitable briefs coming Oliver's way, their income did not match their aspirations, as a result of which, Oliver had come, reluctantly, to rely upon the practical skills of his father in the field of home improvements. Oliver had never been good with his hands, and Vita had reluctantly been forced to admit to her tennis friends that whenever she was late for a match it was usually because her husband had experienced an unfortunate encounter with a hammer or an electric drill and needed driving to the local hospital. He had, she maintained with some credibility, a thicker file than anyone else at the local A and E department.

Oliver had finally given up all hope of being regarded as competent on the DIY front when a flat-pack wardrobe he had erected exploded with all the force of a nuclear bomb as Vita was attempting to load its inner rail with her evening dresses. Oliver blamed her predilection for sequins and gold thread. Vita blamed Oliver. The injury she sustained to her left foot lasted several weeks, though her limp was, he suspected, considerably more pronounced whenever she was in his company.

But it was a lesson learned. It pained him to call in his father (though not as much as the result of his handiwork pained Vita) but financial constraints offered him no alternative. He did not ask Timothy for assistance directly, but instead counselled his mother on the matter, enquiring if she knew of a 'little man' who could do a few odd jobs around the house and who would not charge an arm and a leg for doing so. He hoped that she would rise to the bait. He was not disappointed. Isobel said that she was sure his father would be happy to oblige, and now that he would have more time on his hands it would help to occupy him and stop him becoming too morose.

'Here you are, Timmy.' Vita's voice crackled through the doorway as she brought her father-in-law a cup of coffee. 'I'll leave it on the windowsill. Don't want to interrupt the master at work. I can't tell you how grateful I am.' She patted him on the top of the head and left the bedroom in a cloud of Amber & Patchouli, courtesy of Jo Malone, and a rustle of expensive silk, courtesy of a joint account at Coutts.

How he hated being called 'Timmy'. It was Isobel's fault; she had begun it all those years ago at university, and in the first flush of love he had felt disinclined to demur. Then the moment had passed and it was too late to do anything about it. But the fact that his strident daughter-in-law had picked up on it was a cause for continued irritation. The moment at which he felt he could ask her not to use that diminutive was long gone and, as with Isobel, he was saddled forever with 'Timmy'. At work he was called Tim – a marginally stronger interpretation. Timothy itself implied softness – like the grass of the same name. He suspected he had grown into it – soft and easily trampled. There were times when he felt, in new company, and on his own, of changing the vowel and becoming Tom. Much stronger; nearer to his inner being. He felt like a Tom, not a Tim; even less a Timmy – one letter away, aurally, from 'timid'. Had he grown into his name he wondered? These were pointless conjectures, futile attempts at changing one's character, but they were just the sort of idle, random, meandering thoughts that entered his mind when he was erecting a flat-pack wardrobe – the sum total of the intellectual demands of the day. He sighed. It was stupid to get so worked up. He would only be here for another hour, then they could wend their way back down the A31 and the A3 towards the welcoming skyward-pointing spire of Chichester cathedral.

Isobel had come with him. With only one car between them there was no alternative. She would do some shopping in Guildford, she said, while he got on with the wardrobe and the shelves. It occurred to him that if he had a car of his own he could be more independent. It was an obvious thought, but in the mayhem of the last couple of weeks it was not something that had crossed his mind. What a good idea. Suddenly as screws were threaded into holes and wooden dowels pushed into slots, he began to muse on what sort of car he would have. A sports model perhaps? Hah! He couldn't see Isobel sanctioning that. 'Are you going through a midlife crisis, Timmy?' she would ask. She would see it as expensive and impractical. Which, of course, it would be. You couldn't get anything inside one of those and the boot would be ridiculously small.

But they already had an estate car. A Volvo. Very spacious. Very safe. But not very exciting. A Land Rover would be fun. Chunky. But uncomfortable on a long drive. *Introduce section A to section B, locating dowels C and D into holes C and D.* How could Oliver possibly have failed to make a wardrobe according to such easy instructions when he was presumably capable of holding his own in a court of law and tying the defendant in knots with his clever questioning? It was beyond comprehension.

Of course, he could choose a classic car – something that would remind him of his youth and childhood. Such a car would need to be maintained of course, but he could go to classes and learn everything from maintenance of the internal combustion engine to welding. Yes; that was the thing to do. What about a Bristol? Or an E-type Jaguar? No. Too phallic. A Mark II Jaguar; an Inspector Morse car. That would set the cat among the pigeons. He felt a strange sensation in the pit of his stomach that he thought he recognised as excitement. Perhaps the hours and days would not loom so large and forbidding if he had a project. Even if foreign travel was out of the question he still had choices. It was up to him to make them.

His thoughts were interrupted by a commotion downstairs. Isobel had returned and he could hear her, along with Vita, mounting the stairs. He popped the last of the white plastic discs into the screw hole to mask the head and closed the wardrobe door. A perfect fit. And well made, too. Not one of those cheap flat-packs where nothing seems to fit and half the screws are missing. But then Oliver and Vita didn't really do cheap.

'Oh look, he's finished!' shrieked Vita.

'Well done, dear!' said Isobel. Then, turning to Vita. 'I told you he was good at this sort of thing. It's going to be so useful having him about the house.'

Timothy smiled ruefully. 'Yes. Provided I'm not stuck there all the time.'

'Now don't be grumpy.' Isobel made to pacify her husband. 'You know how you like working with your hands.' She turned to Vita. 'If there's anything else, now or in the future, you only have to let us know and Timmy will pop round and sort it out. Poor Oliver. Never very practical. But then he always did have a more intellectual turn of mind. Where is he today?'

Vita smiled proudly. 'Winchester. Leading for the prosecution. Some ghastly fraud trial. Very boring but quite technical.'

'Oh, he'll be good at that,' said Isobel.

Timothy wanted to say 'Yes, he's good at the boring and technical; it's a shame he's so hopeless at the practical and useful.' But he didn't. Instead he said 'That's all done then. Time we were off.'

'Oh, but you'll stay for tea won't you?'

Timothy made to decline, but not for the first time Isobel beat him to a reply. 'Of course we will. We've nothing to go home for, have we, Timmy?'

'No tennis this evening?' asked Vita.

'No; the nights are drawing in now and we only play in the morning and early afternoon. I'm thinking of taking up bridge.'

It was as if he didn't exist. He had become used to it. It was not as if Isobel really meant anything by it, just that she had become so accustomed to running their domestic life that she took it for granted that she would order the day and he would fall in line. It was his own fault for not being more assertive on that front, but, up until now, he had been content to let such a state of affairs exist. What was the point in arguing over trivialities? It occurred to him that now he was going to be at home more, he might find such circumstances marginally more constraining.

They stayed for tea and he only half listened as the two women shared confidences and complained about the difficulty of finding reliable tradesmen and the joy of bridge parties. His daughter-in-law was not a bad sort. She was well intentioned if a little misguided in her assertiveness – and she took pride in her appearance, too; she had a good figure which she made the most of by dressing smartly, if a little showily – the sort of wife he imagined barristers would regard as a good catch. But oh, that voice! Her strangulated vowels could cut through a force ten gale.

He looked from Vita across at Isobel and mused on the thirty-four years they had spent together. He could remember the number exactly. He still felt responsible for her, a state of affairs which was, he sometimes admitted to himself, laughable since she seemed so capable, so self-contained, so lacking in apparent need of any intervention on his part – except for his useful practical skills. Yet again he chastised himself for being so mean spirited.

What had happened? He was still the same person who married her. He hadn't changed, had he? But Isobel seemed to have grown, somehow; grown into a person he no longer recognised as the girl he had married. Surely that was as much his fault as hers. If he had been more forceful from the outset, more determined to wear the trousers . . . What a dreadful expression.

He had decided at the beginning to take a stand only when the occasion demanded it, and not to make a fuss about every last little thing. As a result of which it seemed that his own authority had gradually, imperceptibly, been eroded; worn away until it was almost non-existent. Yet underneath he didn't *feel* like a mouse. Maybe this was inevitable in a long-standing relationship. He had heard it called a 'Zombie marriage'. Heaven forbid! If you had any sense you just kept buggering on, realising that things changed and you had to accept the fact that the bells and whistles would fade into oblivion after a few years. A chap had to be realistic about these things and settle for pleasant companionship. That would have been fine. But over the past few years even the companionship had seemed strained. He suspected that if anyone had asked her if she enjoyed her husband's company she would have laughed. He was her husband wasn't he? It wasn't something that ever gave her pause for thought.

Was there a particular reason why had they grown apart? Was it simply that they had let communications between them slip into neutral and accepted a kind of banality born of over-familiarity? He felt no animosity towards her. Neither did she towards him, or so it seemed. Just indifference. But on his part there was something more than that: profound disappointment. He doubted if she even realised just how much she took him for granted.

Their relationship had been a happy and intimate one until the children were born. Not that he blamed them in any way, it was just that their presence meant that Isobel was more and more preoccupied with them; their moments together as a couple were more infrequent. He told himself that it was natural – the maternal instinct manifesting itself. He tried to involve himself, but only Rosie, the third child, seemed to relate to him; the other two he found difficult to fathom. He accepted the situation for what it was, and told himself that Isobel would come back to him when the children had grown up and flown the nest. But somehow that never happened. The earlier relationship faded away and they never regained the easy rapport they had had as students. The final indignity came when she asked for separate bedrooms, the better to sleep since his snoring had, apparently, become unbearable. He took it on the chin, but it was a pivotal moment in their relationship.

So why, if things between them were so strained, had he not plucked up the courage and left her? He had stayed, originally, for the sake of the children. Not that Oliver or Alice would have taken it badly if they had separated, but it would have broken Rosie's heart, and separating was not something that Isobel would ever have countenanced. It had probably never crossed her mind. But it had crossed his.

He had never been unfaithful, but there was one work colleague who had awoken within him the kind of feelings that he no longer experienced with Isobel. Not just feelings of physical attraction, but something chemical – shared enthusiasms, shared tastes, shared values, that indefinable rapport that seems greater than empathy alone. He never dared to call it love. The object of his admiration eventually sensed there was little likelihood of him furthering the relationship. She left the firm and moved on. He told himself that it was probably for the best. And yet there was always the lingering, recurring 'what if?'

He looked again at the two women talking – Vita with her blond bob and her expensive dress, Isobel, greying now and a little fuller of figure but still attractive. Just distant from him; seldom if ever seeming to connect.

He suspected – hoped even – that if he had upped and gone a few years ago that it might have hurt her, might have caused her to realise that she did indeed love him. Hanging on to that thought caused him to believe that he had done the right thing. If he had gone – taking off with the woman to whom he was strongly drawn – where would he be now? Would that relationship, too, have palled and become run-of-the-mill? He hoped not. He had to believe that it would have endured as enriching and blissful as it had promised. The experience remained neatly locked away in its mental box. A thing of perfection, to be revisited from time to time and relived, until doing so became too painful and too unresolved. Life, he regularly told himself, was not all about him. There were others to think of, too.

His reverie was broken by his daughter-in-law's exclamation: 'Goodness! Is that the time? I must get on, and I can't hold you up any more.'

The audience, to his profound relief, was over. They could leave and go home. On the way back in the car, with Timothy driving, Isobel said 'She's a bright girl, Vita. Wonderful company. Perhaps now you've more time on your hands we can come up to Guildford and see them more often.'

There was no reply.

'Timmy?'

He was miles away. Dreaming of a Mark II Jaguar.

3

CHICHESTER

NOVEMBER

'Surprises are foolish things. The pleasure is not
enhanced, and the inconvenience is often considerable.'

Jane Austen, *Emma*, 1816

The day started like any other over the past few weeks.
Unremarkably. Timothy made Isobel her early morning cup of
tea and took it into her room at eight o'clock, giving her a peck
on the cheek as she lay back on the pillow. Then he went downstairs and ate a bowl of granola with strawberry yoghurt, accompanied by a mug of coffee made in his new espresso machine.
He laid the *Daily Telegraph* on the table in front of him and
leafed through its pages slowly, bypassing tirades on the evils
of the Labour party, marvelling at the paper's ability to find an
excuse to picture a half-clothed model in spite of it not being
London Fashion Week and trying not to be too dispirited by a
full page on Italian travel.

Eventually Isobel came down in her tennis outfit – a crisp
white blouson and a close-fitting combination of skirt and

leggings ('It's a skort dear,' she told him somewhat impatiently) – that looked reasonably athletic without revealing too much flesh, except between knee and ankle. Her hair was tied back, and under her arm she carried the bag that contained her tennis rackets. 'You haven't seen my balls have you?'

'Sorry?' asked Timothy absently; raising his eyes from the picture of Cara Delevingne and wondering why the model always looked so cross.

'My tennis balls. I can't find them.'

'Over there.' Timothy pointed to a fluorescent metal tube standing on the corner of the worktop. 'Where you left them yesterday.'

'Stupid,' muttered Isobel.

'Sorry?'

'Me, not you. Stupid for forgetting where I left them.'

He folded over the back page and glanced at the crossword, asking, as he did so, 'You back for lunch?' He knew what the answer would be but thought he would ask anyway.

'No. I'll have lunch with the girls at the club. Are you sure you can manage to get your own?'

'Oh, I expect so. I can't decide whether to have baked beans or scrambled egg.'

'Now there's no need to be so dull. There are some sausages in the fridge and a quiche in the freezer. Honestly, anyone would think I neglected you.'

'I thought people played tennis in summer, not in November.'

'Oh, I prefer it at this time of year. It's cooler. We'll manage another couple of weeks yet, before the court gets too slippery.'

Timothy looked up and smiled pleasantly. 'Well, you be careful.' Then he turned back to the paper and mused over the cryptic crossword. It was a remark that would come to haunt him in the weeks and months ahead. Like all remembered trivialities, it would seem to fall woefully short of a suitable farewell. But then what would he have chosen to say if he had realised that he would never see Isobel alive again?

It had happened very quickly, the women at the tennis club said. Without any apparent warning. Isobel and her partner were one set up and leading three games to two in the second set when she slowly crumpled to the ground while preparing to serve. They rushed over to her but could find no pulse. Her partner had tried cardiopulmonary resuscitation, an ambulance was called and she was rushed to the hospital, but there was nothing they could do. A massive heart attack, the doctor said. Mercifully quick. She would not have known anything.

Timothy sat alone in the hospital corridor looking with morbid fascination at the highly polished grey linoleum floor while the world carried on around him. Sounds and sights seemed blurred like distant echoes as doctors and nurses, patients and porters went about their business. Trollies were wheeled into distant wards, nurses squeaked past in sensible shoes, and all the while he sat perfectly still, lost in an alien world.

They had taken him in to see her, for his own peace of mind but also to confirm her identity. She lay there, uncharacteristically still, her face paler than he had ever seen, one eye half open. He raised his hand and gently closed it. The flesh felt soft but icy cold. Tenderly he brushed back a wisp of hair and tucked it behind her ear; as he did so a feeling of grief mixed with fear seemed to rise within him; it was almost choking in its intensity. Never had it crossed his mind that she might die before him. They had talked about it from time to time – idly, sarcastically (she saying that she supposed he would go and find some floozie with whom to spend his twilight years) – but it had all been a joke; neither of them had taken it seriously, and he doubted whether Isobel would have believed that any other woman would have him or would put up with his funny little ways. It was a cruel joke now; a sickening one. His stomach felt empty and for a moment a kind of dizziness overtook him. The doctor grasped his arm and steadied him, then they both left the room, the doctor leading him into the corridor where he now sat, the cup of sweet tea growing cold on the moulded plastic chair beside him.

They were kind and thoughtful, but now he had to stay here while they sorted out the paperwork. Would he like them to call anybody so they could be with him? He said that it would not be necessary. He would speak to his children just as soon as he left the hospital. Reluctantly, Isobel's tennis friends melted away and he sat in the echoing corridor alone.

He could not cry. Now the sick feeling in the pit of his stomach had faded he could not feel any emotion except that of disbelief. Isobel had seemed fine that morning when she left. There was absolutely no indication of ill health. Isobel did not do 'ill', and had little time for those who lay in bed with colds and flu.

Time seemed to stand still as so many things ran through his head. She was gone. He would not see her again. Their time together of late might have diminished in terms of emotional impact, but they were still with each other; still somehow a joint entity, in spite of the absence of open affection. His life, rightly or wrongly, noticed or unnoticed, had revolved around her. Whatever form his day had, that form was dictated by Isobel. Now his life would be shapeless. He had no job, no wife, no apparent future. He was a worthless and insignificant speck in a massive and frenetic world.

He stood up and walked to the end of the corridor where a window looked out upon a bare concrete footpath that ran between two stretches of grass. Walking along it was a young couple, the mother cradling in her arms a white-blanketed bundle. A baby. The building opposite the mortuary in which he found himself was the maternity unit. It was an unfortunate juxtaposition, but then maybe it was a timely reminder that as one life ended, so another began. He remembered, like a bolt from the blue, that soon there would be a new arrival in his own family. Rosie was due to give birth in a fortnight's time. It was a glimmer of hope that might enable him to put aside the self-recrimination that could now so easily manifest itself and send him spiralling into depression. In spite of his worst fears, he hoped that it might be so.

4

CHICHESTER MARINA

APRIL

'I'm still working. I need the money. Money, I've discovered, is the one thing keeping me in touch with my children.'

Gyles Brandreth, 2010

'It's absolutely outrageous!' exclaimed Rosie, pushing the letter back towards her father.

The three of them – Rosie, Ace and Timothy – were sitting at an outdoor table alongside the marina, a mile or so outside Chichester, where brave and early season boaters were negotiating the free-flow of the lock as best they could on a surging spring tide. In an old-fashioned pram alongside them, five-month-old baby Elsie gurgled appreciatively, unaware of the anger rising in her mother.

Timothy had suggested the venue for their meeting. Since Isobel's death he had often come here to walk the pontoons; to lean on the railings by the marina lock and watch the yachts and the motor cruisers as they snaked their way down the

Itchenor reach, eventually disappearing in the direction of The Solent and distant shores. Where would they be going? Not to Samarkand or Constantinople; more likely Cowes or Lymington. It hardly seemed to matter. The very mystery of their voyages to ports less distant than even Cherbourg or St Malo seemed to imbue them with a magical air. Whatever their destinations, more often than not he wished he were going with them. The time had come where he must make his dreams reality, or else settle for the humdrum and the sedentary. And that, he had all but decided, was not something he was prepared to countenance. It was a state of affairs that his son found absurd.

The reason for Rosie's indignation was simple and straightforward – a letter written by Oliver to Timothy, making clear a number of things that the son felt the father ought to know and understand. The letter read as follows:

Fairlawns,
Guildford

28th March 2015

Dear Dad,

It has come to my notice that you are planning a voyage; a Grand Tour as I believe you are calling it. Vita and I fully understand how much you must be upset by mum's death, and we are hugely sympathetic to the fact that you must be feeling very lonely after so many years together. However, we cannot help but feel that such an undertaking is extremely unwise, bearing in mind your age and the circumstances in which we all find ourselves. Such a jaunt would involve considerable expense and you must realise that, as a family, we are none of us at all well found. The frittering away of funds on such a bizarre undertaking is, to put it mildly, somewhat irresponsible.

Foreign travel always seems so inviting but to do it unaccompanied is, we believe, to invite disaster. There are plenty of 'singles' cruises on offer nowadays and many of them are relatively inexpensive. It would seem to us that such a holiday – lasting perhaps a couple of weeks, rather than the months you are planning – would be a safer, more economical and more responsible option.

In these straitened times, when your funds are constrained by lack of a regular income, the cost of living in general and the need to make sure your children (and now your grand-children) are looked after now and in the future, we beg you to reconsider your plan which is, we think you might agree, at best over-adventurous and at worst foolhardy.

Please do not think us interfering. We have your best interests at heart.

Yours sincerely,

Oliver and Vita

'How dare he talk to you like that?' continued Rosie. 'It's your life.'

'And your money,' murmured Ace, keen to show his support but anxious not to be interfering in family matters which were nothing to do with him. He might be the father of Timothy's first grandchild but not being married to Rosie he felt reluctant to overstep the mark.

'Well, he does have a point,' confessed Timothy. 'It *is* a lot of money and perhaps it is irresponsible to spend it in such a way.'

'It is *your* money,' said Rosie. 'Yours to do with what you will. You've helped all of us out enough over the years; I don't know how Oliver has the nerve to be so bolshie – and so rude.'

Timothy smiled ruefully. 'Oh, you know Oliver; that's just his way.'

'Anyone would think he was writing to a client, not his father. I mean, he even signs it "Yours sincerely", not "Love".

'Yes, well . . .'

'Honestly, Dad. If you let him brow-beat you into not going I shall never forgive you.' She glanced across at Ace. '*We'll* never forgive you, will we?'

Ace was reluctantly drawn into the fray. 'If you want to do it, guv'nor, you do it. We can manage.'

'But you're even worse off than Oliver and Vita,' offered Timothy. 'Perhaps I can have a smaller holiday as they suggest. It would cost a lot less'

'Oh Dad! There's nothing wrong with singles holidays; I think they're fab for older folk who are . . . lonely. But you're not old. You're in your mid-fifties – hardly "singles holiday" fodder at all. Club Med is one thing but Costa Geriatrica is quite another.'

'I think you're being a bit harsh,' said Timothy.

'Not as harsh as Oliver. I mean, the bloody cheek of it!'

'Don't swear in front of the baby,' warned Timothy.

'It's not funny, Dad! And I bet Vita goaded him into it.'

'Well, I'm not sure that Oliver would need any goading. But I was a bit surprised by his tone. Your mum and I helped them out a bit over the years – as we did you – but they've never been quite so . . . up front about it before.'

Rosie shook her head. 'It's unbelievable.'

'Well, there we are. I thought you ought to see it. I wouldn't want to call it off without you knowing the reason why.'

Rosie leaned forward in her chair. 'You are not calling it off, do you hear? You've planned this trip and you are going to do it. Ace and I will be as worried as Oliver and Vita, but for different reasons I suspect. We want you to be safe, but if that means you staying at home and doing odd jobs around our houses for the rest of your days then I for one couldn't live with myself.'

'So I'm caught between two children then.'

'What about Alice?' asked Rosie.

'Oh, you know Alice. You saw her at the funeral. Non-committal as ever.'

'It's almost as if she were a distant cousin,' murmured Rosie reflectively. 'I tried to make conversation with her but she just said "yes" and "no". She didn't seem to be able to get away quick enough after we'd had tea.'

'Oh, she has her own way of dealing with things. She gave me a kiss and said she'd be in touch.'

'I bet she won't,' muttered Rosie. Then she said, 'Sorry; I don't want to diss both my siblings but . . . oh . . . they do drive me nuts in their own way: one a virtual recluse and the other a pompous ass.'

'Mmm. Says a lot about me as a father doesn't it?'

'No. It says a lot about them as people. I grew up happily. At least I think I did. What makes them both the way they are . . . well . . . I'll never know. But don't beat yourself up about it, Dad.' She nodded towards the pram. 'You've got another generation to think about now.'

'That's what concerns me,' admitted Timothy.

'Dad; I'd rather she grew up with a grandpa who was fun and adventurous and who came back to us full of stories of his travels and with a glint in his eye than one who stayed at home with his pipe and slippers and whose idea of a good day out was assembling a flat-pack wardrobe.'

'You heard then?'

'I did.

'I can be quite useful you know.'

Rosie leaned forward and kissed him on the cheek. 'If the best I can say about my dad is that he's useful, then it's not just him who has failed as a father, it's me who has failed as a daughter: failed to see that there is more to his life than a loving daughter and a granddaughter who will both dote on him. Everyone needs time to themselves, not in a selfish way, but to be the people they really are. That way they offer far more to those around them – those who can see that a dad isn't just there as a back-stop or a bank, but that he has a life and a personality of his own.'

'And you think that's me?' asked Timothy. 'Without very much evidence to back up your claim?'

'Just because I never said anything about you and mum doesn't mean I didn't notice. I knew what things were like.'

Timothy looked surprised and not a little uncomfortable.

'She wasn't the easiest person to live with, Dad. I know. But I never for one moment thought that you were a mouse, or lacked backbone or even an opinion on things. You saved your opinions for the moments when it really mattered. You were never a pushover. You might think you were, but as far as I was concerned you were a man who knew what his priorities were. You were loyal. You were true, and you kept your powder dry for when it really mattered.'

She smiled, and Timothy noticed that her eyes were filling with tears.

'You are the strong, silent type, Dad.' Then she nodded towards Ace. 'I chose my man because he reminded me of you. Now get out there and have your moment. You've waited long enough.'

Timothy tried to speak, but for the first time since Isobel had died, he felt a surge of emotion that precluded speech. Instead, with trembling lips he simply smiled at his daughter, and then turned his gaze upon the baby in the pram. His own tears made a clear view of her quite impossible.

5

CHICHESTER

MAY

'In preparing for battle I have always found that plans are
useless, but planning is indispensable.'

Dwight D. Eisenhower (1890–1969)

The decision to travel had not been arrived at lightly. For several
months he had found himself in a kind of limbo, where his
daily routine had been undertaken in an almost semi-conscious
state. His appetite faded to almost nothing, and only the
intervention of Rosie in inviting him round for meals and
making sure that his cupboards and fridge were well provi-
sioned prevented him from becoming gaunt of appearance and
skeletal in outline. Ace, too, engaged him in conversation and
made arrangements to meet him for lunch at least once a week.
At first Timothy declined, preferring to be alone with his
thoughts. But eventually good sense prevailed and he admitted
to himself that the period of mourning was getting him
nowhere. Christmas was the catalyst. He was invited to Oliver
and Vita's but tactfully declined, preferring to spend time in

the company of Rosie, Ace, and Elsie his new – and only – grandchild. Vita had made some tart comment about the fact that she and Oliver would now have to take second place to the next generation, but the remark went over his head – or at least he gave the impression that it did so. The truth of the matter was that a festive season of chattering-class drinks parties and false bonhomie interspersed with a leavening of DIY would do little for his self-esteem. He needed company that he knew and loved and felt comfortable with, which would lift his spirits from the lowly plateau they had occupied since Isobel's death.

There was, he knew, too much time for self-analysis, for self-flagellation – it was easy to beat himself up about his failings within the marriage, and now it was too late to do anything about it.

Conscious of his fatherly duties, he visited Oliver and Vita on Christmas Eve to deliver presents – a bottle of 2005 Bordeaux he thought his son might appreciate, and a small hamper of Liz Earle cosmetics for Vita. Rosie had told him the stuff was quite good. He hoped Vita would agree, but her cursory glance at the collection of pots and bottles gave little away. He felt rather let down, but tried not to show it. He was only too relieved to depart for home after a glass of mulled wine, rather than waiting for the house to fill with the friends and neighbours that Vita had suggested he stay on and mingle with. This Christmas would be a strange one; no Isobel to organise the family, and only a Christmas card from Alice. He called her twice, but there was no reply and he became resigned to the fact that she was probably happier in her own world rather than his. Her card sat in the centre of the mantelpiece; an ancient nativity scene by Gerard von Honthorst in which a brilliant light shone up from the face of the Christ Child on to the face of his adoring mother. Another reminder of what might have been.

Over the rest of the Christmas holiday he remained at home but persuaded Rosie and Ace to come and stay. It made sense, he said, rather than the three of them – plus baby – cramming into Rosie and Ace's tiny rented flat.

Seeing that it meant so much to him, Rosie put up little resistance. And there was a greater scheme at work here, too. Timothy decided, after some soul-searching, that he no longer wanted to live in the old family home alone, with its echoes of the past and, on balance, a greater number of unhappy memories than those which would be cherished for a lifetime. The bedroom where he slept alone would, forever, be a reminder of failure on his part. The one occupied by Isobel already made him shudder. He did not want to forget her – never would and never could – but neither did he want to live with a ghost of the past, which seemed still to be capable of admonishing him, of reminding him of his shortcomings.

The task before him was to persuade Rosie and Ace to move in permanently. He would find for himself accommodation more suited to a single man with a fondness for books and the sea. He knew he would have some difficulty in getting Rosie to agree, and that Ace would be unwilling to interfere in negotiations between father and daughter. The deed was done on Boxing Day after the lunch of Christmas leftovers when Rosie had enjoyed a glass or two of a particularly mellow Burgundy. She was not so relaxed that she did not put up a good degree of resistance, but once her father had explained why he wanted to move out (without going into more detail than was strictly necessary) she agreed only on condition that they paid more rent than they did for the flat. Seeing that this would be a stumbling block, Timothy agreed to the slightest increase of their current outgoings and the whole arrangement passed off with considerably less fuss and fretting than he had anticipated.

Rosie had made it clear that Oliver and Alice should be informed of the arrangement, lest they should think their sibling was coming into some kind of windfall and depriving them of their inheritance. Bearing in mind the content of Oliver and Vita's subsequent letter, she was not at all sure that the message had got home, but her brother's attitude and actions never ceased to surprise and vex her; she knew in her heart of hearts that this was a fair and sensible arrangement, and her father was her priority – it was what he wanted and so she (and Ace and Elsie) – would brave the upshot, whatever it might be.

Before all that might happen – and to make its execution more practical – Timothy had decided to put into store what goods and chattels he wished to retain, and to get away for a while so that Rosie and Ace and Elsie could settle in to their new home. He looked at shipboard holidays (ironically the singles cruises that Oliver and Vita would later suggest in their letter) but decided that in spite of his love for the sea they would not be what he needed: time in his own company rather than with others who were in the same boat, both metaphorically and literally. He knew that it was unwise to be totally alone, but just as yet he was unready to be hurled into the midst of a group of similarly lonely souls who would be confined on board a ship with little hope of escape except when in port.

He contemplated renting a villa on the Italian coast, and then, one day, tidying up another pile of books that Isobel had intended for the Lib Dem cause, he came across a small leather-bound volume that she had put on one side, intending to take it to an antiquarian book dealer rather than consigning it to the monthly coffee-morning book stall where it might only fetch a couple of pounds. Its title page explained that the book contained 'Remarks on Several Parts of Italy &c in the Years 1701, 1702, 1703' by one J. Addison. The book was a second edition, dated 1718. Thumbing through its pages, which offered up that fragrance unique to ancient paper, a mixture of mustiness and acrid aroma compounded of antique print and paper, Timothy realised that what he held was a record of 'The Grand Tour' – a voyage undertaken by young men of means in the late 18th century, when they would visit the cities of Europe (Italian cities in particular) with a view to widening their appreciation of the arts, collecting paintings and sculpture, perhaps having the occasional dalliance with pretty ladies, and generally broadening their minds. Such tours could last months or even years. While such a long sortie was certainly beyond his means (in spite of Isobel's life-insurance policy which had brought him a welcome windfall), a few weeks, or perhaps a month or two, of seeing Europe at his leisure awoke within him feelings that he thought were no longer capable of entering his consciousness.

He would put on one side the dalliances with pretty ladies, but he would make out for himself a rough itinerary of places to visit and things to see while 'perambulating within their environs'. Already he was picking up the vocabulary of Mr Addison who found when shopping for souvenirs 'As most of the old Statues may be well supposed to have been cheaper to their first Owners than they are to the modern Purchaser, several of the Pillars are certainly rated at a much lower Price at present than they were of old.' Timothy doubted his own ability to pick up a statue – or even a pillar – for a reasonable sum, or to arrange its transport home for accommodation in his new abode – wherever that might be. But the prospect made him smile. Perhaps a miniature marble head of Michelangelo's David would suffice.

On consecutive evenings he spent time in the company of

Joseph Addison, the poet, playwright, essayist and politician, skipping the more dreary episodes of his travels and the long screeds of Latin, but fuelling himself, nonetheless, with a degree of mounting anticipation when things that caught his imagination were alluded to – the harbour at Monaco, the ruins of Pompeii, the canals of Venice, the Duomo in Florence. He began to map out his own Grand Tour. It was not one that took in all the cities delineated by Addison – Padua and Verona, Ferrara and Genoa, Pavia and Milan – he did not envisage spending the better part of three years away from home; but he drew up a shortlist of the major cities that captured his imagination and arranged them into a rough itinerary: Paris, Monaco, Pisa, Florence, Rome, Naples and Venice. Seven; a lucky number, according to some.

Except for the first couple of stay overs, he resisted the temptation to book all of his accommodation in advance, for that might limit his time in places that took his fancy and condemn him to a longer period than necessary where his surroundings did not appeal or the weather turned against him. It was a brave move – and a move that gave him one or two sleepless nights as the very folly of such an expedition sank in. His natural inclination, born in him after years of domestic economies, was to billet himself in 'cheap and cheerful' hotels, not least because profligacy in the face of his children – and grandchildren – would seem to be depriving them of their inheritance. But then Isobel's life insurance policy had yielded a surprisingly generous windfall. At first he felt it should be left untouched, but then he reasoned that even Isobel would have found such an approach a wasted opportunity. He would not fritter it away, but to make life difficult for himself, both at home and abroad, seemed perverse.

The combination of his pension and the insurance payout

did mean that such parsimony was really unnecessary. With courage and a rare amount of insouciance he decided that there was no need to stint himself. At the start of his trip, at least, he would indulge himself, if not on the scale of those Georgian travellers, then at least in hotels that would be regarded as luxurious. Yet even as he made the decision he worried, and vowed also to arm himself with a list of suitable more modest hotels and *pensiones* before he left and trust to luck; the very thought of it created a churning sensation in the pit of his stomach. It was, he convinced himself, high time that he took a chance on life and on what it had to offer. He had played safe for too long. He could no longer keep on dreaming of travel. Now was the time – with no ties to speak of – to grasp the nettle and fly the nest. Or, rather, to catch a train.

6

ST PANCRAS STATION, LONDON

MAY

'Railway termini. They are our gates to the glorious and the unknown. Through them we pass out into adventure and sunshine, to them, alas! we return.'

E.M. Forster, *Howard's End*, 1910

Timothy would have happily slipped away with little or no fuss, but Rosie had decided that she would see him off and make 'a proper adventure' of it. He limited himself to one large suitcase – wheeled and easily manoeuvrable along station concourses – and one small holdall. Laundry would be done on the way he had assured Rosie, whose personal hygiene was of a fitting standard for a nursing mother. Elsie was left with a kindly neighbour (Ace having been sent on a seminar about coastal erosion), and father and daughter made the first leg of the Grand Tour together from Chichester to London Victoria, then across London to St Pancras station with surprisingly little incident, except for Rosie losing an earring somewhere between the two London stations. It might have been construed as a bad omen, had she not convinced her father that she had never liked them – Vita had bought them as a birthday present for Rosie last year and been careless enough – or tactless enough – to leave them in the Accessorize bag they had been wrapped in at the shop. They were not, Rosie assured her father, of either great monetary or sentimental value.

And so they arrived at the proper beginning of his journey: St Pancras station and the Eurostar train to Paris. Timothy felt the kind of butterflies in his stomach that he could only remember from the days of his university exams, but told himself that this was a good thing; lack of fear and trepidation would mean either that he was not sharp enough to spot potential problems before they turned into disasters, or that his senses were not heightened enough to enjoy possibly the greatest adventure of his adult life. He tried to keep a sense of proportion and balance that lay somewhere between triumph and disaster and to treat Kipling's two impostors just the same.

'Have you got your mobile phone?' asked Rosie. 'I know you hate technology but . . .'

'Yes. And a charger,' replied her father reassuringly.

'And a universal plug – you know, one of those that you can use in different parts of Europe?'

'In my small bag.'

'And your ticket? And your passport? And some euros?'

Timothy reached into his inside pocket and drew out a long, thin piece of card on which were listed within a neatly ruled grid the umpteen things he needed to have with him. Beside each was a neat tick.

'Once a graphic designer, always a graphic designer,' said Rosie.

Her father smiled. 'I suppose so.' He glanced up at the platform indicator. 'There it is. That's me. They say you have to leave half an hour for customs clearance and passport so I'd better check in.'

'Right,' said Rosie, doing her best to sound bright and breezy. She raised her face towards him and planted a kiss on his cheek. 'Have the most wonderful time and make sure you call us regularly.'

'Well, you know I struggle with the mobile. It always seems to have run out of juice when I need it. And I can never work out how to send pictures. They go somewhere but I don't know where.' He looked at her beseechingly. 'I thought I might write, actually. I'll use the mobile for emergencies. And when I need to hear your voice. And it's there if you want to call me, if there's a problem. But I thought I'd do what Mr Addison did and write down my experiences. I could keep a journal, but it seems like more fun to write you letters saying what I'm doing. Would that be all right?'

'If that's what you want; of course.' Rosie brightened. 'I can curl up at night with your words and imagine I'm there with you.'

'I don't know how that will go down with Ace.'

'Oh, he won't mind. I'll share them with him – I won't keep them to myself.'

'I'll make sure what I write is for both of you, then.'

'You could just go to an Internet café and email us – or do Facetime. Or Skype.'

Her father looked at her imploringly, as if she were asking him to master space travel. 'I know I could . . . hopefully . . . but I want to do this journey like Addison did it. Like a proper Grand Tour of old. If I'm connected by this sort of technolog-ical umbilical cord it won't be like it used to be. I won't get the feeling of being cast off on an adventure, heading off into the unknown on a voyage of discovery. It would be . . . just another holiday. Not that we had many of them,' he added reflectively.

'Is that why you're going by train and not flying?'

'Partly. Though he went by coach back then. He sailed more than I will, and went on horseback, at which I draw the line. But I like train travel – I'll get to see more of the countryside that way. It seems more of an adventure by rail, somehow, rather than waiting in grisly airport queues with a seething mass of humanity.'

'Talking of which,' said Rosie, looking about her, 'there's a seething mass of humanity here. You'd better be getting along.'

Timothy let go of his case and his holdall and put both arms around his daughter. 'I won't be gone forever. Just until . . .'

'I know. Just until . . .'

He saw his daughter fighting back the tears, and as he wrapped his arms around her, Timothy, too, found himself prey to her emotion.

'Now don't start,' he said. 'You'll set me off, and that's no way to begin a journey.'

'I know; I'm sorry. It's just that we'll miss you. But I do think you're right to go and I hope you have an absolutely brilliant time, seeing all those places you've only ever dreamed about.' She sniffed back the tears and Timothy pushed his hand into his trouser pocket and withdrew a clean, freshly ironed handkerchief. Gently he wiped away the tears from his daughter's cheeks and pressed the handkerchief into her hand. She raised it to wipe her nose and then said, 'It smells of you. Can I keep it?'

Timothy laughed gently. 'If you want. I've a few more in my case.' He glanced up again at the platform indicator. 'Now I really must go.'

'Yes.' Then a look of remembering came to her face. 'Oh, I've got something for you.' She opened the bag that was slung from her shoulder and withdrew a folded piece of paper which she slipped into his jacket pocket. 'Read it when you're on the train,' she instructed. 'Now go; and good luck.'

He touched her lightly on the cheek, picked up the holdall and set off down the concourse, pulling the suitcase behind him. Rosie watched as her father disappeared into the crowd and could not help but feel a rising sense of loneliness and more than a hint of fear at his departure.

Her father, finally aboard the Eurostar train, and with his luggage stowed in the racks at the end of the carriage that contained his reserved seat, settled back to enjoy the journey. And yet there was, at the back of his mind, a nagging feeling of guilt. Guilt at being alone. Guilt at setting out with the intention of enjoying himself. He had no recollection of ever making a journey of this significance on his own. For almost forty years, Isobel had been by his side, in body if not in spirit. Her reluctance to travel had surprised him when they were first married; it had disappointed him, too, but as time went by it became accepted and he sublimated his own desires in order to please her. Now he could please himself. Funny how it was not quite as simple as that. He reasoned with himself that even after his loss it must be acceptable at some stage to learn to live again; to live for oneself and not necessarily with or for someone else. But then he was rather out of practice.

Only when they had emerged from the Channel Tunnel into France some two hours later did he slip his hand into his jacket pocket and withdraw the folded slip of paper that Rosie had given to him at St Pancras station. Upon it was written:

'Three grand essentials to happiness in this life are something to do, something to love and something to hope for.'
Joseph Addison.
(I got this off Wikipedia so it might not be exactly right.)

And at the bottom of the page:

To which I would add: and a family who love you to bits and can't wait for you to come home safely. Hoping your trip is all <u>you</u> hope it will be.

    All our love, Rosie, Ace and Little Elsie xxx

The trouble with daughters, he thought to himself, is that they have this terrible habit of tugging at your heart strings at the most inconvenient moments. The businesswoman sitting opposite him and tapping away on a laptop looked across at him with an expression of concern as he wiped away a tear from his cheek. He did so with the back of his hand, for he no longer had a clean handkerchief about his person.

7

HÔTEL PLAZA ATHÉNÉE, PARIS

MAY

'My dear Sir, Brussels may be the heart of Europe,
but Paris is her very soul.'

Robert Hardisty, *Travelling Hopefully*, 1975

For most of his Grand Tour Timothy would take pot luck with his accommodation, telling himself that while he could afford decent small hotels or *pensiones*, he could not lash out on the grandest of them all the time – with one or two exceptions. A book he had come across about the Hôtel Plaza Athénée had so captured his imagination that he had decided he would at least begin his Grand Tour in grand style and so he booked into the lavishly appointed hotel with its red awnings and creeper-covered walls that opened into a central courtyard where parasols and tables were arranged to allow the diners privacy and grandeur at one and the same time. So it was that he awoke on the first morning of his great adventure and pulled back the curtains to find the daylight streaming in and a gentle breeze ruffling the leaves of the creeper that embraced his window.

Gone was the worry of the day before; the anxiety of leaving behind his family. Or at least that concern was much reduced, for here he was in Paris – in the springtime – and in a hotel about which, a few months ago, he could only have dreamed. He had not taken a suite (that would have been far too self-indulgent and far too costly) but the room he had booked, though compact, was not ridiculously small and had a plush en-suite bathroom with ridiculously fluffy towels and a wonder-fully comfortable double bed in which he had slept like a top.

For several minutes he leaned out of the window, taking in the bright, clear Parisian light, the echoing sounds of waiters, cutlery and crockery on the tables four floors below, and the distant sounds of a city waiting to be explored. There was a tap at the door and he let in a waiter bearing a tray laden with orange juice, half a bottle of champagne, croissants and fresh coffee. 'But I didn't order breakfast,' he explained, making no attempt to essay the schoolboy French which might have let him down.

'It was ordered before you came, *m'sieur*,' confirmed the waiter. 'There is a card. Enjoy your stay.' The waiter left and Timothy opened the small envelope. It contained a card with the Plaza Athénée monogram at the top. Below it were written the words: 'To send you on your way in style. R, A and E x'.

Timothy shook his head. He slipped the card into the book on his bedside table, alongside the slip of paper that Rosie had given him at St Pancras, then he picked up his mobile phone and texted her the briefest of messages: 'Arrived safely at Plaza Athénée. Can't really believe I'm here. Thanks for being so understanding. All my love, Dad.' He pressed the 'send' button, heard the sound that indicated his message had been despatched and switched off the phone. Though feeling not in the least like Peter Pan, he smiled to himself as he contemplated the beginning of his 'awfully big adventure'.

The streets of Paris at 10am were a bustling microcosm of French life. Was it his imagination or did it really feel so very different from London? Looking up at the towering buildings on either side of broad boulevards he marvelled at the mansard roofs with their fish-scale tiles, the oriel windows, the cupolas and turrets, the shuttered windows, ornate iron-balustraded balconies and the acres and acres of hand-beaten lead. Every doorway seemed to be a work of art, every street was lined with trees through which the morning sunshine winked and glittered its greeting. It all looked so . . . foreign.

The traffic whirring in stertorous bursts around the Arc de Triomphe hooted and honked a welcome – or so it seemed to his fanciful imagination – and he found himself entranced by the bookstalls on the banks of the Seine, with their strings of postcards, mountains of paperbacks, boxfuls of etchings, coins and stamps to tempt those bewitched by this city of romance. He had been prepared to be disappointed; had steeled himself for the fact that Paris might, in reality, be just the same as every other city – like London with a foreign accent. But it was not, and he was instantly and hopelessly seduced by its atmosphere and its history.

Armed with a pocket-sized guidebook – in English – he climbed the Eiffel Tower and gazed out across the city, basking in the spring haze; at the hill of Montmartre, and the River Seine shimmering like a silver ribbon as it snaked through the city. He walked through the mighty portals of Notre Dame, taken aback by its height and dark loftiness, and almost reeling from the thick, sweet tang of incense that hung in the air.

But the thing that struck him most, having entered the

echoing halls of Les Invalides, was the massive scale of Napoleon's tomb – the gargantuan cradle-like sarcophagus of red quartzite that held the body of a man just five feet five inches tall. It towered above the floor on its green granite pedestal as if proclaiming the greatness of the hero within, now entombed in silence.

So eager had he been to take in the sights and sounds of his first foreign capital that he had quite forgotten to eat or drink. The dizziness he felt was due in some measure to the overwhelming scale of the Place de la Concorde and the Jardin des Tuileries, the length of the Champs-Élysées and Boulevard Haussmann, but also to a lack of nourishment. He sought out a small café, ordered a ham and cheese baguette and a coffee and sat for a while, restoring his energy and telling himself that he did not have to see the entire city in a day. He had three nights booked at the Hôtel Plaza Athénée and could then seek out more modest accommodation or move on as the fancy took him. He must pace himself. Today he had been like a boy in a sweet shop, anxious to try everything on offer – to soak up a city of which he had heard so much but which, bizarrely, he had never before visited despite its relative closeness and ease of access via the Channel Tunnel.

His mind turned to the lack of adventure that had characterised his marriage. The fact that Isobel had never really wanted to leave the shores of Britain – a fear of flying and martyrdom to seasickness being her reasons for lack of travelling ambition. And so their holidays, such as they were, were confined to a week or two each year – as far afield as Scotland and Cornwall – and the rest of his time off work was spent pottering at home. But now life would be different, *was* different. Now he could go where he wanted, when he wanted.

And yet, the underlying feeling was one of guilt. Guilt at being released from a life that had been predictable in its routine and totally devoid of anything that could be called adventure. He had hoped that he would feel liberated after so many years of uneventful marriage, but suddenly, having been used to turning round to enquire what Isobel thought of any suggestion, any proposed action, the space she occupied was empty. There was novelty in his not having to seek her approval, and yet a kind of hollowness seemed to pervade everything. He told himself that it was only to be expected; that he would learn to live again without feeling reproachful towards himself and disrespectful to the memory of his late wife. His first day, he had to admit, had been liberating and enriching, despite the strangeness of being alone. As the energy began to return, thanks to the nutritious baguette and the best coffee he could ever remember drinking, so he leaned back in his chair and watched the people of Paris come and go – young lovers, old men with dogs, elegant young women possessed of effortless style, little old ladies with raffia shopping baskets, businessmen with sharp suits and slim attaché cases. A motorcade swept past, scattering a few dried plane leaves into the gutter. The president? Some government minister? Who knew? It was all so . . . well . . . exciting – if he allowed it to be. And he knew he must, otherwise this 'trip of a lifetime' would be wasted.

'*Un autre café, m'sieur?*' asked the waiter.

'Er . . . *non merci. L'addition s'il vous plait.*' The waiter disappeared. He hoped he had got it right. A few moments passed before the waiter reappeared and placed a small silver saucer on the table. A folded bill lay beneath an almond macaron wrapped in tissue paper. He smiled to himself. Even this tiny streetside café had style. Parisian style.

He left a note, sufficient to cover the cost of his lunch plus a small tip, and walked along the banks of the river towards the Louvre. He saw another row of bookstalls and stopped to look. One of them sold artists' materials – oil and watercolour paints, paper and small canvases. The stallholder nodded at him as he expressed an interest – a craggy, unshaven man of middle age with a cigarette dangling from his mouth and a rivulet of saliva in each of the creases that ran towards his swarthy chin. The aroma of Gauloises (or was it Disque Bleu?) had not assailed his nostrils since university days. This was clearly a voyage of rediscovery as well as discovery – the unlocking of memories long since confined to the back of his mind. He sifted through the drawing pads and tin boxes of watercolour tubes and pans, jars of camel- and squirrel-hair brushes, large Chinese brushes made of goat hair, and all the while the stallholder muttered and mumbled under his breath some kind of informative litany that Timothy was beyond assimilating. But it seemed good-natured in its rough and ready way, and appeared not to need an answer, which was just as well.

Another memory was unlocked. He remembered the joy he had once found in painting in watercolours. Why should he not do it again? He had been quite good, once. Had even managed to sell a few in those years of penury early on in their marriage – to friends and work colleagues who were probably just being kind and happy to find a way of helping out the young married couple.

He picked out a 4H and a 3B pencil, a small water bottle, three brushes of varying thickness, an A4 watercolour pad and a small but comprehensive flip-top tin of colour pans bearing the name Sennelier. He lay the paints, the pencils, the bottle and the brushes on top of the pad and asked the stallholder 'Combien, m'sieur?'

'Quatre-cinq euro,' came the reply, followed by a wide and suspiciously insincere grin that displayed an uneven set of nicotine-stained incisors.

Having paid his forty-five euros, and wondering if he really should not have beaten the man down a little, Timothy strolled off towards the famous gallery with his painting paraphernalia in a paper bag tucked underneath his arm.

The glass pyramid he found rather incongruous, and the Louvre itself a seething mass of schoolchildren and tourists. The Mona Lisa was his first disappointment – rather small, dimly lit and difficult to see through a welter of humanity intent on acquainting themselves with the smile of the ages. He was, he decided, rather too tired to take it all in. He would come back on another day – earlier in the morning – and try to beat the crowds.

Back at the hotel he sank his body into a deep bath fragranced with the exotic Plaza Athénée foam and mused on the events of the day. Paris had been all he hoped it would be – the architecture, the people, the sights. His mind reeled at the recollection of it all. It was just a shame that the Louvre had been so crowded, but there were bound to be disappointments along the way. And tomorrow would be different. He knew exactly what he would do. He would take his paints and his watercolour pad to Versailles and see what he could make of the palace and the gardens. He would do nothing else. A quieter day would suit him well.

As he slipped between the sleek cotton sheets that night – having partaken of his first (and last) hotel dinner at exorbitant expense, he vowed to rein in his ambitions, both in terms of pace and extravagance. If he continued at this rate his energy – and his money – would be gone by the end of the week. But as he drifted between wakefulness and sleep, a warm feeling began to come over him. It was a sensation that he had not experienced since Isobel's death. The feeling was that of contentment. He hoped it was not misplaced; that it would not be short lived. And then he drifted off to sleep.

8

VERSAILLES, PARIS

MAY

'Dreams weigh nothing.'

Marie Antoinette (1755–93)

Timothy was ready to be disappointed by Versailles. The Louvre experience had tempered his expectations. And so it was with some delight – and relief – that he wandered around the environs of Louis XIV's extensive palace and grounds, astonished at the scale, the grandeur and the feeling that at any moment the French court of the Baroque might appear around the corner in a gilded carriage; that the Sun King and his Queen might disembark and their subjects fall into low bows before them. The Hall of Mirrors and a four-poster bed topped with white ostrich plumes were images that danced in his mind as he found a bench outside with a good view of the palace and its gardens.

Like the day before, the spring sunshine possessed a warmth that cheered his heart and mind. Billowing clouds moved but slowly across the palest blue sky, and the late morning rays warmed his back as he opened his pad and began to sketch the rough outline of a corner of the palace and the ornate parterre beyond. His draughtsmanship was practised, but his painting a little rusty. And yet before too long the old technique returned and, having discarded the first two attempts, he was quite pleased with what was appearing on the paper. Perhaps he would continue as he travelled through his chosen cities, making a pictorial record of this and that as well as writing letters home. It reminded him to sit down that evening, to write and tell Rosie and Ace that all was well; that he was conscious of not being too profligate, and not trying to do everything at once. Rosie would worry, in spite of the fact that he had warned her of irregular contact, and he had not even rung since his arrival. For a moment he felt guilty, but the feeling evaporated as he became more absorbed by the image of the palace and its garden appearing on the page in front of him.

He was lost within it and in the world of the 17th century when a voice at his shoulder brought him back to present-day reality.

'*Ah m'sieur. C'est magnifique!*'

Timothy looked up with a start to see a smart young woman dressed in black from head to toe – her dark hair cut into a sharp bob, her body encased in a tight-fitting roll-neck sweater, black trousers and boots. She was leaning towards him, holding her sunglasses above her eyes and scrutinising his painting. In her hand was a red leather leash, and at the end of it a rather sad looking pug that did not share its mistress's admiration of his work. The leg of the bench on which he sat clearly offered it greater opportunity and it wasted no time in demonstrating the fact.

The woman sighed and said '*Je suis désolée! Mon chien est grossier!*'

Unsure of the precise translation, but grasping the gist of it, Timothy shook his head. '*Toutes les chien est critiques!*' he offered.

The woman laughed. 'You must be English!'

Timothy looked crestfallen. 'Is it that obvious?'

She smiled. 'Only by your accent.' Her own was of that delicious French kind that he had heard in films – seductive and almost poetic in tone.

The woman pushed her sunglasses on to the top of her head. She gestured towards the empty seat beside him and looked at Timothy questioningly.

'Oh, please do,' he offered.

She sat down beside him. 'It eez a lovely day.'

'Yes,' confirmed Timothy. '*Le soleil brille, et il y a beaucoup de nuages dans le ciel.*'

The woman laughed again. It was a light, rippling laugh and Timothy noticed that her eyes were a soft shade of green, her teeth white and even. She was astonishingly attractive; like something out of a French movie.

'It really is all I remember from school French lessons.'

'Very useful zough,' she responded with mock seriousness.

'It's the first time I've said those words since the school class-room. I never thought I'd have cause to say them again.'

'It eez your first time in Paris?'

He nodded.

'And you like eet? Does eet live up to *expectations*?'

She used the French pronunciation of the word and he began to fall under her spell, before reminding himself that he was sitting in a strange country next to a strange woman and things like this only happened in movies.

'I think it's wonderful. It's so very . . . French!'

'*Ah oui!*'

She sat silently for a moment, staring at his painting of the palace and its garden.

'You 'ave, 'ow you say . . . experience at painting?'

'Oh, not really. I'm a draughtsman – well, a graphic designer, but I haven't painted for years. I thought I'd see if I still had the ability.'

'*C'est trés bon*. It eez very good. You should sell eet.'

Timothy chuckled. 'Oh, I don't think anyone would want to buy it!'

'I would.'

Timothy looked at her sceptically. 'Now you're being too kind.'

'Not at all. Zare eez a market for such views. I know. I sell zem.'

'Really?'

'*Oui*. I 'ave a little gallery just off ze Champs-Élysées.'

Timothy began to think that she was teasing him. Here he was, sitting on a bench in the gardens of Versailles, being accosted by a beautiful Parisian woman old enough to be . . . well . . . much younger than himself – not much over forty at a guess. He had only been here two days and . . . well, he had better be getting along. He stoppered up the bottle of water and began to dry his brushes on a wad of tissue.

'I am so sorry. I 'ave broken your *concentration*. It eez very rude of me. You do not know me from . . .'ow you say . . . Adam.'

He made to placate her. 'Well, Eve, I suppose. But you are very kind.'

The woman held out her hand. 'Francine Faragon.'

Timothy was about to give her his own name, but instead heard himself saying 'Tom. Tom Gandy.' How odd was that? He was stunned at his response, and just a little ashamed.

'It eez a pleasure to meet you, Tom.'

She reached into the pocket of her trousers and pulled out a card. 'I do not give one to every artist I meet here, but I keep my eyes open for zose who can produce saleable work for my gallery. It eez very modest but . . . well, it is my own. I 'ope you do not mind me saying 'ello.'

'Not at all.'

'Zat man over zare,' she pointed to an older man in a navy blue smock and a beret who was sitting at a small easel and holding up his paintbrush to translate the scale of the building, 'He eez useless. Ee sinks he is . . .'ow you say . . . ze gift of God . . . but eez work eez very poor. Very . . . *qu'est ce que c'est "brut"?'*

'Er, crude?' Timothy offered.

'*Oui.* Crude. Not at all liked by my customers.'

She looked back at Timothy's painting. '*C'est delicieux.*'

He felt a bit of a wretch now. He had thought at first that she was spinning him a yarn; throwing him a line, coming on to a gullible tourist. But it did seem that she was genuine; that it was not just him that she was approaching, but any artist whose work was reasonable enough to flog for what he supposed would be a few euros. No doubt as the summer progressed, demand for such souvenirs would increase and how else was she to replenish her stock? That's what he told himself as she turned impatiently towards the pug tugging at the leash and crying, '*Proust! Viens ici!*'

He let out an involuntary laugh. She turned back with an enquiring look.

'Proust?' he asked

'*Oui.* I used to call eem Jacques but as he grew I realised zat whenever we went for a walk 'e just went on and on and on – rambling – and so I call eem Proust.'

Timothy laughed again. '*Parfait!*' There was a brief silence before he added, 'Well, I'm very flattered that you think my work is good enough for your gallery, but I doubt that I shall produce enough to make it worth your while. And I'm not sure I shall be here very long.'

Francine tilted her head on one side. 'Oh?'

He was unsure whether or not he should explain, but his new acquaintance wore an expression of interest that encouraged confession. 'I'm making my way through Europe. A sort of mini-Grand Tour. Visiting cities I've not seen before – mainly in Italy. France is my first stop. I've only been here since yesterday. *Hier*. And I shall probably leave at the end of the week.

'And where are you staying?' she asked.

Timothy smiled guiltily. 'At the Plaza Athénée.'

'*Mon dieu!*'

'Oh, only for one more night; then I shall move somewhere less expensive.'

Francine looked taken aback. 'But you will 'ave to get used to a lower standard of living.'

'Oh, it will be more what I am used to.'

'You 'ave somewhere in mind?'

'Not yet; but I have a little book – a guidebook. I plan to use that.'

Francine looked troubled. '*M'sieur*, I 'ope you do not sink me too . . . too . . . 'ow you say . . . *presomptueux* . . .'

'Presumptuous?'

'*Oui* . . . but I can recommend a small hotel which eez very clean, very reasonable and which has a good breakfast. So long as you do not sink I am being . . . presum—'

'No; not at all. I'd be very grateful.'

'May I borrow your *crayon*?'

In a state of semi-shock, Timothy handed her the pencil and she proceeded to write an address on the cover of his sketch pad.

'If you cannot find it, just give me a ring at ze gallery and I will 'elp you.'

Then she stood up and tugged at the lead to remind the pug that its journey was not yet complete.

'*Au revoir*, Tom. I do 'ope to see you again. If you 'ave any paintings to sell it would be wonderful, but if not I shall quite understand. It 'as been good to meet you. Good luck wiz your Grand Tour. It sounds very exciting.' And with a brief wave, she walked along the gravel path towards the palace gates. Timothy watched her go as if mesmerised.

When he wrote to Rosie and Ace that evening, there was no mention of his encounter with Francine Faragon. Neither did he let on about his use of the name Tom.

9

PARIS

MAY

'The French never care what they do, actually, so long as
they pronounce it properly.'

Henry Higgins in *My Fair Lady* by Alan Jay Lerner, 1956

He knew the moment he woke up that the first thing he would
need to do was find a bed for that evening. The three nights at
the Plaza Athénée had been all he hoped they would be – a
chance to indulge himself a little and to people-watch from the
comfort of an elegant *bergère* in a corner of a sumptuous lounge
in the evening, before dining more modestly at bistros and
restaurants a short walk away. There were limits, after all, and
now he must draw in his horns further still and find more
modest accommodation for . . . how long? Perhaps a week?
Before he moved on? There was still so much to see. He felt he
had barely scratched the surface of Paris and what he had
discovered so far had filled him with delight.

He showered, changed and went down for breakfast, determined to make the most of his last hour in the hotel. At least

he would be able to eat well in Paris, whatever the accommodation, for the street-side cafés seemed to overflow with fresh
brioches and croissants, cheese-and-ham-filled baguettes and
pains au chocolat all to be washed down with delicious coffee.
It was, Timothy decided, something he could easily maintain
on his return home, though it would most probably have a
disastrous effect on his waistline.

He drained his cup, dabbed at the corners of his mouth with
the generous-sized damask napkin and laid it on the table with
a sigh of regret. An assiduous waiter caught his eye. 'Something
wrong, *m'sieur*?'

'No. Not at all. It's just that this is my last morning here and
I've had such a lovely time.'

'Ah, *m'sieur*. Stay a little longer. You will not regret it,' offered
the waiter with a glint in his eye.

'I'm sure I would not but . . . well . . . all good things . . .'

'Pardon?'

Timothy smiled. 'It has been wonderful. A delightful experience. But I have to move on.' He got up from the table and
made to shake the waiter's hand. The waiter seemed a little
surprised.

'You will always be welcome back, *m'sieur*. We 'ave a lot of
guests 'ere, but we like the nice ones best.'

'I'm very flattered. I would love to come back . . . one day.
There are one or two people I'd love to share it with.'

'You will be welcome, *m'sieur*. Most welcome.' The waiter
gave a little bow. Timothy did the same in return, then the two
of them laughed simultaneously and Timothy walked from the
restaurant towards the concierge's desk in the foyer to settle his
bill.

Half an hour later he found himself standing with his luggage
on the pavement outside the hotel, having declined the offer

of a taxi. He had also felt too embarrassed to ask the way to
the small hotel – if it was, indeed, a hotel and not just some
kind of bordello (where did that word come from?) – that
Francine Faragon had recommended. It seemed indelicate
somehow (and a touch embarrassing if he were honest) to ask
the receptionist at the Hôtel Plaza Athénée the way to . . .
what was it called . . . he looked again at the number and the
name that Francine had scrawled above it: the Hôtel La Cocotte,
Rue de la Planchette.

He would not call the hotel, even though she had jotted down
the telephone number, since that would commit him, and it
might turn out to be totally unsuitable. Instead he planned to
walk there. It was not too far away and if he did not like the
look of it there was nothing to stop him from walking on and
finding some other more suitable accommodation.

The Rue de la Planchette was a small turning off the Avenue
de l'Opéra, so at least it was handy – within walking distance
of the sights rather than out in the sticks. At first he could not
find anything resembling a hotel – large or small – and then he
noticed a small bottle-green awning jutting out between a hat
shop and a patisserie. The awning covered a black gloss-painted
door, flanked on either side by ornate iron balustrading on each
panel of which was fixed a small brass sign: Hôtel La Cocotte.
Both signs were highly polished – a good omen. He looked
upwards, above the shops, to see four floors of black-painted
windows, each with a window box of green ivy. It was not on
such a lavish scale as the verdure that furnished the Plaza
Athénée, but the fact that it was, in its way, a miniature version
made him smile.

He climbed the two stone steps and pressed the brass bell-
push to one side of the door. The lock buzzed and he pushed
at the shiny door which yielded in front of him. He walked

forwards into a narrow hallway and found that it suddenly opened out into a small courtyard. The whole area was brightly lit – something of which the outer door and the narrow passage gave no inkling. Looking upwards he saw that he was in a glass-roofed atrium; not a modern construction but one a century or more old, perhaps twenty feet square, no more. In one corner stood a desk, behind which sat an elderly woman with grey hair spun upwards into a kind of candyfloss arrangement. She was dressed in black and a pair of spectacles hung about her neck on a chain, tangling themselves with a string of large malachite beads. She looked alarmingly fierce and, for a moment, Timothy wished he had not plucked up the courage to press the bell by the front door. The feeling in his stomach was akin to that which he had encountered when he had left for university – a mixture of fear and loneliness engendered by unfamiliar surroundings far from home.

The old woman stood up and smiled. '*M'sieur?*'

'*Bonjour.* Er ... *Avez-vous un chambre? Madamoiselle Faragon* er ...' He struggled to remember how to say 'recommended you'. He did not need to worry.

'Ah, you must be the Englishman she told me might come. Tom isn't it?' The woman spoke without a trace of a French accent.

'Goodness! Your English is good,' offered Timothy, relieved, and finding no reason to dispute her assumption.

'I should hope so. I was born there and didn't leave until I was thirty! I married a Frenchman.' The woman offered her hand. 'Pamela Lamont. It's my hotel. It was my husband's. He died five years ago and now I run it alone. So there you are; an instant life story and the door has barely closed behind you.'

Timothy hesitated. 'I see, well ...'

'Francine said you were looking for a room. Was she right?

You see I've only the one left and if you don't snap it up it will be gone by lunchtime. Busy time you see. Paris in the springtime. Oh yes. I only have six rooms and they don't hang around. All en suite. I do breakfast – not full English mind – just pastries and coffee. Or tea. And you find your own sustenance for the rest of the day. How long will you be staying?'

'Er, I thought perhaps a week if that suits . . . I'm not really sure.'

'Cash in advance mind. Or a credit card. Provided it clears. I can't afford to wait until you do a bunk. Not that you look the sort.'

'Well . . . could I see the room?'

'Of course. But you'll have to find your own way up. My legs don't like to climb those stairs more than they have to. Oh no. You can leave your bags here.' She saw the look on Timothy's face. 'Oh, they'll be perfectly safe with me. Go on; up you go. Room eight. Fourth floor – at the top – the door on the right.' She took a key from the board behind her and dropped it into Timothy's hand. It was a brass key attached to a large leather fob; the kind that could not be slipped into a pocket and forgotten about.

'Right. Er . . . thank you.'

'Off you pop then.'

It was rather like being back at school, thought Timothy, but there was something endearing about the old woman and her matter-of-fact approach to life. As he turned towards the staircase, he saw her pick up a copy of French *Vogue* and begin to leaf through its pages.

By the time he reached the fourth floor he was quite out of breath, but he had time to notice that the staircase, though Spartan, was spotlessly clean and the brass handrail atop the black iron banisters had been freshly polished that morning. If the staircase was anything to go by Madame Lamont clearly kept a clean house.

He turned the key in the lock of the door numbered '8' and tentatively opened it. It led into a small room containing a double bed with a brass-knobbed bedstead. Madame Lamont was clearly a martyr to her brasswork (or her cleaner was) for, like the nameplates outside the front door, and the banister rail itself, the brass bed sparkled in the sunlight that slanted in through the window. A white-painted dressing table, chair and wardrobe completed the furnishings of the tiny room, aside from a bedside table and a Tiffany lamp. Another smaller door led to a shower room with a lavatory, bidet and hand basin. It was basic accommodation but clean and tidy. Two Redouté prints of roses decorated the walls. He walked to the window, which was tall, split into two halves vertically and flanked by long white net curtains. He turned the catch and opened the windows inwards. As he did so a cool breeze caught the nets and lifted them gently, allowing in also the distant sounds of the traffic below. He leaned out over the ivy-filled window box and looked to left and right. In the far distance he could see the towers of Notre Dame. It was not a view that could be boasted about, but it was a view nevertheless, made up mainly of the elevations of buildings and shops of different periods.

He closed the windows and looked about him. The room, while not luxurious, had a pleasant feel to it and smelled clean and fresh. It would do him nicely. Already going round in his head were thoughts of moving on. He was not sure how long to stay. He did not want to rush his visit to Paris, but at the back of his mind were thoughts of Italy and the other places on his itinerary. It was becoming clear to him that allowing fate to take a hand, allowing himself to be nudged along at a speed dictated by outside agencies, was easier said than done. And all the while he remembered those he had left behind at home – Rosie and the baby in particular. How his life had changed, and yet something deep inside him had not changed at all. His sensibilities, his feelings of unease and . . . well . . . guilt at surviving when Isobel had died, refused to go away completely. It was something he would have to reconcile himself to if the trip were not to be overshadowed by such negative thoughts. He resolved to work harder at it.

Madame Lamont regretted that he would have to carry up his own suitcase and hand baggage, but suggested that he looked young and fit enough for it not to be a problem. She looked at him curiously when he presented his credit card bearing the name Timothy Gandy. She shrugged and fed the card into her small machine, handing it back to him when satisfied that he was, indeed, the man whose name appeared on the card.

Unpacking felt strange. He had kept most of his things in his case at the Plaza Athénée, feeling that it was hardly worth taking them all out just for three nights. But now, having committed himself to a week with Madame Lamont – feeling that to move on at the weekend might mean more travel problems than if he were to travel midweek – it made sense to settle in properly. He was rather relived she was English. In one way it was a disappointment – a lack of local colour – but in another it was a way of easing himself in gently, and he would not feel the need to speak French the whole time. Not that he supposed he would see much of her. She clearly did not venture up to the top of the house very often, if at all. She had a young girl to do the cleaning, she said, and if he had any laundry that needed doing it would take two days. It should be put in the bag he would find in the wardrobe: the bag marked 'Blanchisserie'. There would be an extra charge, of course.

When he came downstairs after unpacking, Madame Lamont was no longer at her desk. The door behind it was open and he could hear voices from what he assumed were her own rooms – a ground-floor apartment. He could not see very much, except pale blue walls, a blue and yellow parrot in a cage and a comfortable looking white-covered armchair with bright cushions on it. On the far wall was an abstract painting in strident colours: not the sort of décor one would have expected for a woman of . . . what? Seventy? Eighty? It was difficult to tell.

He laid the key on the desk very gently, eased open the front door and stepped out into the street. He had walked only a few yards before a familiar voice greeted him. 'Tom! You decided to give it a try zen?'

Proust was not with her, and today she was dressed in a smart camel-coloured coat with a tie belt, her legs encased in black tights. She wore vertiginous heels, which seemed only to enhance the elegant Parisian sashay he had noticed on their first meeting. She came forward and kissed him on both cheeks, which rather surprised him. Face to face he was able to observe her more closely now, rather than at the sideways angle that the Versailles bench had imposed upon him. Her face framed by the dark bob of hair, he noticed in particular the vitality in her eyes. They were green and framed by long lashes. Her lips the same rich red that he remembered. Her cheeks dimpled when she smiled. All of which he tried to ignore as she enquired, ''Ave you settled in?'

'Yes. Yes, I've just put my things away. Madame Lamont seems very . . . pleasant.'

Francine threw back her head and laughed. 'She is a bit fierce, but she 'as a heart of gold. A great friend. She and Patrice – he was her husband – were very 'elpful to me when I started out.'

'Your gallery is close by?' enquired Timothy.

'*Oui*. Just around ze corner. Come and look when you 'ave a moment.' And then, almost without drawing breath 'What are you doing today?'

'Oh, I thought I might do that touristy thing and take a trip on the river.'

'Ah, *oui*. But do not eat on ze boat. Ze *bateau mouche*. Ze food is not as good as ze little cafés and restaurants. I can recommend one but . . .' She paused and looked a little down-cast. 'I am sorry. I impose too much. You must find your own way . . . It is not up to me to tell you what to do.'

He felt guilty that she should assume she had overstepped the mark. 'No . . . please . . . I am happy to be steered in the right direction. Please don't feel that your advice is unwelcome. It might save me a lot of heartache.'

She brightened. 'As long as you don't think . . .'

'Not at all. It's very kind of you to take an interest.' He tried to lighten the moment. 'Look . . . where is your gallery exactly? I'll take my boat trip today and perhaps I could come and have a look tomorrow.'

'You will?'

He nodded.

'*Merveilleux*!' She raised her hands in relief, and he noticed the long fingers, devoid of any rings, and the dark red, well-manicured nails. 'You see ze little street across ze boulevard? Ze one wiz ze *confiserie* on ze corner? I am down zare on ze right-hand side. Galerie Bleu.'

Timothy looked at his watch and then, somewhat to his own surprise said, 'I don't suppose you would join me for supper would you? This evening?'

At first Francine looked taken aback and Timothy felt himself colouring up – something he could not remember doing since he was a teenager. After all, she might be married. Might have children. Might regard his proposition as completely inappropriate.

'*Mais oui*! Zat would be very nice.'

In the heat of the moment the reality of the situation began to dawn. 'Only . . . er . . . I'm not sure where to recommend.'

Francine shook her head. '*Non*. I will come to *La Cocotte* at *sept heures et demi* . . . 'alf past seven. I know a little brasserie – not too expensive – a short walk from 'ere. Would zat be a good idea?'

'Yes. Er . . . yes . . . if you don't mind, only . . .'

'*Bon*. I shall look forward to it, Tom.' And with that she leaned up, kissed him lightly on the cheek, turned and was gone.

10

CAFÉ LAUTREC, PARIS

MAY

'Every wise and thoroughly worldly wench
Knows there's always something fishy about the French.'

Noel Coward, 'There's Always Something Fishy About the
French', 1933

True to her word, Francine was waiting in reception at the Hôtel La Cocotte shortly before seven-thirty that evening. Well, to be precise, she was not exactly *in* reception, but in the doorway of Madame Lamont's ground-floor apartment, talking to the old lady who was comfortably ensconced within.

They were speaking in French and Timothy could hear, as he descended the stairs, the sound of their voices, interspersed with a rather croaky rendition of 'The Bridges of Paris' courtesy of the blue and yellow macaw, released from its cage and now standing on a perch just inside the door of the apartment. It was a bizarre scene, made all the more unreal by the fact that Timothy wondered how, in just the space of a few days, he had seemingly entered a whole new world. His intention had been to travel as an observer, to keep a comfortable distance, to look at the world as an independent outsider, but quite without noticing it he seemed to have been drawn into these other people's lives.

Tentatively he put his head around the door to indicate his arrival, and Madame Lamont, without getting up from her chair, greeted him with 'Ah, the accidental tourist!'

Timothy smiled, but was slightly baffled by the strange greeting. He managed a slight nod and a murmured '*Bonsoir*'.

'We are confused, Mr Gandy' said Madame Lamont in firm if not forceful tones.

'I'm sorry?'

'We are confused by your name. Is it Tom or Timothy – Francine seems to think it is the former, but your credit card says your name is Timothy?'

Timothy felt a sense of rising unease. There seemed little alternative but to come clean.

'I am afraid I might have been less than straightforward with Mam'selle Faragon.'

Francine looked at him questioningly.

'It's quite simple really. My name is Timothy but I have always felt it was a little . . .'

'Soft?' cut in Madame Lamont.

'Yes. I suddenly found myself . . . when given the opportunity to . . . start from scratch, I suppose . . . to be called Tom. It all seems rather childish now.' He shrugged, hoping to make light of the matter.

'I see.' The old lady regarded him with a beady eye. 'Is that the extent of your deception?'

'Oh yes . . . I wouldn't . . . I mean, I haven't . . .'

Before he could continue Madame Lamont laughed softly. 'I told you he was a genuine chap,' she said, looking at Francine.

Now it was her turn to blush. 'Please, *madame*!'

'Not a very good start, I know . . .' confessed Timothy.

Francine shrugged. 'Oh, it is not a problem. And if you want to be called Tom, zen Tom it is!'

Timothy cut in. 'Well, it all seems rather silly now. I suppose I was trying to start a new chapter, that's all. And it seemed one way of . . . moving on.'

'From what Mr Gandy?' asked Madame Lamont.

'A life I've left behind . . . for a while.'

The old woman regarded him curiously. 'That sounds rather ominous.'

'Not really.' He glanced at his watch, then looked at Francine. 'Shall we be going. I'll tell you all about it over supper.'

'No more . . . *bobards*?'

Timothy looked appealingly at Madame Lamont.

'Fibs,' said the old lady.

'No more fibs. Only the truth.' He gestured towards the door. Francine smiled and shook her head. 'Timosy,' she said softly, under her breath. 'Mmm. It is much easier for me to say Tom.'

'As you wish,' said Timothy, as she slid her arm in his and said, '*Au'voir, madame. À bientôt.*'

'*À bientôt, ma petite.* Oh, and *m'sieur?*'

Timothy turned in the doorway. 'Yes?'

'Be careful.'

Anxious not to make more of the evening than he originally intended – a modest 'thank you' to Francine for sorting him out with new accommodation – Timothy endeavoured to bring a lightness of tone to the conversation. The brasserie she had chosen was one of those small French restaurants redolent of Alphonse Mucha and Henri Toulouse-Lautrec, the walls decorated with posters of La Goulue, and tables lit with pools of light cast by small lamps with deep red shades.

'I thought you might like it 'ere,' she said. 'It is very . . . French, *non*?'

'Very. Somehow I thought you'd go for something more modern.'

She looked a little crestfallen. 'You are disappointed?'

'No. Not at all. It is, as you say, very French, and it is France – well, Paris – that I came to see.'

She looked relieved, then asked, 'Has it lived up to your expectations?'

'Oh, and some.'

Francine looked confused.

'I mean, yes. It has more than lived up to them. I didn't think that anywhere so close to Britain could feel so . . . different, so . . . French!'

She smiled, and the dimples appeared again. 'So, M'sieur Tom, you promised to tell me all about yourself.'

'Did I?' he asked disingenuously.

She broke off the tiniest piece of crusty baguette, which she dipped in olive oil and popped into her mouth. Her eyes did not leave his. The effect was more than a little disconcerting.

'Well, where do I begin?'

'At ze beginning?'

'Oh, it's too long a story really. But I was married, I have three grown-up children . . . oh, and one grandchild – a grand-daughter – just a few months old. My wife died suddenly . . . just last year . . .'

'Oh. I am so sorry.'

Timothy smiled in acknowledgement of her sympathy. 'I had always wanted to travel so . . .'

'And your wife did not like to travel?'

'Not really. No. She was afraid of flying and . . . well . . . she always seemed to have so much to do at home that we never managed to find the time.'

Francine took a sip from the glass of white wine in front of her. 'So you are making up for lost time?'

'In a way. I'd always had this yen . . . this wish . . . to do The Grand Tour – you know, all those young men in the late eighteenth century who went off round Europe to experience the culture and the food and wine . . .'

'And the women?'

'Well . . . yes, I suppose so, though that wasn't strictly a part of their itinerary. It just sort of . . .'

'Happened?'

'Yes.'

There was a mischievous twinkle in her eye as she said, 'Like us . . . just sort of happening?'

He hesitated, unsure of the seriousness of her meaning. 'If you put it like that, yes.'

Francine laughed. 'It is all right, Tom, I am only teasing. It is very kind of you to ask me out to supper.'

He felt a sense of relief at her bursting the bubble and relieving what he could imagine might have been a tricky moment; a moment of getting in deeper than he had intended. Though she was incredibly attractive, and it did feel wonderfully liberating sitting across the table from such a beautiful woman who seemed to be quite enjoying his company. It was something of a novelty.

They dined on asparagus, followed by roasted sea bream. Francine sipped slowly at her glass of Sancerre, and by the time the cheese arrived, Timothy was on to his third glass of claret, his cheeks, he could feel, showing the effects of his indulgence. But he was having such a good time.

The talk was of his planned itinerary, in the main, with

Francine suggesting occasional things she felt that he should not miss – the Ghiberti Doors on the baptistery in Florence, the view of the city from the hills of Fiesole, the horses of St Mark's in Venice.

'I envy you,' she confessed, when his list of cities was completed.

'But you have obviously been to these places?'

'Ah yes; some of zem. But not in . . . good company.'

He regarded her quizzically.

'It was not an 'appy time. Emotionally.'

'Oh?'

'I was wiz a man for eleven years, but 'e was not a good man. I loved 'im very much but . . . ah well. Sometimes life does not turn out as well as could be 'oped for. And now . . . I am content to be alone. Quite content.' She brightened. 'But you were 'appily married?'

'Yes. I suppose so. Yes.'

'You do not seem so sure? For 'ow long were you married?'

'More than thirty years.'

'*Alors!* Zat is a *very* long time.'

'Yes. It is.'

Francine looked at him intently. 'Why do I sink you were not very . . . content?'

Timothy prevaricated. 'Oh . . . thirty years is a long time. Things change. Well, some people do. That's all. I was very lucky. I have three children . . .'

'And you love zem?'

'Of course. Though they are all quite different. My son is a barrister, married. Quite different to me; in temperament I mean. My elder daughter is a librarian in Oxford – self contained, her own person, happy in what she does. I don't see a lot of her, really, which is a bit of a shame but . . .'

'And . . . one more?'

'Yes. Rosie. Living with her partner whom I like a lot. He works with nature – a conservation officer?'

Francine nodded.

'And they've just had a little girl – Elsie. Old-fashioned name. Funny, really, how names come back.'

'And you love Rosie ze best?'

'Oh . . . I wouldn't want to . . .'

'But it is obvious. She is ze one who captures your heart?'

'Is it that obvious? Yes; she's the one. The one who under-stands me; the one I feel closest to. You try, as a parent, not to have favourites, but sometimes you just have to be honest with yourself and admit that you feel closer to one of them than the others. At least, that was the case with me and mine. Not that I wanted it to be that way. I'd have happily been close to all of them but . . . Well, Isobel always used to say that I didn't really try hard enough with Oliver and Alice.'

'And you did not see it zat way?'

'No. I tried as hard as I could, but there comes a time when you just have to admit that you're never going to get any closer. The lines just seem to get crossed. So I tried to work out some kind of compromise; to do what I could when I was asked but not to assume . . . well, Rosie was more loving than I would ever have expected, so I consider myself very lucky really.'

Francine held up her empty glass to the waiter, who swiftly refilled it. 'And Isobel? What was she like?'

'Oh dear. I seem to be treating this as a confessional. Are you sure you really want to sit and listen to all this?'

Francine reached across the table and put her hand on his. 'I would not ask you if I did not want to hear.' She squeezed his hand and then withdrew hers.

'Isobel was bright, sparky, opinionated, devoted to her children and . . . I suppose the truth of the matter is that we drifted into a relationship that was simply convenient.'

'You did not love her?'

'Oh, yes, I did love her. It was just that it seemed almost impossible to get on her wavelength towards the end. I did wonder, sometimes, if she actually noticed I was there. And then I would think that it was me who wasn't making enough effort. Being assertive enough. But it seemed impossible to change things by then. As though I were desperate. So I just settled for what we had; and there were the children to think of. I'm not stupid enough to think that marriage is all bells and whistles – it simply can't be sustained like that – but Isobel and I seemed to have hardly any common ground by the time she . . . by the time she died. If you want me to be perfectly honest, I think I failed.'

Timothy paused and looked away. 'But I'm getting morose. And self-pitying. Not attractive qualities.' He took another sip of wine. 'But life moves on. Life *has* moved on, and here I am on the verge of my awfully big adventure.'

Francine fixed him with a look. 'From which you will 'ave to return at some point and go back to . . . what?'

Timothy met her gaze. 'I don't know. I'll cross that bridge when I come to it. But there has to be more to life than making wardrobes.'

'*Pardon?*'

'Oh, nothing. I'm quite good with my hands, that's all. It is one way of being useful to my children – all of them.'

'I sink you underestimate yourself.'

'Really?'

'You are a talented man. I can tell from your painting. You 'ave the eye.'

'And you? You run a gallery, but do you paint as well?'

Francine shook her head and smiled. 'Interior design, zat was my talent.'

'Was?'

'Oh, I grew tired of tricky clients wiz . . . 'ow you say . . . more money zan taste. So I opened my gallery and now I enjoy myself much more . . . most of ze time.'

'But . . .' Timothy hesitated. 'There is no Monsieur Faragon?'

'Not any more.'

Timothy waited, unsure whether to press the matter.

'We parted a year ago now. He was . . . is . . . an actor. In French films. You would not know 'im.'

'I'm sorry.'

'It is not necessary. Like you . . . but differently . . . we 'ad very little in common by ze end. And I am . . . 'ow you say . . . a one-woman man . . .'

'I think you mean a one-man woman . . .'

Francine smiled ruefully. 'Exactly. Alain was not a one-woman man.'

'Oh dear.'

'Yes. Oh dear.' Francine brightened. 'So now I am a one-dog woman!'

Almost without thinking, Timothy murmured, 'What a shame.' And then, feeling a little embarrassed, added, 'I mean, you deserve . . . well . . . better.'

Francine evinced a mock-frown. 'Proust would be very upset to hear you say zat.'

Timothy laughed. 'Please give my apologies to Monsieur Proust and tell him he is a very lucky dog!'

Francine threw her hands into the air. 'Does he appreciate it? *Non!* He is just as tricky as any man. He does not deserve me, of zat I am sure.'

'Coffee?' asked Timothy.

'*Non, merci.*'

'Mint tea?'

Francine looked at him sideways. 'Ow did you know?'

'Oh, just . . . you look like a mint tea girl, that's all.'

'A mint tea *girl*?'

'Well, I mean, you're young . . . younger than me . . . it's just that . . .'

'I am very flattered. But I am forty already . . .'

'As I said, a girl . . .'

'M'sieur Tom, would you sink me very . . . forward . . . if I asked you back for coffee?'

'Well . . . I . . . no, but . . .'

'Zen please come back for coffee. I live above ze gallery. It is a short walk. I will show you . . . 'ow you say . . . my etchings?'

Timothy laughed. He could not remember enjoying another woman's company so much for quite some time.

11

GALERIE BLEU, PARIS

MAY

'A kiss can be a comma, a question mark or an exclamation point. That's basic spelling that every woman ought to know.'

Mistinguett (French actress), 1875–1956

The first thing he noticed was the large painting on the wall, and its similarity to the one hanging in the apartment of Madame Lamont. 'This is what I imagined somehow.'

'*Pardon?*'

'Your taste. I thought it would be modern, and I was right.'

'Am I so predictable?'

'No. Not at all. Far from it. I mean . . . you dress so stylishly and you have . . . *élan*. What I mean is . . . chic. Yes, that's it . . . chic.'

'Why sank you, *m'sieur*. I am very flattered!'

Timothy felt like some gauche teenager being taken back to his first girlfriend's apartment. 'Oh dear. I'm not doing very well am I?'

Francine smiled. 'Sit down. I will make coffee. I am guessing you would like coffee?'

'Please.'

She disappeared into the small kitchen which led off the large sitting room on the floor above her gallery. They had walked past its inner door and up the stairs, and he had noticed that the gallery was hung from floor to ceiling with various views of Paris – some were abstract in composition, but most were more figurative; the kind of works that well-heeled tourists would be happy to take home as a souvenir of their visit to the city of the Eiffel Tower and the Arc de Triomphe, the Tuileries and the Bois de Boulogne. Sculptures stood on white plinths and cellophane-wrapped prints, for those of more modest means, were stacked on shelves down one side of the gallery.

He looked around him now that he was briefly on his own in her apartment. Two white sofas faced one another across a low Louis Vuitton trunk that did service as a coffee table. Large tea canisters topped with vast cream shades offered a cool glow on glass side tables. Above a glass console table against the wall hung a massive seascape – the effect was that of looking through a vast window above the city and out towards the far, far distant sea – the sky a mixture of pale blue and soft yellow – the kind of clear light that occurred above the ocean in the aftermath of a thunderstorm when the waves had settled once more and the beach was freshly laundered at the hands of nature.

Copies of *Vogue* and *Elle* were neatly stacked on the floor and a marble bust of Napoleon gazed at him with a critical eye from the same sort of white-painted plinth he had noticed in the gallery below. He lowered himself on to a sofa and tried to avoid the emperor's basilisk stare.

'Someone wants to see you,' came the voice from the kitchen. At which point a snuffling and a scuffling of paws on the polished wooden floor heralded the arrival of Proust who looked at Timothy balefully before turning tail and heading for the small round bed that lay underneath the console table. He was, thought Timothy, no more impressed than he had been at their first meeting in Versailles.

Soft music began to play. The words were those of Charles Trenet and *La Mer*. Timothy laughed softly to himself and then said, as Francine walked back into the room with a tray of coffee and mint tea, 'Are you trying to give me the ultimate French experience?'

'But of course! If I 'ad put on ze Rolling Stones it would be . . . 'ow you say . . . inappropriate.'

'Just so.' Timothy leaned back on the sofa. 'I *do* like Paris,' he said with feeling.

'And the Parisians?' she asked.

'Yes. Oh, I've heard all those stories about how Parisians are uncooperative and surly, but in my experience, if you make the effort . . . try to speak the language . . . they are very . . . pleasant.'

Francine came and sat beside him. He was a little surprised, having expected her to sit opposite.

'Pleasant?'

'Yes.'

She handed him a small and delicate mug of coffee from the tray. 'Milk? Sugar?'

'No. Neither. Thank you.' He took the mug and smiled at her. Then, looking around the room said, 'This is very nice.'

Francine picked up her mug of mint tea and cradled it in her hands, then flipped off the black Christian Louboutin shoes she had been wearing all evening and tucked her feet underneath her on the sofa. Her body was wrapped in a small black dress that showed off her figure to perfection; her legs were encased in black tights and a row of small jet beads hung at her neck. He could not remember being so close to such beauty for a long while. It all seemed completely unreal. Her perfume gave him a frisson of excitement which he tried to ignore.

There was a moment of unease until she said, 'Well, Tom, 'ere you are, on ze brink of your adventure. 'Ow do you feel? Are you excited?'

Aware of the double meaning – intended or otherwise – of Francine's remark, Timothy took a deep breath and said, 'Yes; I suppose so. Excited and a little apprehensive. Wondering what will happen along the way and . . . if it will change me, I suppose. Alter my outlook on life.'

'Do you want it to?'

He was silent for a moment. Then said, 'Yes. I do. I don't want to come back the same man I was when I set off. Yes; I do want to change, in that I want to be more positive . . . and to find out a bit more about myself.' He paused, then asked, 'Does that sound odd for a man of my age? It's twenty-some-things who are meant to take gap years and discover themselves.'

Francine shook her head. 'Not at all. You find yourself in different circumstances and you are wondering what ze future holds. It seems to me to be perfectly natural.'

He took a sip of coffee and then said, 'Good. I do wonder sometimes if I'm quite mad. If I shouldn't just settle for . . .'

'Making wardrobes?'

He stopped and looked at her. 'What do you mean?'

'You said earlier about wardrobes. You did not expect me to understand. But I did understand. You must say to yourself zat you are worse more zan a flat-pack wardrobe.'

The red wine had clearly taken effect, for he leaned over and kissed her on the cheek.

'Zat was nice.'

'You've been very kind,' he said. 'And I'm very grateful. You've set me off on my Grand Tour in the best way possible.'

'Ze pleasure was all mine,' she said softly.

Timothy got up from the sofa. 'And now I really must go before Madame Lamont locks me out and I have to spend the night under the bridges of Paris.'

'Zay are not all zay are cracked up to be,' offered Francine as she got up and walked towards the door. 'I will see you down ze stairs.'

'No. Really. I can find my own way out.'

'But I 'ave to lock ze door behind you.'

'Oh, yes. Of course.'

They walked down in silence. The lights in the gallery had gone out now, so all Timothy could see through the inner door were the shadows cast by sculptures in the pale street lights. They made strange, surreal patterns across the gallery land-scape. He turned at the doorway to bid her goodnight, and as he did so she reached up and kissed him on the lips. Slowly. Tenderly. Her arms about his waist. Then she rested her head upon his chest and murmured softly, 'I wish you did not 'ave to go.'

He squeezed her gently and said, 'So do I.'

Then he slowly lowered his arms, paused for a moment and walked off silently into the Parisian night. As he traced his steps back to the Hôtel La Cocotte, the words of Charles Trenet and *La Mer* kept running through his head.

12

MUSÉE RODIN, PARIS

MAY

'People don't talk in Paris,
they just look lovely . . . and eat.'

Henry 'Chips' Channon (1871-1958), Diary, 1951

It was Francine who had recommended the Musée Rodin as a place to visit. She thought he would find the small house in the Rue de Varrenne more to his liking than the crowded Louvre. 'Go just after it opens in ze morning,' she had instructed, and so he did, but with his mind still whirling after the events of the night before.

True to his word he had refrained from using his mobile phone to call home. Part of him worried that he was being selfish, and that he would be out of touch if Rosie – or, less likely, Alice – needed him, but he consoled himself that he had explained to Rosie why that was, and he doubted that Oliver and Vita would give a fig. He found time, before he left the Hôtel La Cocotte, to write his younger daughter a letter.

My Dear Rosie,

I do hope all's well with you. You'll be pleased to hear that so far 'Gay Paree' has lived up to its name. I have been to Versailles, which was astonishingly grand and very atmospheric. I really did feel that the Sun King and his retinue might round the corner in an elegant rococo carriage at any moment and that we tourists would fall into a deep bow as they passed by. The Louvre was a bit of a disappointment. Well, not the museum itself (though I am not sure about the glass pyramid outside) but the welter of tourists. It was so difficult to see <u>anything</u>. The Mona Lisa was something of a let-down, but then I could not really see her above the heads of hordes of students and their 'selfie sticks'. (Am I turning into a grumpy tourist? I hope not.) I will go back at a quieter time of day. My boat trip on the river was a <u>delight</u>, and Notre Dame hugely impressive – gloomy, lofty and reeking of incense (which your mother would not have enjoyed!), but perhaps the most impressive thing of all was Napoleon's Tomb at Les Invalides – absolutely monumental. I could see in my mind's eye that little man lying inside, satisfied that at least in death they had chosen to remember him in grand fashion. His sarcophagus is a massive great lump of red quartzite, hewn into a kind of enclosed cradle which is overwhelming in its magnitude. (I am beginning to sound like a travel guide!)

You will be pleased to know (I hope) that I have bought some watercolours and started to paint again. Nothing too dramatic – just a few views that you (and I) might enjoy looking at on my return – souvenirs of my very own Grand Tour. I will start dipping into Addison's Travels once I reach Monaco – my next stop and his first – but for now I am simply an 'accidental tourist', going where the whim takes me. Today I plan to visit the Musée Rodin which was recommended by someone I met here.

I enjoyed my three nights at the Hôtel Plaza Athénée but am now staying in a much more reasonably priced hotel called La Cocotte. It is small but central and has – unbelievably – an English landlady! I will be here until next Tuesday. I think it best to travel midweek when I can to avoid weekend rushes. My next stop is Monaco and I have, I am afraid, booked three nights in another smart hotel: if one is to see Monte Carlo properly then I think one needs to experience the full effect. (Did that sound like a good excuse?!) I shall be staying in the Hôtel Hermitage, just so you know where I am. I have not booked all my accommodation in advance because that would nail me to an itinerary and I want to enjoy the freedom to move on when I choose and when I feel I have had enough of one place. Though, to be honest, I would be happy to stay in Paris for rather longer than I shall. The boulevards are ravishing in their spring greenery and there is an excitement about the place that I am coming to love.

Don't worry about me, though I do think about you all the time – and Ace and little Elsie. I hope she's doing well and that her teething is not keeping you up all night. I have made a promise to myself that I will bring something back for her that will remind her of my trip when she is grown up – her mad grandfather who suddenly took himself off to travel the world – or part of it - when she was still in her cradle.

So there we are for now. I will write when I reach Monaco and let you know what I think of it. In the meantime I have the music of Charles Trenet ringing in my ears. Do you know him – and his songs? They are wonderfully atmospheric. <u>Very</u> French. Oh, and I met a rather nice gallery owner who bumped into me while I was painting in Versailles and asked if I would agree to sell some of my paintings in her gallery! Can you believe it? She is very pleasant and I may well do one or two that I can leave there. They may raise enough money to buy me an ice cream!

That's all for now. I hope the house is working out OK, and remember that you are always in my thoughts. Although I am enjoying myself I cannot wait to see you all again.

With so much love,

Dad xxx

He popped the letter in a postbox, Madame Lamont having furnished him with a stamp, on the way to the Rue de Varenne, and arrived to find that only part of the Musée Rodin was open due to renovation work. At first he wondered whether it would be worth going in, but admission was free and having arrived it seemed churlish to walk away. He was not disappointed. He enjoyed the intimate atmosphere of the house and was surprised at the sheer quantity of art on display in the various rooms and the annexe where some works had been moved temporarily. Turning a corner he found himself face to face with Van Gogh's painting of Dr Gachet, which was hanging alongside a set of French windows, the sun streaming in over its impasto brushwork. Timothy shook his head in disbelief. It was refreshing, somehow, to see a painting hanging so naturally, rather than in the hallowed confines and restricted light of a gallery. Clearly a century or more of sunlight had done it little harm. The old man's eyes gazed mistily past him, as though he were lost in thought.

Bronze and marble sculptures were displayed everywhere – standing on the floor or raised high on simple plinths. Most impressive of all was the one enormous white marble sculpture that sat in the centre of a kind of loggia, again with the sunlight streaming in and highlighting its contours. The couple sat with their arms entwined, lost in the moment and in their love for one another. He knew the sculpture well, though he had never before set eyes on it in the flesh – or rather the marble. The Kiss. For several minutes he stood rooted to the spot and simply stared – at the angle of the bodies; at the man's hand resting gently on the woman's milk-white thigh. Then he walked slowly around the pallid couple who towered above him, lost in their love for one another, totally oblivious to the world for all eternity.

There was a tenderness to the image that took his mind back to the evening before, not that for much of the morning the memory had been out of his mind. How long was it since he had been kissed on the lips? How long since anyone had shown him that sort of affection? It was too long ago to remember. There came over him, as he gazed upon the two lovers, a mixture of emotions – of sadness at the diminution of physical love that his life had undergone, and of excitement that the tenderness of the previous evening had awoken in him. He half wanted to believe that it might lead to something; half told himself that it was nothing more than a grateful gesture, best remembered fondly then put to one side. In a few days he would be gone and the chances of ever seeing Francine again were minimal. And, anyway, the French were like that, weren't they? The events of the night before would mean no more to Francine than . . . a pleasant interlude with an Englishman. That was all. Wasn't it?

13

MONTMARTRE AND THE BOIS DE BOULOGNE, PARIS

MAY

'*Ce qui n'est pas clair n'est pas Francais.*'
(What is not clear is not French)

Antoine de Rivarol, *Discours sur l'Universalité de la
Langue Francaise*, 1784

For the following two days Timothy did not see Francine. He
thought it best to keep his distance for a while. He took a day to
explore the Left Bank and the cemetery at Montmartre. He had
no idea that so many writers, artists and musicians were buried
there – Hector Berlioz and Edgar Degas, the family of Emile Zola,
the eccentric king of operetta Jacques Offenbach – he of can-can
fame – and the ballet dancer Nijinsky, whose grave was decorated
with the statue of a clown. That, and the tomb of the French
farceur Georges Feydeau seemed to point up, somehow, the
absurdity of the previous day. He walked and occasionally sat and
sketched, then with aching feet and a whirling mind he was content
to spend the evening in the quiet of his room, reading guidebooks

and putting finishing touches to a couple of small watercolours – one of the distant Notre Dame and another view across the cemetery, with Nijinsky's clown in the foreground. It seemed an appropriate image for the first part of his tour.

The following day he left the Hôtel La Cocotte by 9am and went for a stroll in the Bois de Boulogne to clear his head. It would be his penultimate day in Paris. Having planned to leave for Monaco in two days' time, he had booked his train journey and the three nights at the Hôtel Hermitage, having decided against moving on to more reasonably priced accommodation just yet. The plan had worked well in Paris, thanks to Francine's intervention, but such an encounter was unlikely to happen again – an understatement of which he was more than aware – and he felt reassured that for the three days he considered sufficient to take in the sights of the millionaire's playground he would not be tramping the streets with a suitcase looking for a bed in something rather better than a Youth Hostel.

He enjoyed the relative calm of the Bois de Boulogne, and the brisk walk between the water and the trees, but the fine weather of the preceding few days was beginning to deteriorate and he was caught for a while in a heavy shower. The sky looked threatening; there was a distant rumble of thunder and then the heavens opened. He sheltered beneath some towering pines, enjoying the fruity fragrance enhanced by the shower but, despite having taken his watercolours with him, found no opportunity to use them thanks to the rain.

By early afternoon the weather had brightened up and he took out his sketch pad and began to work up a view of water and trees and a distant Japanese-looking folly perched on an eminence. It would take his mind off the events of the previous evening, or so he thought.

He stayed until late afternoon and then, satisfied that the

small painting was finished, he packed his equipment into the canvas bag, slung it over his shoulder and went back to the hotel.

Reluctant to disturb Madame Lamont – for he could hear her moving about in her apartment through the partially open door – he climbed the stairs quietly and let himself into his room. Dumping his painting bag on the floor he opened the long windows to let in some air, washed his hands and face at the basin and then flopped on the bed.

He awoke with a start. He had not expected to fall asleep, but clearly the frenetic pace of the previous few days had caught up with him. He felt weary, though partially refreshed by sleep. How long had it been? He glanced at his watch. It was eight o'clock. He had slept for two hours. He felt hungry, and remembered that he had not eaten lunch. He would slip out and find a small bar or café where he could have a light supper before retiring to bed early. And the following day? What should he do? He could not keep avoiding Francine. Or would that be for the best? Should this relationship – not that it yet qualified for that description – be nipped in the bud?

His mind ran over the events that had occurred back home before he left; of Oliver and Vita's attitude to his departure. What would they think if they knew what had happened two nights ago? What would Rosie think? But then, nothing at all had happened. Why should one kiss take on such significance? It was a kiss – a friendly gesture, that was all. And yet he knew – or at least suspected – that there was more to it than a casual peck on the cheek. Round and round in his head waltzed the memories of his dinner with Francine, but he came to no conclusion.

He got up from the bed and picked up Addison's Travels, but the words seemed too ancient to penetrate his consciousness, littered as they were with Latin epigrams: *Aggeribus socer Alpinis atque arce Monoeci Descendens*. Virg.

He had not studied Latin at school, and his only encounter with Virgil had been the character in *Thunderbirds*. He felt momentarily embarrassed by his ignorance, closed the book and laid it gently on the dressing table.

He was contemplating the likely outcome of the evening when there was a gentle tap at his door. Madame Lamont had not, so far, ventured this far up into the building. He walked over to the door and opened it, to find Francine standing on the small landing. It was clear from her face that she had been crying.

At first she spoke only in French, words that spilled out so fast that he could make no sense of them. He sat her on the bed and offered her a handkerchief, remembering that the last time he had done so it had been given to his daughter on their parting at St Pancras Station. Gradually the tears subsided and Francine blew her nose loudly on his handkerchief, then looked at him apologetically. He gestured that it did not matter and she clutched tightly at the square of fabric, dabbing at an errant tear as it coursed down her cheek.

'Tell me what it is. Slowly,' instructed Timothy.

'I am sorry. I should not 'ave come to you. It is not to do wiz you. Why should you care?'

'Because . . . I am a friend,' he said, wondering at the same time why Francine had chosen to unburden herself to him rather than Madame Lamont, who was not only closer to street level but was also an older and more familiar confidante.

'It 'as not been a good day,' Francine confided.

'I rather gathered that,' murmured Timothy, intending to make light of the matter and jolly her along.

'You do not understand. Two years ago, when I opened ze

gallery, I took out a loan to 'elp me get started. Ze repayments were large but I worked out zat I could afford zem. For ze first year it was not a problem. Sales were good and I managed to make ze repayments and everysing was OK.'

'I see.' Timothy felt that he knew what was coming.

'Zis year, under Monsieur Hollande, sings 'ave not been so good. Sales are down and I 'ave been told zat if I do not pay what I owe by ze end of ze week my gallery will 'ave to close and I will 'ave to move out. I shall lose my gallery and my *appartement* and . . . everysing.' Her eyes began to fill with tears once more.

Timothy took her hand and squeezed it, by way of reassurance. 'Is there nothing you can do? Can they not give you more time?'

Francine shook her head.

'Have you told Madame Lamont?'

Francine looked up at him mournfully. 'Zat will do no good.'

'But why? Madame Lamont is a good friend isn't she?'

'Madame Lamont is my . . . ow you say? . . . landlady. It is she who demands ze rent.'

Timothy regarded her incredulously. 'It is Madame Lamont who is threatening to put you out on the street?'

'*Oui*. She was a good friend but she 'as said zat zere is a limit to friendship and she 'as to make a living.'

'Good God! How dreadful!'

Francine blew her nose again and endeavoured to regain her composure. 'I am sorry. I should not 'ave told you all zis, but I 'ave just come from seeing 'er and I felt I 'ad to tell somebody.'

'But how much does she need? To let you stay, I mean?

'Twenty thousand euros.' For the first time Francine pronounced the diphthong, as if to make the point more forcefully.

Timothy whistled. 'That's a lot of money. When would that take you through until?'

'*Pardon?*'

'If you pay her twenty thousand euros, how long will you be able to keep the gallery open?'

'For anozer year. Sales are getting better; I keep telling 'er, but she says zat enough is enough and she cannot give me any longer. I 'ave tried to pay 'er wiz paintings but she says zat is no longer . . . acceptable.'

'Would it help if I had a word with Madame Lamont?'

Francine shook her head. 'Please do not. I would not want 'er to think that I 'ad told you about it. She would say it was none of your business.'

Timothy got up from the bed. 'Come on. Dry your eyes. We're going out.'

'But . . .'

'No buts; we need to work out what can be done.'

'I do not believe anysing can be done.'

'Well, that's where you're wrong. Come on . . .'

He took her arm and lifted her up from the bed. 'Do you need to freshen up?' he asked.

She nodded.

He gestured towards the bathroom. 'I'll meet you by the front door when you're ready.' And then, ignoring her protestations, he grabbed his jacket from the hook at the back of the door, left the room and walked softly down the stairs. He hoped that Madame Lamont might make an appearance, but the door to her *appartement* was firmly closed and no sounds – not even the squawking of a parrot – came from within.

Over a bottle of Beaujolais in a nearby bar, and the largest platter of cheeses Timothy had ever seen, Francine explained the full story of how she came to know Madame Lamont and how Madame – and her husband who was alive at that point – had come to finance her gallery. Monsieur Lamont, it transpired, was godfather to Francine's former husband, Alain. When the marriage broke up the Lamonts had felt guilty that Francine had been so let down, and did their best to help out by financing the gallery and the apartment above. Then Monsieur Lamont had died.

Alain had refused to let matters rest and had regularly complained to his godfather's widow that Francine herself had been responsible for the break-up and that he, Alain, had never wanted it to happen. It was Francine, he maintained, who had been unfaithful, not him.

'So why has all this suddenly come to a head?' asked Timothy.

Francine bowed her head. 'Because Madame Lamont saw me wiz you last night. She had been out to a friend's for dinner and the car she was in was passing by when we said goodnight.'

'But she can't think that . . . I mean . . . one kiss.'

'She said zat you were an hotel guest who 'ad been 'ere just a few days and it was clear zat I was making a play for you. She said it was ze last straw. She could see zat what Alain said was true and zat she 'ad given me enough chances. It was time for me to go.'

'But that's completely wrong!'

'I know zat and so do you but . . .'

'Let me go and tell her.'

'No. It would do no good. She said as much. Said zat whatever you said would count for nothing. I told her zat you could tell her we were just good friends but she waved me away. She said her patience 'ad run out. If ze money was paid zen she would turn – ow you say? – a blind eye. But if I did not pay, zen I would 'ave to leave.'

Timothy sipped at his wine and thought for a moment. 'What if I were to lend you the money? He said.

14

OPÉRA GARNIER, PARIS

MAY

'I do not mind what language an opera is sung in so long as it is a language I don't understand.'

Edward Appleton (English physicist), *Observer*, 1955

It was, insisted Francine the following evening, to be her treat. She would take him to the Opéra Garnier. It was the least she could do to thank him for his kindness, which was, she kept repeating, '*incroyable*' and '*magnifique*'. Something at the back of his mind told him that he was being rash, irresponsible, foolhardy. But he didn't care. He wanted to help her; had helped her. The money had been transferred into her account and Madame Lamont had remained silent in her apartment, the door firmly closed each time he went down, but the sword of Damocles had been lifted from Francine's head and Madame had reluctantly conceded that she could remain at the gallery for another year.

'What are we going to see?' he enquired.

'Mozart. *Der Zauberflöte.*'

'The Magic Flute? I know it. A bit. Well, some of the music.'

'Do you like opera?'

'Some opera. Not all. I *do* like Mozart, but I'm not into all that heavy stuff, Wagner and the like. And Richard Strauss. It's a bit beyond me I'm afraid.'

'You should keep trying with Wagner,' said Francine, as they walked up the steps of the opera house, her arm through his. The sensation was one of elation; that he had been able to help her; that she clearly enjoyed his company and not, he hoped, simply because he had been able to help her out financially.

'I remember something about Wagner,' he said.

'Mmm?'

'Wagner has wonderful moments . . . but dreadful quarters of an hour.'

Francine giggled appreciatively. 'Whoever said zat needs to try 'arder.'

'Maybe another time.'

They walked up the ornate staircase and Timothy found himself overwhelmed by the décor and the atmosphere. 'It's huge! I had no idea.'

'Look out for ze phantom,' teased Francine.

As they took their seats Timothy felt dwarfed by the grandeur of the place – pillars and pilasters towered like lofty trees, their branches turning into foliate finials; gilt and red plush enveloped them. The stupendous scale of the place – the buzz of the audience stacked in semicircular tiers from floor to the incongruous Chagall-painted ceiling, added to the thrill of being here. The chandelier shone like so many diamonds but none of this spectacle compared, in his eyes, with the person sitting next to him. She wore a milk-white cashmere wrap over a silk blouse and dark brown trousers, her hair shone like jet and her red lips, white teeth and green eyes mesmerised him at every glance.

She smiled at him and squeezed his arm as the lights dimmed and the overture began . . .

He knew, in his heart of hearts that it was all too much, too soon, but he did not care. Her hand rested on his arm throughout the performance; the warmth of it was intense. In the interval they drank champagne in the ornately decorated bar.

'Are you enjoying it?' asked Francine.

'Immensely,' replied Timothy. 'It's amazing. I mean, not just the place, but the opera, too.' He paused, then added, 'And the company.'

Francine lowered her eyes. 'You are very kind. Too kind.'

Timothy put his hand under her chin and lifted her face. 'Thank you for making my stay so special.'

She kissed him gently on the cheek and then looked at him without speaking. Her eyes sparkled as she said, '*Serendipite.*'

'Does that mean what I think it means?' asked Timothy.

'Good fortune. Yes?'

'A lucky chance encounter?'

'Very lucky. For me at least.'

Timothy made no reply, but lowered his hand and briefly stroked hers as the bell rang to signal the end of the interval. They took their seats once more, and it was during the second act that Timothy felt the strangest sensations creeping over him. As the Queen of the Night's soaring aria rent the air, he sensed that somehow that he might have made a dreadful mistake. He had known Francine for just a few days, and here he was with her, their chance encounter seemingly on the cusp of developing into something altogether more serious.

'Verstossen sei auf ewig
Verlassen sei auf ewig

Zertrümmert sei'n auf ewig
Alle bande der Natur'

sang the Queen of the Night in supremely threatening tones to
her daughter.

The words, in German, although unknown to him, somehow
transmitted their message to his subconscious:

'Disowned may you be forever
Abandoned may you be forever
Destroyed be forever all the bonds of Nature.'

He wondered what his children would make of his actions.
Well, if he were honest, realistic, he knew exactly what they
would make of them. Oliver and Vita would be apoplectic. Even
Rosie would find it hard to understand why he had been so
rash as to part with more than fifteen thousand pounds to a
French woman fifteen years younger than he was, whom he
had known for less than a week. They would think that he had
completely lost his marbles; that he was not fit to be let out
alone, never mind to be allowed to gallop off around Europe
on some foolhardy trip. Perhaps he should have offered to invest
in her gallery, rather than simply hand over the money, but then
that would have been to ask for something in return and his
heart would not let him do that. His heart; not his head. Had
he made the classic mistake of letting the one rule the other?
Of course he had, but he had an instinctive feel that this was
the right thing to do. Was he impulsive? Not normally but in
this case most certainly. Was he foolish?

Who could tell? Rash, certainly.

They were thoughts that he did his best to banish from his
mind later that evening when Francine invited him up to her

apartment. Yes, the voice in his head told him it was unwise. But when she turned towards him having closed the door, put her arms around his waist and leaned up and kissed him tenderly on the lips, he knew he was lost. The softness of her skin, the scent of her body and its warmth aroused in him sensations he thought were no longer his to enjoy.

Nipping his lips with her teeth she slid the jacket from his shoulders and began to unbutton his shirt.

Surely she could feel his heart thumping? Her body was pressed close to his, her breath fell softly upon his cheek. This was not happening. This could not be happening. Not to him. He found himself unbuttoning her blouse, his hands slipping inside and caressing the breasts that lay behind a silken chemise. She stood away from him slightly now, her eyes fixing his as she slipped off her blouse, pulled the chemise over her head and stood in front of him naked to the waist. She, too, was breathing heavily now, her lips parted and her eyes unblinking. Very slowly she raised her arms and held them out towards him. He stepped forward and grasped her shoulders, forcing his lips on to hers with a passion borne of years of denial. The gentle undressing became more hurried and more desperate on both their parts, and within a matter of minutes they were in bed and lost in one another. Lost . . . and found.

15

APPARTEMENT GALERIE BLEU AND GARE DE LYON, PARIS

MAY

'*Bon coeur ne peut mentir.*'
(The heart sees further than the head.)

French proverb

In one way the parting reminded Timothy of his departure from St Pancras, and yet in so many others it was quite different. It had crossed his mind to abandon travelling, at least for the time being, and to stay in Paris with Francine. He was a free agent, after all; there was no fixed itinerary to follow. But when they woke up that morning, lying side by side, she had gently stroked his cheek and said, 'I will miss you, Tom.'

He was unsure of the implication. For one dreadful, hollow moment he thought that it might all have been a ploy, simply to get him to part with money, and now that he had fulfilled his role he was surplus to requirements. Then he banished the thought as being unworthy of him – and of Francine. 'I don't have to go,' he had said.

Francine put her finger on his lips. 'You must. You 'ave your plan – your Grand Tour.' And then, as though she was aware of the doubt that might be creeping into his mind, 'I shall still be 'ere when you get back, and I shall want to know all about it.'

He lay on his side, gazing at her, their two naked bodies only inches from one another. He wanted this moment to last; wanted to savour the warmth of her being, the softness of her skin. Slowly he ran his finger down her side, from her ribcage past her narrow waist to her slender thigh, then rested his hand there and remembered, quite out of the blue, Rodin's white marble statue. It was all he could do to hold back the tears – tears of joy and relief at the opportunity to display emotion, to let go, to risk being hurt if necessary.

She leaned forward and gently kissed his forehead, then turned and looked at the clock on the bedside table. It was 7.45am. 'What time is your train?'

He made light of it. 'It doesn't matter. I can go when I'm ready.'

'*Non*. You 'ave your ticket. What time does it leave?'

'Nineteen minutes past eleven.'

She slipped out of bed and he watched her walk naked over to the bathroom. The perfect slender figure – curved in all the right places. His heart missed more than a beat. Never in his wildest dreams did he imagine that he would ever experience such an encounter. Then a sharp stab of guilt as the past hove into view and reminded him of how much his life had changed in just a few short months. She disappeared through the door and he turned over onto his back and gazed at the ceiling, his mind whirling. Should he go or should he stay? Francine seemed quite intent on the latter, but for the time being at least all thoughts of travel had somehow deserted him. What could be better than staying here with this beautiful woman, seeing the sights by day and then making love at night?

His train of thought was broken by her emergence from the bathroom in a pair of elegant cream silk pyjamas.

'Pyjamas?' he said, involuntarily.

'*Oui*. I normally wear zem, but for you I make ze exception.' She smiled, teasingly, and came and sat on the bed. She reached out her arm and stroked a strand of hair from his forehead.

'I can't believe it really,' he murmured. 'Did it really happen?'

She was resting her hand on his naked shoulder now. 'I sink so. I 'ope so.'

'I didn't mean to . . .'

She put her finger on his lips once more. 'I know. I did not mean to either.'

'What a pair we are.'

Her face changed to a worried expression. 'When I say you should go, you must not misunderstand me. I enjoy being wiz you. More zan enjoy . . . But I sink you should go. It was what you set out to do and I would not want to stop you.' Her pyjama jacket was unbuttoned and from where he lay he could see her left breast beneath the silk. He lifted his hand and gently stroked it, looking into her eyes for some kind of sign. She raised her own hand and held his there for a moment, then she got up from the bed and walked towards the window, drawing the fabric about her and opening the shutters to let in the stream of morning light.

'It is a beautiful day. You will see ze scenery all ze way down to Provence.'

'I rather like the scenery here,' he said. And then, risking her scorn he said, 'Come back. For a moment. Well, for rather longer than a moment . . .'

She looked at him, raised her arms in mock disbelief, then

smiled the smile he found so disarming. She lowered her arms and let the silken jacket fall to the floor, then, pushing the waistband downwards, she stepped out of the pyjama trousers and walked slowly towards the bed. Timothy's heart beat so fast that he thought it must be visible through the bedclothes.

'We cannot stay for long,' she whispered in his ear, before showering him with kisses. It did occur to him that it would not look good if he were to expire here, now, in her bed – killed by a surfeit of pleasure at the age of fifty-five in the arms of a French woman fifteen years his junior. But he quickly convinced himself that there would be far worse ways to die.

The journey to the Gare de Lyon was mercifully quick, the bulk of the Paris traffic having abated, but Francine was still visibly anxious that he should not miss his train. She accompanied him to the platform, his mind in a turmoil of emotions – unsure of himself, unsure of Francine, unsure of what the future held, unsure still whether to go or stay. Her questioning at least made him think of other things, albeit temporarily.

'How long will ze journey take?' she asked.

'Just over six hours.'

'Do you 'ave to change trains?'

'At Nice.'

'Could you not get a train to go straight zare?'

'Yes, but not until this afternoon and then I would arrive too late to sort out my hotel. Well, too late to enjoy it at any rate.'

'*Mon Dieu*! Where will you stay? I forget to ask?'

'I've booked three nights at the Hôtel Hermitage. It should be enough to see Monaco. I thought I'd do it in style. In other places, like Florence, I shall look for a smaller hotel. Like I did in Paris. Except that I didn't have to look. This kind person I met found me a small hotel which was perfect.'

Francine smiled. 'It was my pleasure.'

'Oh, and mine. Mind you, Madame Lamont said very little when I checked out. She found it hard to meet my eye, which was unusual for her.'

'I would 'ave come wiz you but . . .'

'Oh, you were better outside in the taxi. I didn't want to complicate matters. I don't think I've ever left anywhere so quickly, but then Madame Lamont had already been paid – she took my credit card the moment I arrived, and I'd done a lot of packing last night – before you came.'

'She noticed your name' said Francine absently. 'When you checked in.'

'Yes.'

'Timosy.'

He looked at her intently. 'It's funny to hear you say that. I've got rather used to Tom.'

'What will you call yourself in Monaco?'

'Who knows? Hector? Vaslav?'

She laughed. 'Why Vaslav?'

'Someone I encountered a couple of days ago. Oh, I almost forgot.' Timothy unzipped the large pouch on one side of his suitcase and withdrew a cardboard-reinforced manila envelope. He handed it to Francine. 'A present.'

'But I 'ave 'ad ze best present anyone could give me. You do not need to give me anysing else.'

'But I promised it to you. When I came.'

She turned back the flap of the envelope and withdrew the roughly textured sheet of watercolour paper it contained. It was blank. Then she turned it over and beheld a small and intricate watercolour of Montmartre – the sky a soft shade of primrose yellow suffused with forget-me-not blue. In the fore-ground, at the foot of a headstone, sat a forlorn looking clown.

'Nijinsky' she murmured.

'For you. For the gallery if you want. Or to keep. I don't mind,' he said, minding deeply that she might sell it when he wanted her to have it as a memento.

Francine shook her head. 'Not to sell. To keep. In my *appartement*. I shall treasure it. It is quite beautiful.'

'Not too sad?' he asked.

'Very sad. His ending was tragic. He went mad. He was a great dancer.' She paused, then smiled and said, 'But he left behind 'appy memories. Just like you.'

The mood was broken by the tannoy playing the four notes that reminded him so much of a television yoghurt jingle back home. 'I must get on or I'll miss it. Or I could . . .'

'You must get on,' she said, sliding the watercolour back into its envelope. Then she grasped his arm. 'I will repay you, Tom,' she said.

Timothy pressed the button to open the train door. It was an agonising moment. He was going and yet he wanted to stay. He had planned this trip, it would be foolish not to continue. It was what he had dreamed of for years; he must leave Paris – and Francine – behind and continue the Grand Tour. But how could it be half as grand as it had been already, thanks to a woman he had known barely a week?

He stepped back from the train, put down his suitcase and holdall, threw his arms around her and hugged her. 'Call me. You have my number. Any time, night or day.'

'I will. I promise. And you must call me. You 'ave my 'ome number.'

He looked at her enquiringly.

'I wrote it on ze corner of your sketch pad.' She kissed him softly on the lips. 'Now go. *Bon voyage, mon cherie.*'

With the words echoing in his head he picked up the case

and the bag and stepped up on to the train. Quickly he found his seat which was on the upper level, though, to his relief, on the same side as the platform. The doors closed and his eyes swept the concourse in search of her. For one dreadful moment he thought that she must have left, but then he noticed her slightly to one side and waved madly. The train began to move. She had not seen him; he would not experience that final moment of eye contact that he would cherish on his travels. And then she spotted him, obliquely from across the platform. She ran along with the train as it began to move steadily away, then she slowed down and stood still as the double decker SNCF carriages gained momentum. The last thing he saw was the tear in her eye as she blew him a kiss and held her elegant hand aloft. Then he settled back into his seat and realised just how much he hated saying goodbye at railway stations.

16

PARIS TO MONTE CARLO

MAY

'The Riviera isn't only a sunny place for shady people.'

W. Somerset Maugham (1874–1965)

The benefit of a long train journey is that it gives you time to think. The problem for Timothy was that his thoughts were a jumble, and the train journey did not exist that was long enough to unravel them and set his mind in order. He had fondly imagined, when he was planning the trip in the comfort of his Sussex home, that he would be calm of mind and anticipatory of every new location on his Grand Tour. He had made absolutely no provision for falling in love. And that was what had happened, wasn't it? Or was he being ridiculous? 'There's no fool like an old fool,' that was the saying. Was he simply living proof of its veracity?

He tried breathing deeply. He looked at his mobile phone. He had told Rosie that he would not be using it except for emergencies, and yet here he was, knowing Francine's number and wanting to call her to tell her how desperately he was missing her. He slipped it back into his pocket. He could not possibly call Francine having told Rosie that he would only be writing. It seemed disloyal. If he picked up the phone now he would be slipping back into that daily habit of twenty-first century life. He must stick to his guns and live this trip as he had told himself he would – in true Grand Tour style.

But this was different. A different relationship. Didn't that make it all right? Wasn't it an absurd affectation to do without the technology of the modern world when it was available at the touch of a button? After all, he wasn't exactly using a quill and an inkwell. No answer was forthcoming.

He watched the scenery flying by – orchards and vineyards, rows of poplars planted alongside arrow-straight tracks, spacious fields and tiny hamlets. There seemed to be very few cities of any size on his chosen route, and not many towns either. The broad extent of the countryside surprised him. He had expected it to resemble the shires of Britain, certainly for the first part of the journey when the climate would be similar, but already it looked . . . foreign . . . even without many signs of industry or habitation. There was a vast, gaunt quality to it somehow, as if the wilder extravagances of nature had been swept away. Then, occasionally, civilisation would re-assert itself and a river, corralled within concrete banks, would snake alongside the railway track before darting underneath it and continuing its journey in another direction.

Lyon – a name he knew; a city at last. Some got off. More got on. The train slid smoothly out of the station. Large walls and warehouses defaced with graffiti (that much at least in common with home) would loom up and then be left behind, to be replaced by wide open fields of grass green or loamy grey that seemed to lack the intimacy of English enclosures, delineated by fences or drystone walls. The sky was pale grey now;

the light watery. It seemed to suit his mood. He would have preferred bright blue sky and brilliant sunshine, but it seemed he had left that behind in Paris, in more ways than one.

A stewardess with a trolley served small baguettes and coffee which he fell upon, not having eaten breakfast. He took out a writing pad and began a letter to Rosie, but his heart was not in it and he found it hard to concentrate. Instead he looked out of the window and watched as apple orchards began to be replaced by olive trees and orange groves and the landscape of Burgundy and the Rhône-Alpes frayed into the warm terrain of Provence and the Côte d'Azur.

It was such an enchanting name: the Côte d'Azur – redolent of shimmering seas and stuccoed villas, of elegant yachts and . . . wizened dowagers with poodles. Would it live up to expectations? Perhaps over the next few days, in the warmth of the Riviera sun, he would be able to put Francine to the back of his mind. Unless he did he knew that what stretched before him were weeks of mooning about like some love-sick youth, of dwelling on the immediate past and being incapable of looking to the future and fully involving himself in what lay ahead. This was his trip of a lifetime; could he cherish the last few days without allowing them to overshadow the future? And yet, like some tiny, niggling voice – perhaps even the ghost of Isobel – there remained the merest hint of doubt about the purity of Francine's motives in befriending him.

Incapable of totally banishing such thoughts from his mind – even though he told himself they were unworthy of him and unfair to her – he reconciled himself to the fact that he had had the time of his life, and if it were to cost him twenty thousand euros then so be it. Nevertheless he hoped, in his heart of hearts, that such was not the case. He wanted to believe in the devastatingly good-looking Parisian who had come into his life so suddenly, transformed his way of thinking, and left as abruptly as she had arrived. Oh, what would the family think? Enough. He must get a grip and buck up.

He took a modern guidebook from his holdall and began to read about Monaco and Monte Carlo: 'an international byword for the extravagant display and reckless dispersal of wealth.' It was a phrase that could well be applied to him for the next three days, staying in one of the principality's smartest hotels. The feeling of guilt that assailed him on account of such self-indulgence – in spite of having rehearsed the arguments before – was not totally overcome by his attempts to persuade himself that he was worth it and that Joseph Addison, being a man of means, would hardly have been accommodated in Monegasque hovels.

It would not have washed with Oliver and Vita. He mused on what his children would be doing while he was 'gadding off' on his travels. Oliver would be strutting his stuff in court, holding his lapels and puffing out his chest. Vita would be playing bridge, or tennis, rather as Isobel had done. No doubt they would discuss his absence over dinner. Maybe not. Maybe they did not think of him at all now that he was out of sight. But that would be unlikely. Oliver was not one to relinquish lightly the enjoyment to be had from disapproving of another's actions, especially when that 'other' was his father.

The moment the thought crossed his mind he reproached himself for giving it credence. Oliver was not *so* bad. Well, actually, he was, but . . . 'Oh, Isobel. If you could see me now,' he thought. And then he banished the notion from his head. It really did not bear any kind of scrutiny. And Rosie . . . and Ace . . . and Elsie? What would they think of his antics over the past few days? Let alone the reclusive Alice. He shuddered. Even his dearest and most understanding daughter would no doubt have been disconcerted by actions that she would have considered totally out of character.

And then he looked out of the window and saw that the train was travelling along the coast. Small waves lapped upon the shore in arcs of sand between the craggy rocks and ochre-painted villas; and the sun had come out.

The next stop was Nice, where he must change for the short onward journey to Monaco. Still the shrill tones of the Queen of the Night's aria echoed in his head. How to banish them? Replace them with another tune, that was the answer. But what? All that seemed to swim through his head was Charles Trenet and *La Mer*. That would not help at all; the memories of Francine would loom even larger; the slough of despond would widen and deepen. He needed to snap out of his wistful, pining frame of mind with a jauntier song. Something ridiculous that would make him think of inconsequential things. But what? In Monaco . . . Monte Carlo . . . Yes. There was a film, years ago, with Tony Curtis and Susan Hampshire. He rather liked her. Very pretty; lovely dark and smiling eyes. He momentarily replaced the so-far indelible image of Francine with that of Susan Hampshire as he cast his mind back to seeing the film while he was still at school. *Monte Carlo or Bust*, that was it. How did the song go – the one sung by the man with the gravelly voice . . . what was his name? Jimmy Durante! Da-da-da da-da . . . yes, that was it. It was all about old cars having a race across Europe. Slowly the words began to surface . . .

'And when we arrive miles ahead of the rest,
Everyone will know that our jalopy is best;
They'll have to admit she's a car you can trust,
So it's Monte Carlo or bust!'

It was such a silly song. Stupid. But the thought of it made him smile. It also reminded him that he had promised himself an old car when he retired – before Isobel's death: something to occupy his retirement, to tinker with and take out for a spin. Other thoughts had forced it from his mind since the life-changing events of last autumn. What if he hired a car – not an old one which might not be reliable – but a convertible and did that thing of driving along the coast. The Grand Corniche. Yes! Brilliant! Joseph Addison would have done it, though on a horse, of course, or in a carriage. He would simply be updating the exercise.

And so, as he disembarked the train at Nice to change platforms for the short run to Monte Carlo, he began to hum the tune to himself, driving out the sentimentality of Charles Trenet and the imprecations of the Queen of the Night with a song so ridiculous that it forbade any kind of maudlin sentiment. At least it gave him something else to think about. The hotel, presumably, would know all about hiring cars. A BMW or a Mercedes? No. A Lamborghini, or an Aston Martin – a James Bond car – something with a romantic name at any rate. Though perhaps not a Ferrari; he had always thought them rather too showy. And then he thought of Francine sitting in the seat next to him, a chiffon scarf over her head and a pair of sunglasses perched on her nose, looking for all the world like Grace Kelly, and he knew that all resistance was futile. He would just have to live with it, and that was that.

17

HÔTEL HERMITAGE, MONACO

MAY

'Presenting a superlative range of yachts for the
discerning client, we pride ourselves in an efficient and
confidential service for those in a position to demand
unrivalled specifications and unparalleled luxury.'

Cockburn Yachts Brochure, 2016

It was with a spring in his step and a song in his heart (albeit
one with lyrics somewhat more prosaic than those of the Queen
of the Night) that Timothy enquired at the concierge's desk in
the extravagantly plush Hôtel Hermitage as to the possibility
of hiring a car for the day. 'Nothing easier,' the porter had said.
If Timothy would just take a look at the leaflet he handed over,
the porter would be happy to arrange for the car to be outside
the hotel the following morning, or the day after that if he
preferred. Both were perfectly possible.

Timothy took the tastefully designed leaflet and parked
himself in a corner of the terrace overlooking the harbour –
a small arc of water crowded with sleek superyachts. He

scrutinised the leaflet and wondered whether to go for a Bentley, a Lamborghini or an Aston Martin. Then his conscience got the better of him for a moment and a frisson of doubt (engendered by the prices to the right of the page) caused him to pause for a moment and consider whether this wasn't just too extravagant. It also crossed his mind that the experience was one he would have preferred to share.

He lowered the leaflet and raised the Ray-Bans from his eyes, the better to take in the outrageously profligate vision in front of him. These were not yachts with sails, but yachts with staff – dozens of them, crawling over their charges which sparkled in the setting sun thanks to an array of nubile girls in figure-hugging polo-shirts and very tight shorts who seemed to be cleaning each and every one them from bows to stern with cotton buds. Some of the yachts had four or even five decks, replete with hot tubs and swimming pools, helicopter landing pads and canopied dining areas almost as large as the hotel terrace from which he viewed them. They lay, cheek by jowl, in the deep blue water at the foot of the rocky embrasure that was Monte Carlo – an arc of rocky terrain upon which houses and hotels were stacked like apples upon a greengrocer's stall.

He sighed deeply and took a gulp of the ice-cold beer a waiter had obligingly put in front of him. As he did so he made a vow: that today would be the last day he felt overwhelmed by guilt. He had worked hard all his life. He had been true to his wife and his children; he had brought them up as best he could. He was 'out on the toot', of that there was no doubt, but if a chap who no longer had any ties to speak of could not indulge himself, and could not spend his money how he wanted to spend it, then what was the point of it all?

He raised his glass to some unseen deity and toasted his

new-found confidence, knowing that in reality such ingrained misgivings could not be banished overnight, but relieved that at least he had admitted such an intention.

The light was just beginning to fade. It would be several hours before darkness fell, but the pink glow that lay above the Mediterranean heralded his first night on the Riviera. He would take a stroll before supper, walk down to the marina and inspect the yachts; there would be a particularly generous array of them right now since the Monaco Grand Prix was just a week away – another good reason for shortening his visit here. And, anyway, he would have been lucky to have found accommodation during the Formula 1 festivities; as it was he had the good fortune to have capitalised on a cancellation.

His luck had really been in so far, hadn't it? Finding that Paris more than lived up to his expectations. Taking up painting again. Meeting Francine – now that was good luck on an epic scale wasn't it? He finished off the beer, went to his room to change and then walked out into the Monte Carlo twilight to take in the sights and the sounds of the super-rich at play.

Although he had planned on a walk around the harbour, it was really more a series of short strolls, since the grandeur of the shipping arrested his attention every few paces. How could anyone afford such vessels? What must they cost?

At the sight of a well-dressed young man in a deep blue blazer and neatly pressed white trousers at the foot of one gleaming teak and chrome passerelle, he felt emboldened to enquire. The man was clearly not an owner since he had a clipboard under one arm and a wad of brochures under the other. Timothy wondered if he would even give an ordinary passer-by the time of day, but decided to take the risk anyway. Nothing ventured, nothing gained.

'Good evening,' offered Timothy, as he walked by.

'Isn't it?' replied the man. 'Beautiful. And should be nice tomorrow too, according to the forecast.' He had a public school accent, which rather surprised Timothy, but then he reasoned that such a qualification was probably necessary at this end of the market – it was hardly the territory of someone who sounded like an East End barrow-boy.

Timothy stopped and nodded at the superyacht that towered into the firmament behind the man; its navy blue hull as shiny as glass, its three milk-white upper decks elegantly tiered and replete with padded seats and glass tables, sliding glass doors giving way to luxurious interiors. Lights glinted everywhere about her as though some fairy godmother had sprinkled her with stardust. 'Quite a beauty.'

'Isn't she?' And then, with a twinkle in his eye, 'Could be yours if you wish, sir.'

Timothy laughed and regarded the man with curiosity. He was no more than twenty-five, thirty at most. Well spoken, clearly from a good family, and yet here in Monte Carlo among the well-heeled jet-set it seemed he was simply a salesman – albeit of very high-end goods. He had a fresh complexion, burnished by the sun and complemented by the freshly pressed white shirt that was a part of his armoury in the quest to impress potential owners of Odyssey, the yacht at the foot of whose passerelle he stood sentinel. His well-ordered mop of fair hair had been neatly cut and clearly he possessed perfect manners as well as having just the right amount of shirt cuff protruding from the sleeves of his well-tailored blazer.

'And what would I have to pay for the privilege?' asked Timothy.

'Oh, I couldn't possibly say, sir. After all . . .'

'If I have to ask the price I can't afford her?'

'Exactly.' Then he looked swiftly over both shoulders, gave Timothy a knowing wink, smiled and said, 'Thirty million euros to you, sir.'

'Good God!'

Warming to his task, and with no sign as yet of anyone turning up to view, the young man said, 'Good value, sir. They *can* go for more than a hundred million. A hundred and fifty is about top whack for the ones I've been asked to shift . . . er, sell.'

'How long do the buyers keep them for? I mean, don't they depreciate like mad?'

The young man warmed to his task, having found in Timothy a willing listener. 'Oh, the people who buy them tend not to worry about depreciation. They'll keep a yacht for two, maybe three years and then buy a larger one, or else have one designed and built. These yachts are a way of disposing of cash rather than investing it. The owners have all the houses and the investments they want. These are indulgences, extravagances.' He shrugged, then said, sotto voce, 'Odd though it may seem to the likes of you and me.'

'Odd indeed.'

The young man held out his hand. 'Archie Bedlington, agent for Cockburn Yachts.'

'Timothy Gandy, free agent, who just happens to be in Monaco before going on to Florence, Venice and Rome.'

'Ah, the Grand Tour.'

'Yes,' said Timothy, relieved not to have to explain further. 'It's nice to meet someone who's heard of it.'

'Did it at school. Well, read about it – all those dilettanti taking in the culture. Didn't know it still happened.'

'I don't think it does . . . much . . . but it's something I always wanted to do and when circumstances changed . . . well, here

I am on the second leg. Paris last week, Monaco this week, then on to . . . well, other capital cities.'

'What a wonderful idea. I wish you luck.' Archie crooked an arm and glanced at the handsome Cartier watch strapped to his wrist. 'Well, that's me done. Another no-show.'

'You mean, someone has booked to come and look around and hasn't turned up?'

''Fraid so. It happens more often than you'd think.' Then, with a wry grin, 'These are busy people you must understand, Mr Gandy. They have a lot to do.'

'Well, I can see that,' said Timothy, looking at the towering vessel behind them. 'A lot of time to spend doing nothing.'

'Fancy a look?' asked Archie.

'Me?'

'Yes. You seem like a respectable type.' He smiled to reassure Timothy that the line was meant to amuse. 'I've nothing else to do, except go and have too many glasses of cold beer. Let me show you around. It's good practice for me; I've only been doing it for a few weeks. I could do with polishing my act. You can play the part of the discerning prospective buyer, though between you and me your accent is rather too good. If you could knock off a few of your aitches you would sound more authentic. And be picky, Mr Gandy – about the most insignificant things.'

'Call me Timothy!' He laughed, and followed Archie up the passerelle – the smartest gangplank upon which he had ever set foot. Suddenly it seemed rather silly to feel guilty at spending three nights in a five-star hotel while these millionaires and billionaires had no compunction about spending thirty million euros on a five-deck superyacht.

The tour of Odyssey was a revelation. There were en-suite staterooms (not 'cabins' Archie informed him) replete with super-sized beds. Bathrooms were an opulent mixture of highly figured marble and mirrors. There were mirrors everywhere, it seemed – on doors, walls and even ceilings – and glossy marquetry doors which, although a touch elaborate, displayed, Timothy admitted to himself, superb craftsmanship.

The saloon (not 'lounge', please, warned Archie) was an ornate confection of gleaming veneer and gilt, replete with cream leather sofas and armchairs arranged around the polished brass and glass tables, which seemed to be the vessel's leitmotif. The whole effect was far too showy for Timothy's taste, but he had to admit that it was spectacular – especially the main stairwell, which possessed a chandelier that stretched upwards and downwards through three decks.

As daylight turned to dusk, so the superyacht's lighting came into its own – twinkling brightly from ceilings, glowing from strategically placed lamps and shimmering from the depths of the upper deck jacuzzi, turning it into an enormous semi-precious stone of turquoise that glistened on the warm teak deck.

A large and impossibly shiny dining table was set for a dinner, which, today at least, would not be served. The china, glass and silverware bore not a single fingerprint, and the glossy cabinetry surrounding the dining area was dotted with ceramics and sculpture which could, Archie explained, be included in the sale if the buyer chose.

'What about the engines?' asked Timothy.

'Oh. They don't often ask about them. Follow me,' instructed Archie, leading the way down several flights of stainless steel stairs that were clearly never seen by the owner and his guests, though their state of cleanliness was immaculate.

The vast engine room had the appearance of a hospital operating theatre, and Timothy said as much. 'Oh; if you want that then the yacht next door has one – but it's rather more expensive at eighty-five million euros,' confirmed Archie.

Timothy was aware that his jaw must be falling lower and lower in amazement at the lavishness and extravagance of the fixtures and fittings alone.

'You're not being very critical,' teased Archie. 'Surely there must be something you don't like?'

'Well, I'm not mad on the colour of the towels in the master bathroom. I've never been a fan of purple.'

'Don't worry, sir. A simple adjustment. They will be changed by tomorrow, and we won't charge for that.'

'Generous,' murmured Timothy.

They finished their tour on the upper deck, having admired the gymnasium, the cinema, the galley facilities and even the crew's quarters – rather more spartan than that of the owner and his guests, though still capable of accommodating eight people in what to most of the population would be regarded as luxurious if compact accommodation.

'What about staff?' asked Timothy.

'Oh, we can organise that,' confirmed Archie, reassuringly. 'They are full time and the wages bill will be in the region of a quarter of a million euros per annum. 'Of course, if you wish, we can arrange for Odyssey to be chartered when you are not using her, to help defray costs, but most of our owners don't like to have anyone they don't know on board.'

Timothy shook his head. 'Astonishing,' he murmured.

'Have one of these,' said Archie, holding out a generously proportioned full colour brochure showing the deck layout of Odyssey, pictures of all the main staterooms and shots of her both underway at sea and at anchor in some azure blue Caribbean lagoon, surrounded by her 'toys' – the two jet-skis, a speedboat and various other floating fripperies especially laid on for the amusement of her owner and his guests.

'I hope you don't think . . .'

Archie shook his head. 'Just a souvenir. It's nice to take someone round who is impressed by what they see and admiring of the craftsmanship, rather than a prospective owner who is . . . well . . . rather spoiled and difficult to impress, if I'm honest.'

As they left Odyssey and made their way down the passerelle, now lit with a row of lights that made it safer for tipsy passengers to disembark, Timothy said, 'So now you go and have your cold beers and do the same tomorrow in the hope that someone turns up?'

''Fraid so,' replied Archie. 'Come and join me. A thank you for being my guinea pig.'

'Well, I don't want to impose . . .'

'Honestly. I could do with a bit of civilised company.'

Timothy found it hard to disappoint his new-found acquaintance and after a short walk found himself jostling with Archie for a beer in a bar just across the road from the marina. The beer was cold but the noise level was such that after a few minutes the two of them found themselves laughing at the impossibility of any kind of conversation. Timothy shook his head in disbelief and asked, 'Have you eaten?'

'Well, no . . .'

'Why don't you come to supper?'

'Oh, I couldn't possibly . . .'

'As a thank you for showing me round. I'm staying at the Hermitage.'

'Goodness!' said Archie. 'Perhaps you could afford this yacht after all.'

'Not when I've paid the hotel bill,' said Timothy. 'And I'm only staying for three nights. Say about nine o'clock? I booked a table on the terrace and I'm sure they won't object to me having company.'

*

Archie turned up at the Hôtel Hermitage punctually at five minutes to nine, but then Timothy would have expected no less. He greeted his new acquaintance in the hotel lobby and led him up to the terrace which offered a fine view of Monte Carlo at night and the yachts that were now in full entertaining mode in the harbour below. A warm breeze gently ruffled the ivory linen cloths that adorned the tables.

'Drink?'

'Oh, yes please.'

Archie had changed from his working clothes – the smart blazer and the neatly pressed trousers – and now wore cream chinos and a white linen shirt. A pink cashmere sweater was draped over his shoulders. Timothy could detect a whiff of what he suspected was rather expensive aftershave – not oppressive but clearly exclusive.

'Another beer? With conversation this time!' enquired Timothy.

'What are you going to have?'

'Well, to be honest, I was going to celebrate my arrival on the Riviera with a cocktail. A Margarita. Join me?'

'Well, if you're sure?'

'A stiffener, that's what P.G. Wodehouse would have called it. To set us up after the day we've had – me travelling and you selling . . . or not selling . . .'

'Oh, it happens. I've learned not to take it personally.'

They sat at the table indicated by the waiter, who brought two large menus at the same time as the cocktails.

'Here's to you – and to a successful sale tomorrow,' said Timothy, raising his glass.

'I won't hold my breath,' said Archie. He lowered his glass having tasted the cocktail and said, 'God! I needed that!'

'So how do you come to be selling yachts in Monte Carlo? It's not a particularly obvious choice of career for someone with a public school education.'

Archie smiled ruefully. 'Is it so obvious?'

'Well . . . to be honest, I was just guessing . . . I didn't mean to be rude.'

'Well, you're not wrong. Stowe. Then . . . well, I rather bottled out of Uni. Didn't seem the right thing for me. Not really academic. I like people but I'm not mad about exams. I travelled for a year – in Africa. Did some charity work out there and then came home and looked around for a job. I did a bit of this and that – estate agency work, public relations. You name it, I've tried it, I suppose. And then an old school friend offered me this job with his family firm.' He shrugged, as if to say 'And here I am', then he took another sip of the Margarita and asked, 'But what about you, Mr Gandy . . . Timothy? How come you have the time to travel? You're not old enough to have retired.'

Timothy – grateful for the genuine compliment – recounted, as briefly as he could, the circumstances that had led to his apparently carefree peregrinations. He explained about taking up painting again, and intimated that at least two of his children thought he was out of his mind. Archie seemed to sympathise, as though he had found in Timothy a like-minded soul intent on doing his own thing despite the apparent disapproval of other members of the family.

'You should come and live out here,' said Archie.

'Heavens, what a thought.' Timothy looked out over the glittering harbour and thought how beautiful it looked. 'Do you enjoy it?' he asked. 'More to the point, do you like selling boats?'

'Well, I've not been doing it long, but it beats selling houses in Fulham. It's warmer for a start. But then the clientele is . . . challenging!'

'So how many yachts have you sold so far?'

'Two.'

'Oh!'

'I know it doesn't sound many, but it takes a fair bit of persuading in most cases. Well, not persuading exactly, but making it clear to the potential buyer that this is the yacht for them. I rather like the challenge of convincing a man with a lot of money to part with some of it. And we *are* talking about a lot of money – it takes weeks, months, even years sometimes to seal the deal.'

'Is it always men?'

'Almost exclusively. Most of them self-made, so it's not easy to pull the wool over their eyes. You just have to . . . well . . . make them think they are making a really wise decision. Ensuring their privacy. And, of course, there's the macho thing – they always seem to want a larger one – and a newer one – than their rivals.'

'And what about you? Can you have much of a social life?'

'Are you serious? I could be out every night being wined and dined if I wanted – or wining and dining clients on my expense account – but I value my liver and try to pace myself.'

'It strikes me that you've got your head screwed on, and thank you for making an exception tonight. I'm learning a lot . . .'

The waiter came to take their order, and over scallops and smoked salmon, lamb cutlets and cheese, the two chatted amiably about their ambitions (Archie) and their travel plans (Timothy). Archie, it seemed, was in no rush to settle down. He had enjoyed several relationships but none had survived more than a few weeks; superyachts, it seemed, were a considerable – if not a durable – attraction. There was a possibility of a relationship developing, he said, but he was happy for the time being, to be alone – and in spite of the fact that his parents found his lack of a career plan baffling and frustrating in equal measure they had resigned themselves to letting him get on with his life, hoping that sooner rather than later common sense would prevail and he would settle down to a permanent relationship and a steady job in the city. As he remarked to Timothy, he was happy to let them labour on under the illusion, even though at the moment there was little or no sign of such a state of affairs coming to pass.

'So what *do* you want to do when you grow up?' asked Timothy over coffee, making it clear with a knowing wink that the later part of the question was meant teasingly rather than as any form of criticism.

'Not sure. I just need time to think,' replied Archie. 'I'm only twenty-six. I'm not in a rush. I just want to see a bit more of the world before I settle down to . . . well, who knows? Something in the charity sector probably. I spent two years helping in a school in Ghana. Hard work and a real eye-opener. I just feel in need of a bit of a break right now, and this is at the other end of the spectrum. It absolutely appalls me sometimes, the amount of money involved, compared with the poverty in Africa. I think what these sort of sums could achieve out there – it would be amazing.'

He was lost for a moment in reverie, remembering what he had seen and what he had experienced, and then brightened again. 'But I want to experience the extremes in life. I think it will make me more rounded; help me to decide what best to do; to make a difference. I suppose I'm indulging myself at the moment; a bit like you in a way – though for a different reason, and at a different time in my life. I get well paid out here, the weather is good and although the company is a bit limited I like the challenge of persuading people to part with huge sums of cash. They can afford it and if I can sell one yacht a month then I'm not doing too badly. Does that all sound completely contradictory?'

'It sounds to me as though you know exactly what you're doing. But it must be difficult reconciling what you saw in Africa with the level of luxury and indulgence here.'

'Oh, it is. But funnily enough, I think of all the people – the craftsmen – who have built these boats. They may be sold to billionaires with more money than taste, but they are providing employment for men and women with real skills – carpenters and electricians, cabinetmakers and glaziers. It's just that rather weird way the world works. You might not approve of superyachts but you have to admit that they are a valuable part of the economy.'

'Well, if you put it like that . . . and they really are amazingly built,' admitted Timothy, expansively, having enjoyed rather more of the bottle of Pauillac than his companion. 'But absolutely, ridiculously, outrageously extravagant.'

'Could you live on one?' asked Archie.

'Yes. Yes, I think I could. For a while – leaving out the purple towels . . . and the hideous chandelier . . . until the Lotus-eating life began to pall. I couldn't sit about and do nothing all day.'

'Do you think you could sell one?'

'Nooo! Not in a million years. I wouldn't know what to say.'

'Oh, I think you underestimate yourself. You're very companionable . . .'

'Thank you!'

'No. You are. I think our high net worth clients would warm to you.'

Timothy held up his hands. 'I'm really not looking for a job! But thank you for the testimonial! I'd be a rotten salesman – no confidence on that front whatsoever.'

'But they don't really want the hard sell, you see. You just have to be pleasant and good company.' He paused for a moment, hesitating, then said, 'Why don't you come with me tomorrow? Keep me company on my eleven o'clock appointment. You don't need to say much. Just be there. It'll only take a couple of hours at most. I'd be glad of the reinforcements.'

'Oh, I couldn't possibly . . .'

'Just be yourself. You wouldn't have to pretend to know much – but you really appreciated the workmanship and . . . well, you needn't go in the master bathroom with the purple towels.'

In the downy comfort of the vast bed in his opulent room at the Hôtel Hermitage that night, Timothy lay with his eyes wide open for a while, wondering if he were quite mad. Beneath him, in the far distance, courtesy of the open window, he could hear the murmur of traffic and the occasional sounds of conversation, despite the lateness of the hour. Had he lost his reason or was he just enjoying a new-found freedom? How long could this outrageous adventure last? And what was she doing now? Where was she? And who with? Could she, too, be lying back on her bed in her Paris apartment wondering what he might be doing? Around and around swam the events of the past few days until his eyelids became heavy and he drifted off into a deep and dream-filled sleep.

18

THE MARINA, MONACO

MAY

'When I hear a rich man described as a colourful character, I figure he's a bum with money.'

Jimmy Cannon, *New York Post*, 1955

Standing at the bottom of Odyssey's gleaming gangplank the following morning, and trying to remember that it was more correctly called a 'passerelle', Timothy wondered what on earth he had let himself in for. He could be cruising the Grande Corniche in an Aston Martin or a Lamborghini, but he had still not made up his mind which one to hire or on which day he wanted to make the trip, or whether it was just an extravagance too far. He was also – untypically – rather excited to be out of his comfort zone. But then what had he got to lose? He didn't have to do anything except be himself. And if he was asked what he did and why he was there, Archie said that all he needed to do was call himself a consultant.

Which is what he was. (The fact that he knew bugger-all

about boats mattered not at all, apparently. The key was to remain calm, companionable and pleasant.)

It did occur to him that so far he had seen little of Monaco other than the marina, but then this was at the heart of it all and in a couple of hours he could take himself off to look at the Prince's Palace high upon its rocky eminence, and the botanic garden on the cliff face, or sort out that car . . .

His musings were interrupted by Archie who was standing at the other side of the passerelle. 'I haven't told you who we are showing round.'

'No.' Timothy felt more than a little uneasy, like a schoolboy about to be found out by the headmaster for pretending to be something he wasn't.

Archie looked at his clipboard. 'Mr and Mrs Ballantyne. From Aberdeen. He's in second-hand cars. Started out working for his father thirty years ago, then took on the business and developed franchises all over the south-east.'

'Missionary work,' murmured Timothy.

'Sorry?'

'A Scot making his money down south. So do they tell you all this? Do they say "I'm Mr Ballantyne and I can afford your boat because I have second-hand car franchises all over the south-east"?'

Archie frowned in admonishment. 'We do a little background research to weed out the time wasters.'

'And Mr Ballantyne is likely to be able to afford her? The boat I mean.'

'Well able. He's valued at a couple of hundred million.'

Timothy whistled. 'So what do I do? I mean, where do I stand?'

Archie laughed. 'Stand where you want. Don't overcrowd them, don't pressurise them – not that you would – and just make sure they enjoy themselves looking round, and that they notice the quality of the fittings and the facilities – just as you did when you went over her yesterday.'

Timothy nodded as if to convince himself. 'Right. It's just that I don't want to get in the way, and when it comes to the nitty-gritty I'll make myself scarce.'

'Oh, don't worry; I'll suggest to him when we get to that point in the proceedings that we go and sit down in the study next to the saloon, but it might not even come to that. He'll most likely say that he wants to think about it and give me a call. What's most important is that they have a good time. The steward has put the champagne on ice. That should get them in the mood.'

Timothy was about to ask whether or not he should dispense the drinks when heavy footsteps at the end of the wide and stately pontoon heralded the arrival of Mr and Mrs Ballantyne.

The husband had the proportions of a retired prop-forward: fifty-something, fifteen stone, broad shouldered and barrel chested. He was dressed in a navy blue polo shirt that had some difficulty in containing his torso, and a pair of pink Bermuda shorts that finished just below the knee. His calves had the circumference of Timothy's thighs, and on his feet were a pair of pink suede loafers. He walked with a kind of swagger, lurching from side to side, and his tanned, shaven head glistened in the sun. There was, about him, an aroma of cologne rather too heavily applied. He did not look espe- cially happy, his expression being like that of a bulldog that had just swallowed a wasp.

Mrs Ballantyne, on the other hand, was a shapely thirty- something blonde of the kind that might have been drawn by Donald McGill on a saucy seaside postcard of the nineteen fifties. Her generous bust was supported and enhanced by a

turquoise, low-cut swimming costume over which she wore
Bermuda shorts that matched those of her husband in colour,
if not in cut. Over her shoulder she carried a large flower-cov-
ered bag of the sort that might contain a towel on a trip to the
beach. Timothy tried to suppress a smile as she teetered along
the pontoon in a pair of vertiginous white high-heeled sling-
backs, her tanned arms dripping with gold bracelets; at her
neck a Tiffany pendant. Her hair had clearly taken a considerable degree of work that morning, for it was piled up and
interlaced with a pink chiffon scarf. Diamanté-studded Bulgari
sunglasses covered half her face and completed the vision.

Timothy cast a sideways glance at Archie who studiously
avoided meeting his eye.

'Mr Ballantyne?' enquired Archie, offering his hand.

'S'me,' replied the man.

'Mrs Ballantyne?'

The woman giggled and pushed her sunglasses up into the
confection of hair and chiffon. ''Ello! Nice to meet you. You
must be Archie.'

'That's right.'

Mr Ballantyne took off his own sunglasses and tucked one
arm of them into the top of his polo shirt, before scrutinising
Archie from top to toe and back again. Then he asked with a
scowl, 'So this is her then is it?'

'This is her,' confirmed Archie, raising his right arm to indicate the majesty of the vessel standing before them. 'And this
is my colleague, Timothy. We'll be showing you round this
morning.'

It was now that Timothy began to feel slightly sick, a sensation not improved by the vice-like handshake of Mr Ballantyne
who crushed Timothy's knuckles so hard that he wondered if
he would ever paint again.

'Nice to meet you I'm sure,' trilled Mrs Ballantyne, shaking Timothy's hand with a feeble grip more akin to that of a life-less corpse.

'Shall we go aboard?' asked Archie.

'Rude not to, mate. Rude not to. Up the gangplank?'

'The passerelle, yes,' confirmed Archie.

'Passer-what? Oh yes; flashy names for everything you lot. Mind you, I can't see you owning one.' He prodded Archie in the ribs with a finger that, on its own, could have inflicted severe damage on most normal-sized mortals. 'I bought my first Ferrari at nineteen, sunshine. When did you buy yours?' And with that he strode purposefully up the gangway, which bounced so much that it threatened to catapult the rest of the party into the harbour. Mrs Ballantyne followed him, simpering gently and clinging – wisely – to the handrail, while Archie shepherded them forward and Timothy brought up the rear, massaging his right hand in an attempt to restore the flow of blood to his fingers.

To look at Mr and Mrs Ballantyne, thought Timothy, no one would have imagined that they were worth two hundred million pounds. Yes, Mrs Ballantyne's jewellery was showy, though osten-tatious rather than obviously valuable. But then he supposed that multi-millionaires were, in reality, just like everyone else – two arms, two legs and assorted sensibilities and tastes.

Mr Ballantyne waved away the offer of champagne from the young steward who stood like a footman to one side of the saloon, but his wife accepted with a 'Ta ever so', and sipped at the contents of the glass as she looked about her at the opulent fixtures and fittings. 'It's ever so nice, Trevor. Lovely cushions.'

Mr Ballantyne looked at Archie and raised his eyes heaven-wards. 'Got a beer, sunshine? I'm parched.'

Archie nodded at the steward who turned on his heel and exited to locate the required beverage, returning moments later with a cut glass tumbler filled with the foaming brew, along with a napkin which Mr Ballantyne waved away.

'I hope this is cold,' he said, raising his glass before taking a long draught followed by a sigh of satisfaction.

'And you're from Aberdeen?' asked Timothy.

''Riginally.'

'But not for some time?'

'My old man was Scottish; I've lived down south since I was . . . what? . . . five. Expanding the business, you know? Branches all over Essex.' He nodded at his wife. ''S'where we met.'

'Ah, I see. Yes. That would explain it.'

'Right. Before we go any further let's make one thing clear: I'm not a pushover, I know what I'm looking at and I don't have more money than sense. Before I leave I'll want to know running costs, crewing details, engine capacity, cruising speed and how many toilet rolls get used every week. Is that clear?'

'Perfectly,' said Archie with, thought Timothy, impressive sangfroid.

'Right. Where do we start?'

Archie went into full salesman mode, which, thought Timothy, was impressively understated and perfectly pitched considering the tirade which had just emanated from the prospective purchaser. So compelling was his gentle exposition that there were moments when Timothy wondered whether he should not actually invest in Odyssey himself. He quickly got over the fleeting sensation and remembered to smile a lot, to improve the atmosphere and encourage the Ballantynes to feel comfortably at home.

As they toured the vessel on a carefully worked out route, designed to create the best possible impression as well as involving moments of surprise and revelation, Timothy (who had so far had to do very little other than look pleasantly decorative) noticed that Mrs Ballantyne drifted away from the main party from time to time – peeping around corners and opening cupboard doors. It was the sort of thing wives did, he remembered. It was clearly the same with superyachts as it was with houses.

When they came to the dining room, Mr Ballantyne, along with Archie and Timothy, walked forward to take in the view, while his wife lingered over the table.

'What's that?' asked Mr Ballantyne, pointing out of the forward window.

Archie followed the line of Mr Ballantyne's outstretched arm and endeavoured to see what had caught his eye, hoping that it was not another yacht which he might consider was better suited to his needs. Timothy, however, chanced to look in the opposite direction at this point, and as he did so, he noticed Mrs Ballantyne picking up a pair of silver salt and pepper grinders from the dining table and slipping them into her shoulder bag. He could not believe his eyes. He turned away for a moment, then looked back again, but the salt cellars were, indeed, absent from the table and Mrs Ballantyne was now studiously examining a large painting of a horse which adorned the bulkhead above the side cabinets. Seeing Timothy looking at her she said, airily, 'Lovely painting. I like 'orses, don't you?'

'Yes. Yes, I do,' responded Timothy, unsure of what else he could say or do.

If he pointed out that Mrs Ballantyne had lifted two pieces of silver from the table and put them in her bag what would happen? All hell would break loose. Archie would lose a sale. Perhaps it was just Mrs Ballantyne's little problem; one that her husband might be aware of. Or maybe he had no idea.

Either way it was a revelation unlikely to make for a happy outcome.

Timothy felt a cold sweat breaking out on his forehead; he reached into his pocket for his handkerchief and lightly dabbed away the perspiration.

'Warm day,' he said to Mrs Ballantyne, by way of explanation.

'Yes. It's Monte Carlo,' she replied with, he thought, the merest hint of sarcasm.

Archie was in full flow now, turning back from the window and suggesting that they walk below to explore the guest suites and their facilities. 'Lovely,' said the multimillionaire's wife, holding tight to the shoulder bag that concealed her booty and running her finger along the top of one of the polished surfaces as though to test its smoothness.

They moved off in the direction of the companionway that led to the bedroom suites on the deck below, and Timothy wondered what on earth he should do. He decided that the best course of action would be to observe Mrs Ballantyne closely for the rest of the tour, but covertly so that she did not notice his presence. Accordingly, he hung back a little, wondering where the steward and stewardesses were. Clearly they had melted into the background; he supposed that if too many of them were in evidence at a viewing then the effect might be intimidating as well as implying a hefty wages bill.

The party was now in the master bedroom suite and Mr Ballantyne was enquiring in his bullish way about the number of stewardesses in Odyssey's complement. Timothy hovered outside, just round the corner. He had spotted a Lalique statuette of the Greek goddess Mercedes on a console table opposite the entrance to the suite and managed to position himself so that he had a clear view of it through a perforated screen, while not being visible himself. The voices of Archie and Mr Ballantyne echoed from within as his wife came out of the master bedroom, glanced to left and right and then picked up the statuette, slipping it into her bag to join the salt cellars.

Timothy's heart beat faster. What should he do? What could he do?

As Archie and the prospective owner – if that's what he was – came out of the master bedroom, Mrs Ballantyne joined them and followed in her husband's wake making simpering noises about the beauty of the yacht.

'S'all right,' he admitted. 'A bit on the pokey side, but it might just do. I presume we can arrange for a refurb?'

'Of course,' reassured Archie, managing somehow to avoid any hint of either impatience or obsequiousness in his tone.

The tour was almost complete now, and the four of them made their way onto the upper sundeck where, at last, a stewardess had appeared with a silver tray of coffee and another bearing canapés which she placed on a low table at the centre of an arc of deep-cushioned seats striped in nautical blue and white.

Archie motioned them to sit down, which Mr Ballantyne did with alacrity, lowering his vast bulk into the depths of a cushioned seat and tucking into the canapés – one after another – as the stewardess poured the coffee. 'Have you another beer, love? A cold one,' he enquired with his mouth full of smoked salmon. 'Archie and I need a serious conversation.' The stewardess smiled and went off in search of more liquid refreshment.

Mrs Ballantyne asked if she might use the ladies' powder room, at which point Archie said, 'Of course. Timothy, could you show Mrs Ballantyne to the master bathroom suite?'

'Yes. Yes, of course,' replied Timothy, his mind racing. He indicated the way, holding out an arm, and Mrs Ballantyne giggled a little and walked in the suggested direction, clinging tightly to her shoulder bag all the while.

As he showed her into the master bedroom suite and closed the door behind her, Timothy took stock. He had seen her put at least three things in her shoulder bag. She might have taken more. The bag did now seem heavier than it was when she came on board, but he doubted that anyone else would notice. What were his options? He could say nothing and, when the couple had left, tell Archie what he had seen, but he could not imagine that Archie would thank him for that; the goods having gone. He could confront Mrs Ballantyne now, on her own, rather than in front of Archie and her husband, giving her the chance to come clean and admit what she had done without involving anyone else. If the items were returned he would not say anything; but how public spirited was that – releasing her to offend again? And would she be likely to convince her obviously critical husband to buy a boat upon which she had been caught stealing things?

There was no more time to think; Mrs Ballantyne had 'powdered her nose' and as he stood in the companionway considering the alternatives the door of the master suite opened and she stepped out with her bag still clamped firmly to her shoulder. Before he could say anything she asked, 'Shall we join the gentlemen?' and walked purposefully along the companionway towards the afterdeck and its refreshments.

Timothy followed in her wake tapping his hand against his thigh in an effort to hasten some conclusion about a plan of action.

As they came out on to the afterdeck where Archie and Mr Ballantyne sat, the latter looked up and asked, 'What do you think of it then?'

'I think it's lovely, Trevor. Probably just what we want. It's very nicely . . . er . . . appointed.'

'Very nicely. With a few adjustments,' her husband agreed.

'Nice loos.'

Could these people really be multi-millionaires mused Timothy? Were they even married? But then Archie had assured him that checks were carried out on prospective buyers and so the Ballantynes had clearly passed muster.

Timothy had a flash of inspiration. 'Mrs Ballantyne, would you care to try the hot tub?' He gestured towards the foaming pool of water immediately behind them. 'It's the perfect temperature and we've prepared it especially.'

Archie looked at him blankly.

'Oh, I don't think . . .' mumbled Mrs Ballantyne.

'Oh, but you must,' insisted Timothy, leaping up and handing her the topmost monogrammed towel from a large pyramid of them stacked on one of the cushions. 'It's part of the tradition.'

'Oh . . .'

'Yes,' said Timothy, pointing to the monogram. O for Odyssey. 'Lovely, aren't they?'

'But I . . .' Mrs Ballantyne hesitated.

Archie's mouth was now open, his concentration on the job in hand having been momentarily broken.

'You have your swimming costume on, after all. We can even arrange for you to try the shower in the master suite afterwards.' Timothy was getting into his stride. 'Do you know, Mrs Ballantyne,' he said, conspiratorially, 'all the serious owners we have shown around have told us that looking at these things is simply not enough. Not when one is investing such a significant sum. And I quite understand their concern. In fact,' he looked meaningfully at Archie, 'Mr Bedlington and I can always tell the serious owners from . . . well, dare I say it . . . the time wasters. Those who really are potential buyers don't let us get away with anything. They want – quite understandably – not simply to look at what's on offer but to experience these things for themselves – something your husband has amply demon-strated with his comments and his questions.'

Mrs Ballantyne looked uncomfortable. Archie looked incred-ulous, clearly regretting inviting this lunatic on board and wondering what he might do to ease things along, and endeav-oured to gather his thoughts and move the conversation along. To no avail.

Mrs Ballantyne murmured, 'Well, yes, I quite see that . . .'

'If you'd like to pop into the changing room there – it's the single door to the left of the glazed double doors – I'll ask the stewardess to bring you another glass of champagne when you return and you can sample the delights of the jacuzzi, hot tub thingy, while you sip your Laurent Perrier in the Riviera sun and Mr Bedlington and I talk to your husband.'

Helpless to resist, Mrs Ballantyne rose and, with the bag still firmly clamped to her shoulder, she walked towards the changing room.

Archie shot Timothy a warning look and went back to smooth talking Mr Ballantyne, hoping that this was the end of Timothy's attempt to pass himself off as a salesman.

Mrs Ballantyne emerged two minutes later with the bag still in place and a towel wrapped around her waist. Reaching the edge of the hot tub she slipped off the towel, displaying a fine pair of tanned legs, and with great care deposited both bag and towel on the rim of the tub before lowering herself into the water.

Having separated her from the bag, albeit by no more than six inches, Timothy had to work out his next move. Archie, now assuming that the midday sun had gone to his new friend's head, doggedly continued to talk to Mr Ballantyne about the finer points of Odyssey hoping that shortly the prospective owner would decide upon a course of action that would eventually lead to his acquisition of the vessel. It would then be a matter of completing things, hopefully without Timothy sticking in his oar, and bidding the couple – and his mad acquaintance – farewell.

Mrs Ballantyne, now submerged in the azure waters of the hot tub, reached out for the proffered glass of champagne and began to look a little more relaxed. Timothy stood up and said, 'Canapés! That's what you need, Mrs Ballantyne, to finish off the experience.' It was all Archie could do to suppress a groan.

Timothy walked towards the hot tub, holding out a tray of smoked salmon and caviar blinis.

'Oh! Thank you! Don't mind if I do,' warbled Mrs Ballantyne, warming to her experience. She took a caviar-encrusted blini and popped it into her mouth, just as Timothy turned and managed to catch the rococo silver handle of the tray in the loop of Mrs Ballantyne's bag, sending it toppling from the rim of the hot tub on to the freshly scrubbed teak deck.

For a moment the earth stood still, but the silver salt and pepper grinders and the Lalique statuette did not; they rolled from the open mouth of the bag and across the deck, landing at Archie's feet.

It was difficult to work out in quite what sequence the following things happened, but they caught Timothy's attention in the following order: Mrs Ballantyne screamed and rose, like a siren, from the bubbling azure waters. Mr Ballantyne leaped to his feet and, with all the power of the prop forward that he once was, pushed Archie backwards so that he did a reverse somersault from the padded seat onto the teak deck, looking at the world upside down and further disturbing his equilibrium. A young stewardess came running up the outer stairs to see what the fuss was about, but noticing the form of Mr Ballantyne hurtling towards her, with all the power and momentum of a double-decker London bus, she demonstrated her belief in the fact that discretion is the better part of valour and neatly side-stepped into the saloon.

With the speed of a gazelle and the elevation of a dolphin, Mrs Ballantyne exited the hot tub, leaped over her now empty bag and ran like an Olympian in the opposite direction to her spouse. Another stewardess, clearly more familiar with the equipment in the vessel's gymnasium than her colleague, stood in her way, at which point Mrs Ballantyne vaulted the handrail, let out a scream and fell twenty-five feet into the water of the harbour, pausing for the merest instant before executing an efficient front crawl towards the farthest pontoon.

Having seen off the stewardess, Mr Ballantyne lost no time in making for the steps that led to the lower deck, being himself either a poor swimmer or distrustful of his ability to perform a similar gymnastic feat to his wife and commit his ample frame to executing a somersault towards the briny.

Archie, dazed but now upright, found his feet entangled with the straps of Mrs Ballantyne's bag, so the only thing standing in the way of the charging bull that was Mr Ballantyne was Timothy.

Never brawny, Timothy had learned from an early age that speed and quickness of thinking could, on occasion, be a substitute for muscle. Standing to one side he gave the impression that he was about to allow Mr Ballantyne to pass unimpeded, but at the last moment he stuck out his right leg and sent the monstrous frame sprawling across the deck. Swiftly Timothy sat on the man's back, grabbed the shoulder bag which Archie had tossed aside having freed himself from its clutches and, twisting the handles, neatly fastened the large man's hands behind his back. Unwilling to be cowed, Mr Ballantyne flicked back his leg and caught Timothy just above the right eye, but by now Archie had regained his composure and sat on the man's legs to prevent any further flailing.

Their quarry vanquished, the two men looked at each other with wide eyes, while a torrent of abuse poured from the mouth of their prisoner and the two stewardesses ran off down the pontoon in search of police assistance. A distant clock struck midday.

19

LE GRANDE CORNICHE, MONACO

MAY

'Get out the jalopy and polish the wheels
She's got to be the smartest of the automobiles;
Polish the paintwork and clean off the rust
They won't see out chassis for dust.'

Ron Goodwin, *Monte Carlo or Bust!*, 1969

It was, said Archie, the very least he could do. Cockburn Yachts would foot the bill. But Timothy insisted that it was not something that should be done alone and so he would only undertake it if Archie would take a day off and come with him, and, anyway, were such a smart company likely to hire out a car to a man with a black eye?

So it was that the two men found themselves cruising the Grande Corniche in a Bentley Continental, the wind in their hair and the Riviera coastline beckoning them on.

'We're a bit like Thelma and Louise,' said Timothy.

'Who?' asked Archie.

'Never mind. And hopefully the outcome won't be the same.'

Archie assumed that the noise of the wind in his ears made it difficult to understand what the older man was saying.

On they went, through mountainous clifftop hairpins, along sleek stretches of road, the sea shimmering like a vast sheet of metallic foil beneath them. The only thing missing, thought Timothy, was Francine, but he did his best to overcome the yearning for her company, and thoughts of the previous day's events helped to push her, for the time being at least, if not to the back of his mind then slightly to one side.

'Why are we going this way and not the other?' he asked Archie.

'This way's more interesting. The road east towards Menton is not quite so spectacular.'

'So we're heading to Nice?'

'Not as far as Nice. I have a friend in St Jean Cap Ferrat and we're going there for lunch.'

'Goodness, you do know how to treat a guy!'

Timothy was at the wheel of the luxurious convertible, not driving excessively fast, but at a speed that gave him the most tremendous pleasure; taking care on the ridiculously acute hairpin bends, and trying to keep his eye on the road as well as the ravishing scenery. 'I feel like James Bond,' he said.

'You look a bit like him – must be the black eye.'

Timothy dug his companion in the ribs and reflected on the fact that although he had known Archie for only a day, there seemed to be a greater rapport between them than he had ever experienced with Oliver. The thought saddened him a little, and he put it out of his mind.

They stopped every now and then in a lay-by to take in the view, with Archie pointing out places of interest or villas of note, and after a couple of hours, on Archie's instruction, they dropped down towards the peninsula of Cap Ferrat and swept up a crisp gravel drive that lay between rows of pencil cypresses. At its end sat a pale peach-coloured villa, to its left an expansive terrace that gave on to an olive grove which sloped away to the south. The view of the Mediterranean was breathtaking; it glinted like so many diamonds in the noonday sun and Timothy stood still for a moment to take it all in.

'Beautiful; absolutely beautiful. I can see why you want to live and work here.'

'Not bad is it?' boomed a voice from the terrace.

The two men turned in the direction of the voice and beheld a woman of advanced years in a wide straw hat and a swimming costume over which she wore wide silk trousers of soft pink and a diaphanous floral shift. She was standing with her arms stretched wide in welcome, and Archie, accepting the invitation, walked forward and flung his arms around her, kissing her on both cheeks.

'Hello, Auntie. Lovely to see you.' Then, extricating himself from her firm embrace, held out an arm in indication and said, 'This is Timothy.'

'TIMOTHY!' she boomed again. 'The hero of the moment! Come here and give me a hug you wonderful man!'

Feeling that to decline would border on rudeness, Timothy did as he was bid, and found himself engulfed in a firm and surprisingly fragrant embrace.

'Mwah, mwah!' She kissed him noisily on both cheeks, exactly as she had done with Archie, and then held him at arms' length as if to examine him. 'Well, I'm surprised you had it in you, Timothy. I was expecting someone much more sturdily built bearing in mind your heroic actions.' Her voice was aristocratic; her manner warm and welcoming.

'Not heroic at all, really. Just lucky.'

'Nonsense. Archie told me all about it on the phone, and

now you must give me the full story on the terrace. Come on!' She turned and strode purposefully, if a trifle inelegantly thanks to a combination of weight and age, to the stone terrace perched high above the olive trees and orange groves, with barely another villa in sight between its green mantle and the shimmering blue waters of the Mediterranean. Again Timothy found himself arrested by the panorama before him.

'Quite a view, eh?' Sit yourselves down and let's have a drink.' She pointed to the large cane armchairs with their comfortable-looking cushions striped in yellow and white that were arranged on three sides of a square beneath a large square parasol of bottle green.

As the hostess flopped in her own chair – a peacock-like construction with a huge circular back that was positioned in the centre of the row of seats facing the sea – she rang a small silver bell on the table next to her chair and shouted, 'Jonathan! JONATHAN! Drinks please!' At which a small man with slicked back hair that was rather too dark for his years appeared through the French windows. In spite of the heat he was wearing black trousers and a white cotton jacket with brass buttons that reached up to his chin. It was as though he had been waiting around the corner expressly for further instructions. 'Of course, milady. What would you loike?' The accent was east London; strangely foreign in such a seemingly exotic location.

'Gentlemen?'

'A cold beer please, Auntie.'

Timothy nodded. 'That would be lovely.'

'Two cold beers and my usual please, Jonathan.' The little man bowed and disappeared whence he had come, negotiating the sill of the French windows with some care.

'Oh this *is* lovely. So *nice* to see you again, Archie. And to meet you, Timothy.' She stopped abruptly. 'Goodness! All this chatter and I haven't introduced myself, and I don't suppose Archie has told you who I am?'

She looked quizzically at Timothy who smiled weakly, as if to confess the deficiency.

'He never does. Just brings people here – and not often enough I might add – and I then discover they haven't a clue who this mad old bat is or why Archie knows her.'

Timothy grinned and wondered what was coming.

'Rosamund Hawksmoor. Friend of Archie's late grandmother. Not really an auntie at all, though he always calls me that. You can call me Rosamund.'

'Right,' was all Timothy could manage, feeling unable at the moment to say anything more positive in the face of the welter of conversation issuing forth like a cataract from the voluble old woman. She was, he guessed, in her late seventies, maybe early eighties. Her face was heavily wrinkled but possessed of fine cheekbones and a long, elegant nose. She wore rather too much mascara, which was not skillfully applied, and her lips bore traces of bright pink lipstick. The large pair of sunglasses was now pushed up on top of her head, which was generously furnished with a well-ordered cottage loaf of silver-grey hair. She had clearly been a devastatingly good-looking woman in her younger days – was still good looking now thanks to the bones – and had the palest, brightest blue eyes Timothy could ever remember seeing. This was a woman clearly comfortable in her own skin and in her own surroundings, which she seemed to take a delight in sharing.

'Have you lived here long?' asked Timothy, as Jonathan the butler returned bearing a tray on which sat two cold beers and what looked like a dry Martini. He placed them carefully on the table in front of his mistress and her guests and retreated once more into the cool of the villa.

'Goodness, yes. How long, Archie?' Then, before Archie could answer, 'Thirty years I should think. All of Archie's life anyway.'

Timothy took a sip of the beer and looked out to sea. 'I've never been anywhere more beautiful,' he said.

'No. A lot of people say that. And I've never become complacent about it. My husband and I bought it when he retired. He took early retirement, you know. Big mistake. Life needs a sense of purpose. He died three years later. Very sad. I rather felt like giving up.' She hesitated for a moment, as though the ghost of an earlier life had unexpectedly returned to haunt her. Then she brightened. 'But I didn't. In the words of Winston Churchill, I kept buggering on.'

Timothy felt a pang of recognition, but had no time to dwell on it before his hostess continued: 'I decided that I needed a sense of purpose, too. I write, you know. Fiction. Novels. Pot-boilers some call them. Bloody cheek! It takes effort, and dedication − sitting down on your own with a wonderful view to distract you. It's not easy. But I've been doing it for twenty years now. Sell quite a few.' She took a sip of the dry Martini, as if to fuel herself. 'Write in the mornings, enjoy the afternoons, that's my way of life.'

Archie cut in. 'Auntie is amazingly successful. She's been translated into . . . how many languages?'

'Oh, about thirty. Love is the same the whole world over, you see. It breaks down barriers.'

'So you write romantic novels?' asked Timothy, warming to the old woman and her uninhibited manner.

'If that's what you want to call them. I write about people − ordinary people in extraordinary situations. People and their relationships. No two are alike, and yet all of them have common factors. It keeps my mind active. The alternative would be too many of these,' she lifted the glass and took another sip.

'Amazing,' said Timothy.

'Not really. Lucky; that's what I am, though I do find that the harder I work the luckier I get.'

Timothy smiled at the old battleaxe. Here she was, her life sorted. She had coped with the loss of her spouse and come out the other side. She had managed to get the balance right – working hard and yet clearly enjoying life to the full.

'So come on then. Tell me all about it. This episode where our two heroes apprehended the villains in the marina at Monte Carlo and saved the day. It's rather appropriate that it's called Port Hercules isn't it?' She laughed softly at her own little joke and took another sip of the iced martini.

Archie shook his head. 'I was completely taken in. It was Timothy who rumbled them.'

'Well, I saw the woman pinch the silver salt cellars and put them in her bag; what I couldn't work out was how to let Archie know what had happened, because he was ensconced with this enormous guy who turned out not to be a multi-millionaire but a serial burglar.'

Rosamund chipped in, 'But I thought you vetted people before they arrived.'

'We do,' confirmed Archie, 'but these two were crafty, they forged their identities. The real Mr and Mrs Ballantyne really are worth a couple of hundred million, but we discovered later that they were still in Aberdeen. These two were . . .'

'Imposters!'

'Exactly.'

'Wonderful word isn't it? You don't hear it used much nowa-days, but then what with credit card fraud being so common I suppose they just call it "stealing your identity".'

'Well, whatever they call it, Auntie, it's still going on, and the false Mr and Mrs Ballantyne are now locked up at Prince Albert's pleasure, if that's what they call it over here.'

'So what did you do, Timothy? Tell me all.'

Over a second beer, and Rosamund's single Martini (she was true to her word about resisting temptation), Archie and Timothy explained the events of the previous day, Timothy taking great delight in recounting Archie's incredulous expression when he himself went into overdrive and suggested to the false Mrs Ballantyne that she try the hot tub.

'And the black eye?'

'Oh, a wayward kick I'm afraid. I forgot to pin down his legs, but when Archie came and sat on them we had him under control. Mind you, the language was a bit fruity.'

'Ha! I'll bet it was. You'd robbed him of his livelihood. Mind you, he sounds a bit of an evil so and so.'

'He was a heavy, I'll say that for him,' confirmed Timothy. 'If I'd known he had previous for GBH I'm not sure I would have got in his way.'

'And were they really married?'

'Brother and sister apparently. From the East End of London.'

'Didn't their accents give them away?'

'Oh, come on, Auntie,' chided Archie. 'You know that three-quarters of my clients speak like that. And he had this story about having been brought up down south. It seems so obviously implausible now but at the time it seemed they were like so many others I show round – self-made types. He gave the impression of knowing what he was looking at – and for – and you simply can't tell from someone's accent what they're worth.'

'No, I suppose not. Though I'm glad to say that people like that do not impinge on my life – even my fictional one. It's not that I'm a snob—'

Their conversation was interrupted by the emergence of Jonathan from the French windows. 'Luncheon, ma'am,' he murmured respectfully.

Rosamund drained her glass and motioned the two men to follow her around the corner of the terrace to where a table had been set. It was laid almost as opulently – though considerably more tastefully – as the one on Odyssey. Small bowls of cream and white flowers were arranged down the middle among crystal goblets, damask napkins, gleaming cutlery and fine silver-rimmed bone china plates. A basket of freshly baked rolls stood in the centre.

'Help yourself – they're home grown,' instructed Rosamund, indicating a bowl of plump olives.

'This is wonderful,' murmured Timothy, aware that all he seemed to be able to offer in the way of conversation was a string of vacuous superlatives.

Over a lunch of fresh lobster, crisp Mediterranean salad and similarly crisp white wine, Rosamund grilled Timothy on his background, his life at home and his future plans. After an hour and a half he felt drained, though strangely relieved of some kind of burden, as though telling his story out loud to a sympathetic listener older in years than he himself, was, in some way, cathartic. It struck him that in recent times at least he had enjoyed, mostly, the company of younger people. It was, most certainly, invigorating and life-affirming, but it made a change to feel that he was not the eldest member of the company for a while, not the one who had to be wise and sensible, to advise and to warn; the one with the most responsibility resting upon his shoulders; though people who were 'responsible' seldom gave away large sums of money to a person they had known less than a week. He brushed aside the thought, which was now beginning to pester him after the fashion of a persistent mosquito.

The conversation (for it was two-way rather than a monologue), and the example set by the indefatigable Rosamund, reassured him that there could be life after loss, and that one should not be surprised when opportunities presented themselves, even if they came from an unexpected direction.

Throughout it all, he was aware that Rosamund, in spite of her overwhelming hospitality, seemed to be quietly sizing him up. It was almost as though she could see into his mind; into his heart. It was something that ordinarily would have disconcerted him and would have led to him excusing himself from the table for a while to let things blow over, but in this instance he felt strangely comforted by it; as though he had found, in some way, a kindred spirit. Time would tell.

20

VILLA DELPHINE, ST JEAN CAP FERRAT

MAY

'All my wife has ever taken from the Mediterranean – from that whole vast intuitive culture – are four bottles of Chianti to make into lamps.'

Peter Shaffer, *Equus*, 1973

The conversation over lunch continued in varied fashion, covering everything from the price of real estate in Monaco to the mixture of inconvenience and excitement that would be provided by the Grand Prix.

'Will you stay for it?' asked Rosamund of Timothy.

'Oh, no. I'll be on my way before then. I like old cars but I'm not much of a fan of Formula 1 or 2 or whatever it is. They seem to me like nothing more than a swarm of noisy wasps going round and round in circles.'

Rosamund nodded. 'I couldn't agree more. So where is your next stop on this Grand Tour.'

'Pisa.'

'Oh dear.'

'Why "oh dear".'

'Well, I've always felt that there's nothing much to it. The leaning tower leans but that's about it. And it's swarming with tourists who get frustrated that they can't climb it any more. Take it from me, it's frightfully disappointing.'

'Oh,' said Timothy with a note of dismay in his voice. 'I was thinking of staying there a week.'

'Good God! I wouldn't do that. You'll have seen everything there is to see in fifteen minutes, unless you're an architect with a morbid fascination in subsidence.'

'Oh.'

'I'm sorry to have put a dampener on it. Do go if you want – to tick the box on your list.'

'Well . . . no . . . if you think it will be a let down . . .'

'I'm sure it will. I don't know anyone who has a good word to say for it.'

'Right.' Timothy found himself at a loss not only as to how to continue the conversation, but also as to the next stop on his itinerary.

'Have you booked a hotel there?'

'No. I haven't booked anything from now on. I wanted to get my trip under way knowing that I had sorted my accommodation for the first couple of locations – I've been a bit extravagant on that front, a bit indulgent – but then I wanted to move on as I felt like it, rather than having to stick to a fixed itinerary.'

'Well that's a blessing. Where was your next stop going to be?'

'Florence.'

'Ah, Firenze! Now that's a different kettle of fish altogether. I'd go straight there if I were you. Give the leaning tower the old heave-ho. You could spend a week or more in Florence and not see everything.'

Archie, who had sat quietly during the conversation of his two companions now chipped in with, 'Auntie don't be so bossy!'

'I'm not being bossy, I just don't want Timothy wasting his time on some uninspiring heap of faulty architecture, that's all.'

Archie shook his head and grinned. 'That's the trouble with Auntie; she finds it so difficult to be assertive!'

'Archie, why don't you go and have a swim so that Timothy and I can have a good talk. Go on!' She motioned to the steps that led down from the terrace where they were sitting. 'You'll find towels in the pool house; and swimmies if you're feeling modest.'

Archie sighed heavily. 'I thought you weren't meant to swim straight after eating?'

'Poppycock. It's been scientifically proved that there is absolutely no foundation to that argument. Now run along.'

Archie did as he was instructed and left the table with raised eyebrows directed at Timothy. 'Don't let her brow-beat you.'

Timothy smiled. 'I won't.'

They watched as he descended the steps among the myrtle and lavender, agave and citrus until finally his head bobbed from view below the scattering of jagged rocks that bordered the gravelly path. A minute or two later they heard a splash which indicated that he had entered the water.

It was then that Rosamund asked, 'So, Timothy, what are you running away from?'

In spite of his suspicions that she was a perceptive soul, the directness of her enquiry took him by surprise. 'Well, nothing that I'm aware of.'

'Oh, everyone is running away from something. Take Archie. He's finally escaped the clutches of his mother. She's a dear friend but far too possessive. Wants him to settle down with a nice girl and get a job in the city. I keep telling her, he'll settle down with who he wants, when he's good and ready and not before. Best thing he could have done, coming down here. He knows where I am when he needs to sound off about something.'

'And does he?'

'Not very often, no. Keeps himself to himself most of the time. Not anti-social, just self-contained. A bit like you I suspect. Am I right?'

Timothy sat silently for a moment and then said, 'I suppose.'

Rosamund patted the back of his hand as it lay on the armrest of his chair. 'Believe me, I know what it's like. I've been there, even though it was a long time ago now. It gets better. It never goes away completely, but you find a way of moving on . . . slowly. The alternative is a waste of a life.' She thought for a moment and then said, 'But, forgive me, I don't detect . . . profound grief on your part. Am I right?'

'I . . . well . . . we'd been married more than thirty years . . .'

'Happily?'

There was a pause before Timothy replied. 'Contentedly.'

'Resignedly?' she nodded to herself. 'I see. The bloom had worn off. It does that.'

'We were different,' he said, with a note of defensiveness in his voice.

'Ah . . . "we grew apart".'

'Something like that. The old cliché I suppose,' he said, his tone a mixture of guilt and resignation.

'It happens. And you stayed together because of the children?'

'Pretty much. Though I don't think that Isobel thought there was anything wrong at all. If she'd have known how I felt I think she'd have been completely mystified. Disbelieving. Incredulous.'

'Oh, I think she would have known. She might have chosen not to let you realise it but . . .'

'She never said anything.'

'Defence mechanism. It works for the ostrich. Stick your head in the sand and you can convince yourself that nothing is wrong. It's an irritating analogy, and very unfair to ostriches, but you know what I mean.'

Timothy managed a weak smile. 'I do.'

'So now you are undertaking your grand tour feeling a mixture of relief and guilt.'

Timothy looked her in the eye. 'You're very perceptive.'

'It's my job, Timothy. It's what I do. I try to make sense of the silly minutiae of life and weave them into stories. Just stories. But they have a kernel of truth in them. They're touchstones in a way. They might not have the sophistication or complexity of Proust but they appeal to a certain market.'

The mention of the author's name struck a chord. Francine had been at the back of his mind rather than the forefront for a few hours. How could that have been? Now, here she was again, along with her snuffling pug – or preferably without it.

Rosamund noticed the change in his expression. 'Have I said something inappropriate?'

'No. Not at all. I was just thinking of someone.'

'And that's the next danger, of course. At your age.'

'I'm sorry?'

'Falling headlong in love with someone quite unsuitable.'

Timothy fought for something to say, but failed, and found himself doing a passable impersonation of a goldfish gasping for air.

'Oh dear. I fear I've touched a nerve.'

'No. I . . . well . . .'

'Forgive me. I didn't mean to pry. It's nothing to do with me.

We've only just met and I am far too nosey for my own good
. . . and anyone else's. Would you like coffee?'

'Thank you.'

'Come on.' Rosamund levered herself up from her chair with
some difficulty and led the way back to the terrace where they
had sat for drinks. She flopped down in her peacock chair, the
cushions fresh-plumped in her absence, removed her sunglasses
and reached for a large straw hat which she placed on her head,
tilting it to keep the sun from her eyes. 'You must think me
very rude,' she said, when she had settled herself. 'I don't get
a lot of practice at conversation. Jonathan's discourse is somewhat limited – mainly to the areas of catering, housekeeping
and the two-fifteen at Lingfield. And after lunch or dinner it's
non-existent.' She made a drinking motion with her right hand.
'I have friends popping by occasionally – Archie drops in when
he's nothing better to do – so when someone like you arrives I
tend to jump in with both feet.'

'I really don't mind.'

'Just be careful, Timothy. A single man like you on the Riviera.
You represent the perfect prey for a certain type of woman.'

'Oh?'

'Yes. There are plenty of old widows out here – present
company excepted,' she added with a wink, 'who'd be delighted
to be squired by a handsome fifty-something man of means
with no apparent ties.'

'I'm not sure about the means. I'm pretty small fry when it
comes to the likes of Monaco residents.'

'Oh, they have the means, they just don't have the men – men
who are not simply after their money.'

'And I have a family back home – three children – grown up
– and a granddaughter.'

'But they have their own lives now?'

'Yes.'

'You don't seem to realise . . .'

'What?'

Rosamund laughed softly. 'Have you looked in the mirror recently?'

'I'm sorry?'

'You're a very good-looking man. And you're available.'

Timothy demurred. 'You're very kind, but I think you exaggerate.'

'Not much; believe me. But I'm not here to clip your wings; to cramp your style. You enjoy yourself. You're a free agent. Just be careful.'

'That's funny.'

'What is?'

'You're the second . . . mature woman . . . who's said that to me in the space of a week.'

'Well, it must be sound advice then, mustn't it?'

Their conversation was interrupted by the arrival of Jonathan whose nose had now assumed the colour of a ripe plum. A wisp of the slicked-back hair had freed itself from the effects of his brilliantine and dangled just above his right eye. He had clearly enjoyed a glass or two while his mistress had been lunching with her friends. He said nothing, but having deposited the silver tray on the low table in front of them he veered off, placing more reliance than previously on the frame of the French windows.

Rosamund ignored her butler and fixed Timothy with her beady eye. 'So what will you do when all this is over? When your trip comes to an end? When you've visited Florence and Rome and Venice and had your fill of culture. What does the future hold.'

'I don't know,' he murmured softly. 'I really don't know.'

'No. I didn't think you did.'

He felt deflated now. As though he had been rumbled. As though the Grand Tour he had planned had been nothing more than a ruse to mask the passing of time and delay his facing up to the future.

'Has something happened?' she enquired casually. 'Since your trip began, I mean.'

'Oh, just an encounter, that's all.'

'With a woman?'

He nodded.

'Ah, I see.'

'What is it they say? There's no fool like an old fool?'

Rosamund smiled. 'Don't be too hard on yourself. You've a lot to work out over the next few weeks and months. Years even. Don't reproach yourself over what's past, and don't let an interfering old woman like me prevent you from enjoying yourself. Just take your time, that's all. Take your time and grasp life with both hands, if that doesn't sound like a contradiction in terms.'

Timothy thought for a moment or two, then he asked, 'Are you a good judge of character, Rosamund?'

'I'd like to think so. I should be. I've had enough experience.' She laid her hands on her lap, and Timothy noticed the large liver spots and the soft, translucent quality of her skin. A slender gold wedding ring encircled the third finger of her left hand, a large rounded chunk of amber graced the middle finger of her right.

'Have you ever met anyone who made you act . . . irrationally? Who made you question your own judgement?' he asked.

She looked thoughtful, then said, 'Once. When I was very

young. And once while I was married. I let myself get rather carried away when I should not have done and . . . well, we all make mistakes don't we?'

'Did you recover from it?'

'Eventually.'

'Did it make you more cautious?'

'For a while. And then I decided that one can't play safe all one's life. It's a bit like the Grande Corniche really. If you take all the bends at low speed you'll be quite safe, but there are moments when you want to take them faster and have a bit of a thrill. I don't think there's anything wrong with that, do you? Provided you don't lose control completely and hurtle over the precipice.'

Timothy did not answer. He was looking out to sea, wondering if that's all it had been – a bend taken rather too fast. And then Archie came up the path from the pool, a towel around his neck. 'Shall we motor back then? Dinner's on me tonight.'

Rosamund got up from her chair with some difficulty and said, 'Why don't you show Timothy the garden before you go? I just want to pop inside and freshen up. I'll see you in a few minutes.'

Timothy got up as she did and, as she disappeared into the cool and shady confines of the villa, Archie led him down the path between the aromatic cypress trees towards the garden and the olive grove, the citrus orchards and the lily pool. Hot, dry gravel crunched beneath their feet, and all around them cicadas engaged in ceaseless rasping conversation, interspersed by the occasional sound of a wave breaking on the shore below. If this was not Eden, then he could not imagine what was.

21

LE GRANDE CORNICHE

MAY

'Enjoy while you can the exhilarating feeling of driving
with the wind in your hair. In time it will pass.
That's the hair, not the feeling.'

Thomas Maunder, *Passing Clouds*, 1992

Archie drove back so that Timothy could admire the view. He
slipped a CD into the Bentley's stereo and Timothy laughed
when themes to the James Bond films began to fill the air
around them, punctuated by the roar of the 4-litre V8 engine
and the occasional tragic cry of a seagull. It was good to feel
the wind in his hair, to lay his head back and let the sun smite
his face as Tom Jones, Shirley Bassey and Matt Monro provided
a fitting musical accompaniment. It intrigued him how much
music had been a part of his trip – a soundtrack to the series
of events that had happened along the way – first Charles Trenet,
then Mozart's Queen of the Night aria, the simple silliness of
'Monte Carlo or Bust!' and now the Bond themes.

They chatted for a while and then a conversational silence fell between them; an easy, comfortable silence, though filled with John Barry's soaring strings, the engine's growl and the wind whistling in his ears. The mixture of excitement and apprehension he had experienced over the last few days had hitherto been a novel sensation; now it seemed to be his constant companion. Since meeting Francine he had found himself filled with a kind of nervousness he thought had been left behind in adolescence. It made him uneasy and yet it lifted his spirits to new heights, even though he suspected these feelings would betray an evanescence that would, in the long run, prove his undoing. This was not reality; this was the stuff of dreams. This was not a real world – well, not real to him. His was a world of responsibility and steadiness, not of excitement and unpredictability. He had begun this adventure willingly, thoughtfully. Why did it seem to be spiralling beyond his control? Perhaps it would settle down now. He must get a grip; must reason with himself and put Francine to the back of his mind as she had no doubt done with him. It was a fling; nothing wrong with that. He hoped that she had not simply used him, but knew that he had to be prepared for that to be the case, and yet –

'Penny for them . . .'

The voice seemed to come from far away.

'Sorry?'

'Penny for your thoughts, that's what my mum says.'

It was Archie's voice. They were snaking their way down into Monte Carlo now, one minute away from and then towards the setting sun – a fiery, coppery orb intent on slipping into the sea in the next half hour or so. The spectacle was breathtaking, but then he was becoming used to astonishingly beautiful views. They reinforced his belief that beauty was a worthwhile goal in almost any field – art, music, sculpture, even graphic design. He had tasted just a fraction of it so far in his quest to follow in Mr Addison's footsteps; Italy would be where the richest of pickings would be found. All that was yet to come. He knew he should dislike Monaco, for its flaunting of wealth, its show-iness and the type of people it attracted, but he found that he could not. He had seen only a snatch of it so far – the marina in Port Hercules and the apartments that loomed up around it – but although he could see it for what it was – little more than a craggy-edged harbour on a rugged coastline peopled with tax exiles – it did somehow possess a certain charm. Tomorrow he would explore the botanic garden that clung to the cliff face, and have lunch alone up by the Grimaldis' impressive looking palace. Maybe then he could take a more objective view.

'I don't know if they're worth that much,' he replied.

'Try me.'

'I was just thinking how my life has changed in the space of a week or so.'

'For the better?'

'Who knows?'

'What will you do tomorrow?'

'Explore a bit. I haven't seen much yet. I've been too busy selling boats – or trying to.'

There was a sudden note of dismay in Archie's voice. 'Oh God! I never thought! You're meant to be on holiday. I'm sorry if I've taken up too much time . . .'

Timothy turned to look at him; this tanned youth with his open-necked pink shirt and his white Bermuda shorts; quite a catch for some dishy girl. He was good looking, thought Timothy, in that public school sort of way, with his shock of fair hair and high cheekbones, pale blue eyes and – now that the Riviera had become his home – a healthy tan that was reminiscent of honey rather than the desperate mahogany of so many Mediterranean grandes dames.

'You haven't taken up too much time at all. You've opened my eyes. I've had adventure – probably rather too much of it yesterday – and I've discovered the delights of Cap Ferrat. Why should you apologise for that?'

'Well, I just thought—'

'Well don't. I'll have plenty of time tomorrow to wander round the square, risk a few pounds in the casino and go and look at the plants clinging to that cliff. You can get on with selling your boats.'

'Don't remind me.'

Timothy laughed.

'Oh, and talking of reminders,' said Archie, 'Rosamund asked me to give you this when we'd left. I almost forgot.' He pulled a crumpled envelope from the right-hand pocket of his shorts and passed it to Timothy. 'She said it might be helpful.'

'I'll open it when I get to the hotel. If I do it now it will probably blow out of my hand, the rate you take these bends.'

'I thought you wanted a bit of a thrill. There's no point in crawling.'

'That's what Rosamund said,' murmured Timothy.

'What? I can't hear you for the wind and the music.'

Timothy pocketed the letter, leaned back in the seat and looked out over the sea, the better to savour his final moments on the Grande Corniche. The music now was Nancy Sinatra. Why was it that whenever his thoughts seemed to wander, the music could pick up on his mood and encapsulate it? This was getting too frequent to be comfortable. As Archie steered the Bentley down towards the marina, he shook his head as if trying to dislodge the very thought from his brain.

'What is it?' asked Archie.

'Nothing. It's nothing.'

'Something wrong with the music? Don't you like this one?'

'It's not that I don't like it, it's just that sometimes the music I listen to seems to fit the moment rather too well.'

They pulled up outside the Hôtel Hermitage, and as Timothy alighted and walked towards the shiny glass doors, he heard the words of the song fading away behind him. As the song said, maybe you really could live twice.

22

HÔTEL HERMITAGE, MONTE CARLO

MAY

'Advice is seldom welcome; and those who want it the
most always like it the least.'

Lord Chesterfield, *Letters to his Son*, 1748

It was not until he had washed and changed that Timothy
remembered the letter from Rosamund that Archie had given
to him. He wondered when she had had time to write it, and
then he called to mind the fact that she disappeared into the
villa while Archie was showing him the garden. She had hugged
him before he left, then held him at arm's length, a hand on
each of his shoulders. He could recall quite precisely what she
had said: 'Sometimes, Timothy, it is later than you think. Good
Luck!' And then she was gone. He would miss her. He wished
they could have talked for longer.

He looked at his watch – a quarter to eight. He had agreed
to meet Archie at eight outside the hotel. They would eat, he
had been told, at a rather exclusive restaurant.

He tore open the envelope and removed the folded sheet of thick writing paper it contained:

> Villa Delphine,
> Cap Ferrat

My Dear Timothy,

Forgive my familiarity today. It is rare for me to meet someone whom I feel is on the same wavelength (even if years younger!) and so I was perhaps tempted to be more candid than was polite. But I wish you well on your Grand Tour. It is brave of you to undertake it. I also want to thank you for being so nice to Archie. He is a special child of whom I am very fond. What I did not tell you during our conversation is that he was rather badly treated by his father, who expects such a lot from him. Nothing violent, you understand, just what I suppose nowadays we would call 'mental cruelty' – setting standards – and having expectations – that are rather hard to live up to. It has left him rather bruised, though his upbringing has trained him, also, not to show his feelings. I'm never sure that this is altogether a good thing. Archie is heir to a large estate (not that he <u>ever</u> speaks about it) and his parents worry that he might meet someone who has a nose for that sort of thing – the <u>wrong sort</u> of someone, that is. It is something of which I know he is aware and I fear it makes him cautious in relationships. Too cautious sometimes. As you and I know, you have to give a little in order to receive.

Why I should tell you all this I am not sure, but I am a great believer in gut instinct – it seldom does one a disservice. Archie has few friends, and the fact that he brought you here counts for a lot. There seemed to be a kind of ease between you, which I don't think I imagined. I have seldom seen him so relaxed in another's company. I wouldn't want you to run away with the idea that he is some kind of wastrel or ne'er-do-well, living a lotus-eating life in Monte Carlo, which he most certainly is not. He will find himself eventually. He could very easily opt for a life of leisure but he chooses not to, even if his choice does not accord with that of his parents who would pack him off into the city if they could. It would, I am sure, be the end of him.

So this is really a thank you letter. You may feel it unnecessary (I am sure you do, since you seem a very pleasant person) but I wanted to say that today you brightened both our lives.

Would you forgive me if I ask of you a favour? It is not one that I can ask of Archie directly, in that he will feel beholden if I do, but if you could somehow slip into the conversation how much I value his visits to me? The life of a writer is, perforce, a solitary one, and there is just so much inspiration and stimulation one can get from a glorious view. I would not ask this were circumstances somewhat different. Without going into sordid – or self-indulgent detail – suffice it to say that I shall not be around for much longer. Archie has no inkling of this, and neither would I want him to, but if you can somehow drop into the conversation just how much I enjoy his company I would be profoundly grateful. It brings into my life a kind of vitality, which is otherwise sadly lacking.

As for you, Timothy, I apologise if I lectured you. It is a failing I try to overcome – usually unsuccessfully. But then sometimes I see what I feel others cannot (or which others have the sense to keep to themselves, you might say!). Please do not torture yourself with feelings of guilt. Neither regret the things you do in your fifties – and later – which might seem rash, frivolous and sometimes irresponsible. Provided they do <u>no harm to others</u> they should be cherished and enjoyed to the full. It is so trite to say that 'life is for the living' but all too often we feel that a state of sadness is where we really belong. It is not.

That said, the one thing I have learned in my long life (I am ninety-two – don't whatever you do tell Archie; it shall be our secret!) is that no amount of money, luxury and privilege is any guarantee of contentment. That is something which must come from within. It is the most elusive of qualities – contentment – but one to strive for and to treasure. It is more realistic than happiness (which is, by its very nature, transient) and more rewarding than either fame or fortune. Trust me – I have experienced both.

Sorry. I did not intend to lecture – <u>again</u>! – simply to encourage you in your endeavours to find yourself. For that, I imagine, is your goal. Travel, you will discover, most certainly broadens the mind, but the people who journey 'to find themselves' generally return home to discover that they have been there all along. Does that make sense? Probably not.

But good fortune to you my friend. You deserve it (and I hope I have not bored you to death . . .)

Yours most sincerely,

Rosamund Hawksmoor

It was a quarter past eight before Timothy made it down to the lobby of the Hôtel Hermitage. He did so with a mixture of feelings.

23

YACHT CLUB DE MONACO, MONTE CARLO

MAY

'Everybody my age should be issued with a 2lb fresh salmon. If you see someone young, beautiful and happy, you should slap them as hard as you can with it.'

Richard Griffiths (actor), *Independent*, 2006

How do you tell someone that their auntie is dying and would like to see them more often without actually giving the game away? It was a problem that occupied Timothy's mind as he met Archie in the hotel lobby and apologised for his lateness, which he put down to the shower not working. It was then all he could do to stop Archie from approaching reception and complaining that in such a smart hotel such a thing was completely unacceptable. He explained that he had already done so, that the concierge was hugely apologetic and that the hotel would deduct something from the bill. He felt hot under the collar at this deception but squared it with his conscience by telling himself it was all done with the best possible motives.

That, and the modus operandi he would adopt that evening in ensuring that Archie did not neglect his 'auntie' over the coming weeks, were temporarily put out of his mind when Archie said, 'I hope you don't mind, but I've invited someone else along for supper. I'd like you to meet them.'

'Oh . . . right . . . well . . . are you sure you wouldn't rather be alone?'

'No! I mean, yes, I'm sure. I'd rather like your opinion.'

Timothy stopped in his tracks. They were walking towards the yacht club, the lights of the marina twinkling around them in the warm night air; boats gently tugging at their moorings accompanied by the musical 'ping' of halyards on alloy masts. 'But I'm not qualified to advise you . . .'

'Please! It's just that I'd value your opinion, that's all, and I don't think I'm ready yet for *dinner à deux*.'

'You mean it's someone new? Someone you've not been out with yet?'

'Yes.'

'What will they think? I mean, you inviting me along as a . . . chaperone?'

'Oh, they won't mind. They're not thinking of it as a date. More of a business meeting.'

Timothy looked baffled. 'I don't really understand.'

'The thing is, it's a potential client, and . . .'

'And you'd like the potential client to be something more?'

'Well . . . yes. But we're not meant to fraternise with the clients and so I thought that if you were there . . .'

'It might look less like a date and more like a business meeting?'

'Exactly.'

'Does this client know that you . . . I mean . . . have they shown any sort of . . . interest?'

'I think so. Well, I'm not sure. The answer was "yes" when I suggested we meet over dinner – but then I did say we'd be accompanied by my colleague.'

'What?!'

'I didn't think you'd mind. Well, I hoped you wouldn't. It would be really helpful. I'd really appreciate it . . .'

Timothy shook his head. 'I thought my days as a superyacht salesman were behind me.'

'You won't have to do anything, or say anything – technical I mean.'

'That's just as well; I can't think that my opinion on the purple towels would be of much value.'

'Oh, I've had them changed. They're cream now.'

'Well, at least I've had some positive influence on sales.'

Archie looked at him imploringly. 'Would you mind? It would only be for an hour or so. Then we can go on and have a drink on our own. It's just that I'd feel a bit more . . . well, confident if you were there.'

'You? Lacking in confidence? You're a salesman! Of superyachts!'

'Yes. I know. I can do that bit all right; it's just that when it comes to relationships . . . well . . .'

Timothy laughed softly. 'What are you like? Have you looked in the mirror recently? You're a handsome young man with a charming manner and you don't have the confidence to ask someone out when you could probably have your pick . . . ?'

'That's the problem. I'm not a very good picker.'

'So I've heard.'

'Mmm?'

'I said I don't believe a word.' Timothy sighed deeply, then slapped Archie on the shoulder and said, 'All right then, go on.

But don't blame me if it all goes pear-shaped and your client rumbles me for what I am.'

'What; a good friend?'

'No. A fraud. But thank you for the compliment. I mean, for goodness sake, you've only known me for a couple of days.'

Archie smiled. 'I know. Ridiculous isn't it? But it's just that . . . you know . . . I get on well with you, even though you're much older. Sort of . . . soulmates.'

'I wouldn't go that far. It's an overused word, I reckon. Why don't we just settle for . . . *sympatico*?'

'Is that better? Less intense?'

'Probably. Come on then. Talking of intensity, let's see how this all pans out. I'll tell you something, Archie Bedlington, you live up to your name when it comes to not letting go.' He began walking towards the shiny door of the Yacht Club de Monaco which is where Archie had indicated they would be dining.

'What do you mean?'

'Didn't you have *The Observer Book of Dogs* when you were a boy?'

'Before my time I'm afraid.'

'Hey! Any more cracks like that and you'll go on your own. The Bedlington terrier is renowned for being spirited, good-tempered and affectionate. And being a terrier it never lets go. Ring any bells?'

Archie grinned. 'I'll take that as a compliment.'

'It's also very intelligent and it was originally bred for hunting vermin.'

'Oh; not sure about that.'

'No. You stick to the good-tempered and affectionate bit and muggins here will endeavour to sniff out the vermin.'

'Thank you! I knew I could rely on you.'

'Hopefully.' Timothy shook his head resignedly. 'Come on, Casanova. Let's go and meet this "dishy girl".'

Archie opened his mouth to reply but Timothy was already striding through the door of the yacht club, and it was all Archie could do to keep up. Before he had a chance to explain, the steward had greeted Timothy, offered his hand to Archie and was guiding them to the table saying 'Your guest has already arrived M'sieur Bedlington.'

The two men sat down opposite the client, who held out a hand in greeting. 'Hello, Archie.' Then, turning to Timothy, 'I'm Sebastian Fraser. My friends call me Basty.'

Of the myriad thoughts that passed through Timothy's mind in the next few moments, the one that did him greatest credit is that he told himself it did not matter one jot that Archie's new friend was a man. What did it matter? The important thing was that he should find someone worthy of him. Someone who would make him happy. Someone who would make his life complete. The fact occurred to him that Archie might have assumed there was more to their own relationship than Timothy had envisaged, but it was an idea that bore no close scrutiny at all. What was tricky was that he was now sitting at a table with two handsome young men and playing gooseberry.

He wondered if Rosamund had known of Archie's preference and decided not to allude to it in her letter, or if she thought that in doing so it might influence his own relationship with her honorary nephew. No. Surely she understood him better than that; she would know that Archie's tastes in . . . companions . . . would not matter to him one jot. At least he hoped that was the case. And now here he was, sitting opposite two extraordinarily handsome young men and feeling – to be perfectly honest – slightly uncomfortable.

'Good to see you,' said Archie to the other man as they shook hands diffidently.

'And you.'

Oh dear, this was going to be even harder than Timothy had thought. What to do? What to say? How to act? He tried to look relaxed, but felt that the expression on his face was a mixture of the inane and the uncomfortable.

'Shall I order drinks?' he asked, anxious to appear useful.

'I've ordered a bottle of Krug,' said Sebastian.

'Lovely,' said Archie.

Timothy sat back into his chair, choosing to avoid an opening conversation that dealt with the weather and the scenery. It seemed decidedly pathetic in the face of the current situation.

The two young men smiled at one another, and Timothy was aware of a certain nervousness between them. A lack of ease. He could remember such atmospheres from his own youth and early courtship of assorted females; courtships which had all ended as they had begun – rather pathetically and frequently unresolved. He must intervene and jolly things along, otherwise it seemed likely that Archie would let this opportunity slip through his fingers.

'So are you a regular visitor to Monte Carlo?' he asked Sebastian.

The young man turned towards him and smiled pleasantly. 'Yes. Every year. For the Grand Prix.'

'Ah, yes. Busy time here I expect.' He was aware of the banality of it all but it seemed preferable to an uneasy silence.

The waiter arrived with champagne flutes and an ice bucket containing a bottle of Krug, whose cork he popped carefully before half filling three of the flutes sitting on the silvery tray.

As the waiter plunged the bottle into its ice bucket and left the table, Sebastian raised a glass and said in Archie's direction, '*Salute!*'

Archie raised his glass in reply and took a sip. 'Delicious,' he said.

Timothy took a large gulp from the third glass and began to feel desperate. He wondered if it was his own presence that was making the conversation so stilted. He was just about to wax lyrical about the newly opened Yacht Club and the astonishingly opulent fixtures and fittings when his two companions got to their feet. He wondered, for a moment, if they were about to call it a day and leave, when a voice behind him said, 'Sorry I'm late. I got held up in the traffic. It's dreadful at this time in the evening.'

Timothy turned and beheld an angel. She was dressed in tight white jeans and a floppy white sweater. Her long blond hair, shining like gold, tumbled over her shoulders. She shot Timothy a devastatingly wide smile, patted Sebastian on the top of the head indulgently and then said, 'Archie I am *so* sorry. I asked Basty to be here to meet you when I knew I was going to be late. You must think me very rude.'

Archie, his cheeks flushed, stammered a greeting: 'No. No. Not at all. We were just having a drink . . . I mean, we've got a glass here for you.'

'Wonderful!'

A waiter glided in from nowhere and slipped a chair beneath the vision of loveliness as she lowered herself into it and raised her newly filled glass. It was all accomplished in a single motion, as if by magic or sleight of hand, and Timothy, suddenly aware that his mouth was wide open, closed it and managed a feeble smile.

The angel lowered her glass, sighing at the pleasure of her first sip and said, to Timothy, 'We've not met.'

Temporarily lost for words, the gap was filled by Archie who said, 'Sorry; this is . . .

'Tim. Tim Gandy,' offered Timothy.

Archie looked across at him with an enquiring expression, then confirmed, 'Tim's a friend. We were meeting for a drink and . . .'

'Yes,' confirmed Timothy. 'I'll be off in a minute.'

'Oh, stay for a while. It's a shame not to enjoy the fizz together,' said the angel, shooting Timothy another smile which had the same effect upon him as the first; that of complete paralysis of words and movement. He noticed that her eyes were pure turquoise.

'Well, you might stay but I've things to do,' said Sebastian, rising from the table and offering Timothy his hand. 'Good to meet you, Tim. I'll leave you in the capable hands of Archie and my sister.' He turned to Archie and added, 'Make sure she's home before midnight; you've no idea what she turns into at the witching hour.'

'Beast,' said the angel, and slapped her brother on his bottom as he retreated from the table giving the assembled company a knowing wink.

Timothy leaned back in his chair, confused by the events of the last couple of minutes, almost drowning in the delightfully gentle fragrance that surrounded Archie's new companion and trying his best not to be overwhelmed by her beauty.

Archie, noticing Timothy's bewildered expression said, 'Forgive me. You two haven't been introduced. Serena, this is Tim Gandy. A very good friend of mine.'

The angel, who could not have been more appropriately named in Timothy's opinion, stretched out her hand and said, 'Good to meet you, Tim. Are you the chaperone?'

'No; not, not at all . . . I just . . . We were . . .'

Serena broke into a giggle. 'Just teasing. Archie has told me all about you. You're really rather special.'

'I don't . . . well, I mean . . . we only met a few . . .'

'Please. Don't be embarrassed. And you must stay for supper.'

'Oh, I couldn't possibly . . .'

'I insist.' She turned to Archie 'We insist, don't we?'

Archie nodded his agreement, and Timothy wondered if it was more out of politeness and an unwillingness to disappoint the angel than out of a genuine wish for his company.

'But I thought –'

Archie leaned towards the angel, kissed her softly on the cheek and said, 'I'm afraid I had to tell Tim a bit of a fib. I said you were a client. I knew if I told him the truth he wouldn't come.'

Timothy said, 'You mean . . . ?'

'I knew you wouldn't want to play gooseberry but I wanted you to meet her. Serena and I bumped into each other a couple of years ago. When I was out in Ghana. We both went our separate ways afterwards – felt we needed to see a bit more of life – but we kept in touch. She works for Formula 1, along with her brother, Sebastian. She looked me up when she came out here. She's been away for a couple of weeks – in the UK – and just got back.'

'I see.' Though, if Timothy were to be frank, the facts seemed to be clouded in sea mist.

Serena made to clarify the situation. 'We both have families who are rather picky. We're not sure they'll approve and so we're just playing it by ear for a while. My brother – Sebastian – knows about our relationship, but no one else so far.'

'But why the secrecy?' asked Timothy. 'All parents can be tricky to deal with . . .'

'Yes,' confirmed Serena, her expression one of resignation. 'But both Archie and I are in . . . an unusual situation.'

'So I understand.' Timothy spoke slowly, his face showing a perfect apprehension of the status quo. 'You are both . . . well . . . quite wealthy, and both sets of parents are concerned that you should not commit yourselves to anyone' – he thought for a moment, searching for the most diplomatic approach before adding – 'who might be taking advantage.'

Archie regarded him wide eyed. 'How did you know?'

'Conversations with a certain auntie,' confided Timothy, taking another sip of champagne.

'I see.'

'But,' Serena interjected, 'you don't know about me.'

'I just sensed as much.'

'Is it so obvious?'

'Not ostentatiously so. I can just tell, that's all. From your good manners, your dress, the way you speak, the way you carry yourself.' He realised that he might have overstepped the mark. 'I'm sorry; I don't mean to be rude or impertinent, it's just that sometimes it is patently obvious about someone's background, and in other cases – as Archie and I discovered yesterday – it is not so transparent. Am I right?'

Serena and Archie looked at one another, then back at Timothy before Archie confessed, 'Yes. Absolutely.'

'Then why are you worried? If you are both in the same boat – sorry; no pun intended in the Yacht Club of Monaco – then surely all will be well with both sets of parents. But then I might be jumping the gun. Assuming things.'

Serena took Archie's hand in hers and said, 'We hope we can manage to convince them, but we don't want to rush things. We just want to enjoy some time together before we—'

Archie cut in, 'Make it official.'

'Well, good for you. I hope everything works out.' He looked at Serena and felt the merest hint of jealousy – at the pair's advantage of youth, and at Archie's ability to land such a catch. He drained his glass and got to his feet. 'Now then, your offer of supper is very kind, but if you two haven't seen each other for a couple of weeks I don't think you need me here at all. But it's been a delight to meet you, Serena.' He leaned forward to shake her hand, at which point she rose to her feet and kissed him lightly on the cheek. The warmth of her face and the scent of her perfume were intoxicating.

'You're a very lucky man, Archie.' Then, to Serena, 'And you're lucky, too. Take care of each other. I'll see you before I go.'

'Have a good day tomorrow,' said Archie. 'And thank you. For everything.'

Timothy waved away the compliment. 'I did nothing; apart from help you apprehend a couple of criminals. All in a day's work guv'nor,' and he mock saluted before leaving the two of them to their tryst.

As he walked back to the hotel in the twinkle of the evening lights, to the music of lapping wavelets against the sleek yachts, the envy of the moment subsided and he felt a warm benevolence towards the young couple. It was good to think about someone else's relationship for a change, rather than his own. He hoped that the two of them would make a go of it in the face of tricky parents, and hoped also that he had not been so intimidating as they appeared to be to the suitors of his own offspring. How different were Oliver and Vita, Rosie and Ace to Archie and Serena, and how different their circumstances? But love was love, wherever it fell. And Alice. Would she ever find love?

His thoughts returned to Rosamund and her injunction that Archie should not leave it too long before he visited her again. Before he left Monte Carlo he would intimate as much to her honorary nephew, and also explain that he could think of no better person to share the news of Archie and Serena's relation-ship than that wise old bird.

Then he laughed to himself about his earlier misconception in assuming that it might be Sebastian who had captured Archie's heart. Would it have mattered if he had? Happiness was the thing, wherever it was to be found. That was what Rosamund, that mistress of the romantic novel had vouchsafed to him, and he was not in the least inclined to contradict her. Perhaps, in the future, he might meet her again. He did hope so. There was something about the old woman that struck a chord within him; that made him feel she understood the complexities of life, loves and the universe. Well, maybe not quite that much, but certainly more than he did himself. He might be middle aged, but he knew, from his experiences over the last few days, that he still had a lot to learn.

24

JARDIN BOTANIQUE, MONTE CARLO

MAY

'All that I desire to point out is the general principle that
Life imitates Art far more than Art imitates Life.

Oscar Wilde, *The Decay of Lying*, 1891

It was not a bad painting but he felt, as was so frequently the
case, that it did not do justice to its subject. Still, at least it was
a souvenir of sorts, so long as Archie did not mind receiving it
as a memento of their meeting rather than regarding it as
something of an insult. Anyway, Archie would be far too polite
to say so and, as everyone knew, it was the thought that counted
– more than the skill of the brushwork. As usual Timothy did
himself a disservice. He was a better artist than he gave himself
credit for. He was, as his daughter Rosie would occasionally
tell him, better at most things than he gave himself credit for.
Not that it ever changed his opinion of himself.

The craggy slopes of the Jardin Exotique de Monaco had
offered a calming antidote to the freneticism of the previous
few days and Timothy was able to indulge himself in solitude

and reflect on his journey so far. It had been an eventful adventure with more than its fair share of incident. At home in Sussex he had few friends. He had never really thought about it before, but since leaving on his Grand Tour he had talked with people and understood more about them than he could ever remember doing at home. It was not that he was anti-social; at least, he didn't think so. It was just that his world in Sussex seemed so much smaller than the one he had encountered since he set off. There were work colleagues who occasionally asked him and Isobel around for a meal, but the occasions were rare and frequently one-offs. He preferred not to brood on the reasons why, for fear of coming to the conclusion that he was a dullard and his wife too intense. His ability to block out such negative thoughts was something of a survival mechanism, as was the comfort he found in his own company on the rare occasions when he was allowed to be alone.

Over the past few days he had surprised himself at his ability to socialise, and to feel comfortable in doing so. And yet he had been sociable at university and in the earlier days of his marriage. Perhaps he had just got out of the habit and dwindled into a quiet, introspective husband. Whatever the reasons, he could not deny that the more outgoing nature he had rediscovered over the past few days was stimulating. He felt buoyed up; alive; and his time with Francine had lifted him to heights he had not experienced for longer than he cared to admit.

He thought of her as he sat among the towering cacti and the palms of the botanic garden, each and every one of them clinging for dear life to the precipitous rocky slope. He wondered how the gardeners managed to work among their charges, so steep was the cliff face, and then his curiosity was answered when he saw two of them abseiling down a particularly steep part of the garden with ropes and harnesses, pruning shears and saws. Horticulture here could most certainly be described as 'gardening on the edge'.

In the morning he had walked up to the cream-painted palace of the Grimaldis with its white-uniformed guards and their albino English policeman's helmets with scarlet plumes. He wondered who had invented such a quaint hybrid of a livery – half English, half French, totally Monegasque. He sketched one of them against the archway, and from time to time the guard looked sideways at him. Whether this was out of curiosity or suspicion he could not decide. His sketch completed he walked to the rim of the canon-fringed square and gazed out from its exalted vantage point over the panorama that presented itself – a vista that took in not only Port Hercules and its yachts which, from the lofty eminence, seemed like model boats below, but also the incongruously commonplace football stadium to the right and the flats and apartments stacked cheek-by-jowl behind it up the steep slopes of the principality.

It was, he concluded, the strangest of places, in spite of – or perhaps because of – its magnetic qualities to those who had so much money that they chose to come here to protect it. He mused on whether in the face of such riches he would feel drawn to safeguard them by living in the human equivalent of a beehive, but decided, after very little deliberation, that the countryside he had left behind in Sussex – and England with its variety of terrain and generous provision of varied landscape – beat it hands down.

Looking out over the sea his thoughts turned to Archie and Serena and their future. Serena who? He had not been told her surname and hardly felt in a position to ask. He felt sorry for Archie, burdened with a father whose strictures must have been stultifying. Perhaps more information about Serena would come out in conversation when he said goodbye to Archie, which he must do that evening. Florence – Firenze – beckoned, and

Monaco – described by Joseph Addison as being 'well fortified by Nature'; a portrayal with which Timothy could not argue – would be left behind.

He felt a tinge of sadness at his imminent departure. He had not expected, when he set out on his adventure, to be drawn into other people's lives. And yet first Francine, then Archie and Rosamund Hawksmoor had all made a great impression on him. An impression which, in one case at least, he hoped would develop into something more durable. No; in more than one case. He might still be in thrall to Francine – whose imagined life he mused upon for many hours of his day – but he would also feel a sense of regret if Rosamund and Archie were to become nothing more than a distant memory, never to be encountered again. And Serena; such a revelation. The image – and the scent of her – lingered with him still. He smiled at the recollection of the previous evening, of his misconceptions in relation to Archie and Sebastian and the apologetic look on Archie's face when he confessed to having not mentioned Serena for fear of putting him off meeting a girl who clearly was the creature of his dreams. How satisfying. At least Archie's life might now be set on an even keel – Mr Bedlington senior permitting – even if his own were not.

He packed up his paint box and pad, slipped them into the canvas satchel and set off down the rocky path of the botanic garden for one last, luxurious bath in the Hôtel Hermitage. It might be the last indulgent evening of his Grand Tour. Tomorrow, in Florence, it would be time to come down to earth and seek out more modest accommodation, the better to make his funds last a few more weeks. Funds; now £15,000 less than they were when he set out. It did not matter. There was still more than enough to carry him through his trip, and enough, he convinced himself, to see him into retirement. That word again. Then Rosamund's enquiry came back to haunt him. 'What are you running away from?' He had not thought of it as running away; more running towards. He put the notion to the back of his mind. It joined a varied collection of other jumbled thoughts that were, right now, best left unresolved.

It was, said Archie, the very thing for the wall in his pocket-sized apartment, and would remind him of some of the best days he had spent out here in this rocky retreat where money was as plentiful as seawater and good friendship as rare as snow. Timothy was touched at his new friend's response, and over a beer in one of the small cafés around the square (Timothy feeling the need to lower his expectations in the face of a more modest stay in Florence) they clinked glasses and vowed to stay in touch.

'Talking of which,' said Timothy, seizing the appropriate moment, 'I think Rosamund would like to see more of you.'

'I know,' agreed Archie with something of a grimace. 'I keep meaning to go but something always turns up.'

'She's got your interests at heart, you know, and she really wants to see you happy.'

'She told you that?'

'Amongst other things, yes.'

Timothy thought for a moment. 'She won't be there forever, and she's a fascinating woman. I think she's rather lonely. It's none of my business . . . and I certainly don't want to interfere but . . . well . . . just try and pop in a bit more often, eh?'

'You sound like my father. Well, actually you don't. He wouldn't have put it like that. Come to think of it, he wouldn't have said it at all – he doesn't really approve of Aunt Rosamund. Not his sort of person.'

'Well she's certainly mine. I hope I've accrued as much wisdom as she has when I get to ninety-two.'

'What?!'

'Oh, bugger. She made me promise not to tell you and now I've blown it. Don't you dare tell her I let it slip or she'll think I can't keep a secret. I really wouldn't want that.'

'I knew she must be getting on for eighty but . . .'

'Well, there you are. All the more reason to keep an eye on her.'

'Yes. Yes indeed. I will. I promise.'

Timothy looked thoughtful. 'I hope I'm as good company as she is when – if – I get to that age. And . . . I don't know whether I should say this . . .'

'What?'

'Well, it's none of my business, but don't get too hung up about what your father thinks of your life. It's yours to live. He's had his chance. The only regrets I ever have in my life are those of omission, not commission. It's the things I haven't done that I bemoan, not the things I had a bash at and which didn't quite work out.'

Archie listened intently as Timothy continued. 'Don't try too hard to please your parents. Be yourself. Especially when it comes to love. There you are. Parting wise words. Your aunt gave some to me and I give some to you. Where would we be without hand-me-downs?'

Archie leaned back in his chair and said, 'I'll miss you.'

Timothy smiled gratefully. 'Oh, you're very kind. I've had a great time – better than I ever thought possible in Monte Carlo. And talking of pleasant things, I have to say I was very impressed with Serena.'

'I'm glad. I'm pretty impressed with her myself. Can't understand what she sees in me.'

'Take it from one who has mastered the fine art of self-deprecation that it's not worth going there. Just be grateful she does and try to make her happy.'

'Oh, I will.'

'When will you tell your parents?'

'Oh, some time later in the summer. When we've plucked up the courage. For now we just want to keep on enjoying ourselves. It'll be great over the next few weeks when she's here a lot, but then when the Formula 1 caravan moves on, she'll have to follow. That's the time when we'll have to make a decision.'

'For one or other of you to give up your job?'

'Yes. Serena says she's happy to but I'm not sure that I shouldn't move on. Perhaps we both should, but we're not sure to what just yet.'

'Well, in the words of Mr Micawber, something will turn up.'

'Are you always fatalistic?'

'No. Well, I never used to be, but I think I'm getting that way. Sometimes you can plan things too much. You spend all your time focusing on something, assuming that things will pan out in a certain way, and then life reminds you of its fragility. One thing changes and all those plans come tumbling around your ears.'

'Oh dear. I'm sorry.'

'No; no, I wasn't talking about me. Well, not *just* about me. It's simply that it doesn't do to be inflexible in your plans, that's all. Be open to opportunities that sometimes come from the most unexpected directions. The important thing is that firstly you can recognise them and secondly that you have the courage to run with them.' Timothy stopped abruptly, then said, 'I'm beginning to sound like your auntie. Or an Agony Aunt. Another beer?'

Archie looked at his watch. 'Would you mind if I didn't? I've said I'd meet Serena. We're being taken out on someone's yacht for drinks. Pleasure, not work. Is that OK?'

'Of course it's OK. Heavens above! You don't need to apologise, or to explain. Have a great time.'

Archie drained his glass. 'I don't know what to say, really. I've had the most amazing few days, and it's all down to you. Just think, last week we'd never met and now – '

'It seems as though we've known one another for ages.'

'Yes. Funny isn't it.'

'I think life works like that. Some people you can know for years without really knowing them at all, and others you can meet and . . . click . . . there's . . . well . . . a sort of instant rapport.'

'Standing at the bottom of a gangplank?'

'Passerelle. I've learned a lot over the past few days, and not just about boats.'

'Me too.'

The two men stood up at the same time, leaned forward and hugged one another.

'Keep in touch,' said Timothy.

'And you. You've got my number and I've got yours, though I promise not to make a nuisance of myself.'

'Don't even think about it. Call when you want.'

Archie made to leave.

'Oh,' said Timothy, 'I forgot to ask . . .'

'Yes?'

'Serena.'

'What about her?'

'What's her surname?'

Archie smiled sheepishly. 'Derwentwater.'

'Any relation to . . . ?'

'Yes. Daughter of the Earl.'

'I see. Well then . . .' Timothy lifted both arms into the air.

'What?'

'Stands to reason doesn't it? I don't think you're going to have much of a problem with your father.'

25

MONTE CARLO TO FLORENCE

MAY

'Don't you agree that, on one's first visit to Florence, one must have a room with a view?'

E.M. Forster, *A Room with a View*, 1908

On the seven-hour train journey from Monte Carlo to Florence (wisely, as Rosamund Hawksmoor would have insisted, avoiding a stopover at Pisa) Timothy put aside the ancient copy of Joseph Addison's *Remarks*, and pulled from his holdall the other books he had brought with him – an ancient Baedeker of Italy, a current guidebook and a battered paperback copy of E.M. Forster's *A Room with a View*. Its half-title page bore Timothy's signature; not the one recognisable today, honed into shape by a career in graphic design, but one made in the loopy hand of his youth. The date gave away his age at the time of first reading – seventeen. How long had he waited to undertake a journey, the seed of which had been sown almost forty years ago? Before long he was lost in the story of Lucy Honeychurch (whose face seemed to be that of Serena Derwentwater) and her older cousin and chaperone Charlotte Bartlett (and here Francine came, unbidden, into the frame; heaven knows why, for their respective temperaments could not have been more disparate). Whether he would be lucky enough to find a room with a view he knew not, but in between reading he would stare out of the train window across the Italian countryside, marvelling at the rugged grandeur of the landscape and diving into the comfortable pages when the scenery became dreary and industrial.

From time to time the Italian coast hove into view, then the train would snake inland. Like some schoolboy trainspotter he noted the stations they passed through – those where the train slowed enough to jot down their euphonious names: Ventimiglia, Sanremo, Imperia, Diano Marina, Alassio, Finale Ligure Marina, Savona, Genova Brignole, Rapello, Chiavari, La Spezia, Massa, Viareggio and the last stop before Florence, Pisa Centrale – the latter with no view of the fabled leaning tower. The list seemed almost like a Catholic litany – musical in its vowelled grandeur. The sort of list you could set to music. He found himself humming 'La Donna e Mobile', but stopped when he looked up and saw, in the seat diagonally opposite, an old and gnarled Italian gentleman peering over the top of a copy of *Il Tirreno* and regarding him warily. Timothy smiled nervously and went back to *A Room with a View*, his eye lighting on the line: "'Life', wrote a friend of mine, 'is a public performance on the violin, in which you must learn the instrument as you go along.'" He closed the book and looked out of the window.

Only an hour to go now; he would be there by late afternoon. Time to check the guidebook and remind himself of the hotels he had marked as suitable bases for his stay. There were three, and the map indicated that they were all within walking distance of Santa Maria Novella station. Why was it that everything in Italy sounded so romantic? Even the mainline stations. There really was a world of difference between the sensation experienced on hearing the words Santa Maria Novella and the effect upon the ears of St Pancras.

Timothy was lucky. And not for the first time. The very first small hotel he tried – in a tiny street off the handsome Via del Calzaiuoli – had a room vacant. *Colazione*, the Italian version of the Continental breakfast, was included, said the owner – a plump and balding gentleman with horn-rimmed glasses and a swarthy complexion. He did not smile but seemed pleasantly civil and responded to Timothy's fractured Italian in equally fractured English. Timothy explained that he would like a room with a bath for five nights (a figure he had settled on as being long enough to take in all the sights before moving on to Rome). '*Va bene*,' confirmed Signor Pollini (his name was painted on a Toblerone-shaped piece of wood that sat on the small counter in the hotel lobby: Alberto Pollini – *Proprietario*.

The formalities completed, Timothy took the tiny rattling lift to the second floor to discover that it was, indeed, a room with a view – of sorts. Stick your head out of the window and look to the right and between the sloping tiled roofs you could just see the outline of the terracotta-coloured Duomo. As views go it might not have impressed Miss Bartlett but it was good enough for him, and he would not be here much, except to bathe (well, shower, since the room did not have a bath) and to sleep. He transferred the contents of his case and holdall to the heavy wooden wardrobe and chest of drawers – one against each wall – and sat on the bed to test its firmness. It seemed comfortable, and both the bed-linen and the towels in the minute loo and shower room were spotlessly clean. The rose-and-trellis-covered wallpaper he could live with, and when it was dark he would forget it was there.

With the window open, and in the fading afternoon sun, he heard the bells that would be an accompaniment to his life for the next five days: deep, sonorous bells and light, airy carillons. They seemed to emanate from every tower and campanile. Single bells, twin bells and bells in uneven numbers, but not rung as in English churches in any particular order – at least that's how it seemed. They chimed randomly. It was all very . . . Italian. He looked at his watch. It was 6pm. Time for a stroll before eating . . . where? Anywhere. He did not need to plan. This was Florence, the city of art, of flowers, of love, depending on where you searched for advice.

He walked out of the tiny Hotel Gandolfo and into the street, to be greeted by a buzz of traffic that took him by surprise. Cars and buses, cycles and motor scooters fizzed about him like bees, and he found himself dodging from left to right in order to preserve his life. At first he found it disconcerting – he had expected such bustle in Monaco but not, somehow, in Florence – but once he had become used to the energetic methods of transportation he reminded himself that this was not the city of Miss Honeychurch and Miss Bartlett. Their Florence was the Florence of a century or more ago; the Florence of pedestrians and horse-drawn fiacres. The horses, the long skirts and the starched collars were long gone. *A Room with a View* had been written in 1908. This was the Florence of today; a city rich in history but with its own vibrant personality, intent on breaking out of a stultifying historic mould; capitalising on its art and its traditions, but at the same time offering its own twenty-first century take on them.

He walked around the outside of the Duomo, resisting the temptation to get up close and inspect the doors of the baptistery. He would do that tomorrow. For now he would admire the city at arm's length, absorbing its general atmosphere rather than examining the particular. He walked along the banks of the Arno, astonished at the Ponte Vecchio and the honeycomb network of windows that opened on to the river from the dwellings stacked higgledy-piggledy upon it like an agglomeration of dolls' houses. It was all a heady brew. This was Italy – rich in history, musical in language and every bit as lively this evening as any city on earth.

He leaned on a stone balustrade and looked around him at the variety of buildings that seemed to be shouldering one another aside to get at the light; a warm, Mediterranean light that enhanced the yellow ochre, raw sienna and burnt umber that were the natural palette of the architecture of Florence. His thoughts turned, once again, to Francine. How he would have loved to have been here in her company. And then, like an arrow to the heart, came the thought of Rosie and Ace and Elsie. How selfish he had been of late. How preoccupied with new friends in new places. A pang of guilt swept over him. He would write to them tonight; after supper.

Slipping down side streets and narrow alleyways he came upon a small bistro filled with Italians – a good sign. A small cloth-covered table on the pavement was being vacated as he approached. He sat down on one of the ancient metal chairs as a waiter in a black waistcoat and long white apron began to clear the used crockery and sweep crumbs from the white napery. 'Menu, *Signor*?' he enquired.

'*Si. Grazie.*' The waiter nodded, and within the hour Timothy had enjoyed the best spaghetti carbonara he had ever eaten, and two glasses of extraordinarily heart-warming Barolo. The bill paid, he ambled slowly back to the Hotel Gandolfo in the fading light and, sitting on the edge of the bed with writing paper laid on his watercolour pad he began to write his letter home:

Hotel Gandolfo,
Firenze

My Dear Rosie, Ace and Elsie,

I am so sorry not to have written more regularly. I mean to and then events overtake me and I get carried away which is, I know, what I am here for, but I should still find time to keep you in the picture . . .

He had got thus far when he put down the pen and thought for a moment. Having made it clear that he wanted to communicate by letter as would have befitted a Grand Tourist in the 18th century, something within him – a yearning to hear a voice from home – made him put aside the paper and pen and reach for his mobile phone. He gazed at it. It was not just that he despised the modern world's reliance upon it – that no one under the age of thirty appeared to be able to walk down a street without gazing, mesmerised, at the little screen in their hands – but also that its abilities and intricacies were by and large beyond his compass. He pressed a button on its side and waited for the screen to light up. He dialled the number. The phone rang at the other end. It rang for almost a minute, but there was no reply. Not even an answering machine. He pressed the button to end the call and laid the phone on the bed. For the first time on his journey – his 'adventure' – he felt completely alone.

26

HOTEL GANDOLFO, FLORENCE

MAY

'I love the language, that soft bastard Latin,
Which melts like kisses from a female mouth,
And sounds as if it should be writ on satin
With syllables which breathe of the sweet South.'

Lord Byron, *Beppo*, 1817

The *colazione* at the Hotel Gandolfo was a modest affair but one which tasted all the more delicious because he was, at last, in Italy and it was fresh: fresh rolls, fresh coffee, fresh pastries and fresh fruit. Timothy fell upon it as though he had not eaten for days – the previous night's spaghetti carbonara but a happy memory.

It was served in a small room at the rear of the hotel where four small tables were equally spaced around its perimeter. A single man – an Italian business traveller by the looks of him – occupied one of them, and the table by the window, at which lace curtains framed the view of the stuccoed caramel-coloured villa opposite, was taken, after Timothy had been ushered to his own seat in a corner, by two elderly ladies, guidebooks in hand. They nodded politely to him as they entered the tiny room (the businessman being absorbed by a dull wad of computer printouts) and began to converse with each other in rather upper-class English accents in between asking for tea, rather than coffee, in a hybrid Oxford-Italian. Timothy remembered the tradition of English diplomats being instructed to speak a foreign language with a pronounced English accent so as to preserve the superiority of their native tongue. He kept his eyes on his own guidebook, not the modern one this time but the ancient Baedeker after the fashion of Miss Honeychurch in the E.M. Forster novel, and listened as the two ladies mapped out their itinerary for the day. If nothing else, he could avoid the places they seemed intent on visiting.

The two were, he gathered from piecing together snippets of their conversation, widows whose husbands had passed on some time ago and who holidayed together each year to sample the culture of various cities they had never visited before. It stung him that they were actually engaged on the same mission as himself, albeit in annual installments rather than all in one go.

Eavesdropping on the waiter's form of address, it appeared that one of them was a Mrs Winder and the other a Mrs Dawes. He tried to suppress a smile behind his Baedeker and even wondered if the two ladies were travelling under pseudonyms. He dismissed the thought as being far too fanciful. They were dressed in sensible trousers and silky shirts – one cream and one pale grey – with the regulation string of pearls at the neck. The grey-shirted lady was grey-haired with a bun (Mrs Winder), the other had a blond bob (Mrs Dawes), and both were smartly coiffed, clearly determined not to let standards slip even though they were on holiday. Their one concession to vacation seemed to be the wearing of their shirts outside their trousers.

He did his best to avoid their glances, but found at one moment that eye contact was inadvertently achieved and Mrs Dawes remarked on the age of his guidebook.

'Yes,' said Timothy apologetically. 'I have a newer one upstairs but I was just seeing how it was done all those years ago.'

'What year would that be?' asked Mrs Winder.

'The turn of the century.'

'Around 1908?' she asked teasingly.

'Yes.' He flipped the guide open at the title page. 'It's from 1904 actually.'

'So that could be the very one then, couldn't it?'

'I'm sorry?'

'The one that Miss Lavish chastised Miss Honeychurch for reading at breakfast.'

Timothy adopted a mock frown. 'Oh, dear. I fear I've been rumbled.'

'Oh don't worry Mr . . . er . . .?'

'Gandy. Tim Gandy.'

Mrs Dawes cut in, 'It's part of the fun really isn't it? Are you going to Santa Croce?'

'Yes. I suppose so. But I'm not sure when. And I hope there isn't a murder when I get there.'

'Oh, quite, quite!'

The two ladies laughed heartily, and when their laughter had subsided they introduced themselves. 'We're old friends. We go on holiday together since our husbands died. I'm Sylvia Winder . . .'

'And I'm Vera Dawes. No comments please!'

'Even if we do sometimes say "Mind the Dawes",' added her companion. 'She's a bit clumsy, you see.'

As if to prove the point Mrs Dawes dropped her knife onto her plate with a clatter and her napkin slid to the floor. Sighing, Mrs Winder said, 'See what I mean?'

Timothy smiled kindly. 'Are you here for long?' he asked.

'Only for a week,' confirmed Mrs Winder. She appeared to be the organising one of the two, Vera Dawes seeming to be in her thrall and seldom initiating a conversation; rather contenting herself with adding her two-penny worth when Sylvia Winder had commented on something. 'We have our lists of sights to see and try to do a few each day, but it's so tiring and Vera has asthma so we don't like to do too much in case it overtires her.'

'I'm quite healthy otherwise,' chipped in her companion, defensively. 'I managed the Uffizi yesterday and that's quite extensive.'

'Yes, you did very well.'

'Worth a visit?' asked Timothy, intent on going there anyway.

'Oh, yes; certainly. You mustn't miss it.'

'Any favourites? Paintings I mean?'

Sylvia Winder's face lit up. 'Oh, da Vinci's Adoration of the Magi. It was much larger than I had expected. I have always loved it. I have a postcard of it at home and I put it on the mantelpiece each Christmas. It was wonderful to see it in the flesh. And talking of flesh, there's Botticelli's Birth of Venus, don't miss that. Very special; so clear, so alive. She seems to be staring straight at you.'

'And of course there's *my* painting,' added Vera Dawes, proudly. 'The *other* Botticelli.'

'Yes,' said her companion impatiently.

Timothy looked at them both enquiringly. 'Your painting?'

'Yes,' said Sylvia with a sardonic tone to her voice. 'The Primavera.'

Mrs Dawes giggled like a schoolgirl.

'Just her little joke,' added Sylvia wearily by way of clarification. She then made to put the conversation back on an even keel: 'And of course you must see Michelangelo's David.'

'Oh yes. We went to that first,' said Vera. 'It's at the Accademia. Very majestic. It's huge you know.'

'Yes,' said Sylvia, frowning. 'We were there, unfortunately, when a Women's Institute party from Yorkshire were visiting. There we were, quite in awe of the Master's achievement, admiring the perfect artistry, when one of them said in a very loud voice (and I think you can guess just which part of his anatomy they were admiring, Mr Gandy), "If that's David, I'd like to see Goliath."'

Timothy tried hard to suppress a smile, said, 'Oh dear,' and masked his face by taking a sip of coffee.

'And where will you go, Mr Gandy?'

'To the Duomo first I think. I want to see the baptistery doors, and then to sit inside the place and drink in the atmosphere.'

'Are you staying long?' asked Sylvia. 'Will you have time to see Firenze properly?'

'I hope so. I'm here for five nights so I can hopefully take my time and take it all in. Funnily enough my Baedeker has an itinerary for five days – suggesting where to go and in what order – but I'm not sure I shall follow it. It looks rather frantic.'

'Yes; that's the trouble; there's too much here really and we don't want to miss anything important do we?' Sylvia pushed her chair away from the table, stood up and said, 'Come along, Vera. We've a lot to see and before we know where we are it will be lunchtime. Mustn't dilly-dally.'

'Oh, yes. I mean, no, we mustn't.' Vera rose less rapidly than her companion and brushed rather a lot of crumbs from her trousers, the napkin now residing under the table. She nodded at Timothy in acknowledgement and said, 'Perhaps we shall see you tomorrow morning, Mr Gandy?'

'Oh, I should think so.'

'We're not late to bed. We tend to have a light supper at around six . . . er . . . in the little café across the road if you feel like joining us.'

'Oh, that's very kind, but I'm not sure what my plans are for later.' Then, seeing that Vera Dawes looked slightly disappointed, he added, 'But if I'm around I'll definitely look in.'

Her companion was in the doorway now. 'Vera! Do come along!'

'Yes, yes. I'm on my way.'

Timothy felt rather sorry for Vera Dawes. He went back to his Baedeker and immersed himself in the world of Florence from a century before. At the back of his mind was the feeling that the conversation he had just had could lead him into yet another alliance. It was time, he thought, that he kept himself to himself, lest the ladies should be transmogrified into the Misses Honeychurch and Bartlett and he should find himself in the unfortunate role of the irritating if well-meaning Mr Emerson. He shuddered at the thought.

'The FIRST DOOR, the oldest of the three, on the S. side, opposite the Bigallo, was completed by *Andrea Pisano* in 1336 after six years of labour. The reliefs comprise scenes from the life of John the Baptist and representations of the cardinal virtues. The bronze decorations at the sides are by *Vittorio Ghiberti*, the son of *Lorenzo* (1452-62); above is the beheading of John the Baptist by *Vinc. Danti* (1571).'

With the Baedeker in his hand, Timothy stood and gazed at the doors and their astonishing bronze reliefs. The book he held was over a hundred years old; that in itself gave him a thrill – to think that some Edwardian tourist had, perhaps, stood where he was standing now, with this very book, gazing at the bronze reliefs. But the age of the panels themselves – around six hundred years old – and the doors, even older – was almost incomprehensible.

What had been going on in England back then? Who was on the throne in 1403 when, said the Baedeker, the panels on the second door showing '28 reliefs from the life of Christ' were begun? He racked his brains. The date seemed familiar from school history lessons. It was not as memorable as 1066 and 1215 but it had something to do with the death of a king. Which one? The Shakespearean one . . . Henry IV, that was it. He was killed at the battle of . . . somewhere. Salisbury? No. Southampton . . . Shrewsbury, yes! Fourteen-o-three. That was more than a hundred and fifty years before the birth of Shakespeare. It was a time frame almost impossible to assimilate, yet the craftsmanship, the quality, the durability of those panels was there for all to see. It made his modest attempts at water-colours pale into insignificance.

He kept his canvas bag closed all day, fearful of reminding himself of his own artistic shortcomings. Instead, he remained in awe of the artists and craftsmen whose work had stood the test of time and which would, God willing, last for another half millennium: Brunelleschi's gigantic dome and its painted interior of The Last Judgement left him with an aching neck and an aching heart, so astonishing was it in both effect and execution.

The Duomo and the baptistery explored, he walked the full length of the Via Calzaiuoli towards the Uffizi but, having learned the folly of not eating during the day, and the light-headedness that was sure to be a consequence, he bought a ham and cheese-filled ciabatta. It was wrapped in crisp grease-proof paper that made it somehow more special than if it had simply been popped into a paper bag. He walked on for a few hundred yards before taking a seat near the Arno to watch the world go by.

So this was Italy; the country he had dreamed of for so many years and whose language he felt had a musicality like no other. A country of delicious food, exquisite music and superb scenery. The sky above him was clear blue; the water below an earthy brown; the buildings all around him possessed of an unparalleled elegance and the simple bread and cheese and Parma ham tasted, as a consequence, like the food of the gods. He was here at last after half a century of life, sitting on the banks of the River Arno and taking it all in. To his embarrassment, and his surprise, he felt the tears prick his eyes. He rubbed them away and savoured his simple alfresco lunch. Or, as they would have it in this part of the world, *il pranzo*. Yes, even his lunch had a melodic ring.

This was how he imagined it would be when he had set off on his tour. Solitary pleasure; a chance to take things at his own pace and to let the wonders of Europe unfold before him. And then he saw her. At first he thought he must be imagining things. It was just a glimpse, then she disappeared behind a bevy of umbrellas outside a street café. He stood up and leaned sideways to get a better view. No; it must have been his imagination. He sat down slowly, convinced that his mind was playing tricks, but a few minutes later she emerged from the café carrying a cup and saucer and a plate. She took a seat at one of the tables perhaps fifteen or twenty yards away. He blinked to clear his eyes, the better to focus, then got up and walked towards her.

As he approached her table she looked up and removed her sunglasses. Surprised, then smiling weakly she said, 'Hello, Dad.'

27

FLORENCE

MAY

'Children begin by loving their parents; after a time they
judge them; rarely, if ever, do they forgive them.'

Oscar Wilde, *A Woman of No Importance*, 1893

The fact that he had never understood her added to his confusion. Since her mother's death, Alice had been conspicuous by
her absence. Now, here she was, far from home – light years
away from her beloved Oxford – not only removing herself from
her local comfort zone, but going out on a limb in a different
country. It was as unreal as it was unexpected.

'What are you doing here?' he asked, with little thought to
the unwelcoming tone in his voice.

'Hoping to bump into you,' she said softly. 'Do you mind?'

'I . . . well . . . it's just . . .' he found himself completely lost
for words. A myriad of jumbled thoughts ran through his head,
before he lighted on what he suspected was at the root of her
visit. 'Did Oliver send you?'

'No.'

He felt a pang of remorse at his unjust assumption, if, indeed, it were unjust. 'But, I don't understand.'

'Oliver didn't *send* me, but he rang me and told me what had been going on.' Alice could read the confusion on Timothy's face. She continued: 'The bank have been in touch. Apparently there has been a massive withdrawal on your account.'

'But what's that got to do with Oliver . . . or you?' And then, 'Why didn't the bank get in touch with me? I've got my phone.'

'They tried. Apparently it's not working. Have you tried using it?'

'Well, I rang Rosie yesterday but there was no reply.'

'What time did you ring?'

'Early evening.'

'Bath time for the baby most probably. They would certainly have been in. I think your phone must be on the blink.'

Timothy sat down beside her. 'Hang on; can we just go back a bit? I haven't seen you since your mum's funeral, and then only briefly. You hardly said a word . . .'

'I was upset.'

'We were all upset. Then you shuffled off back to Oxford and you've not been in touch since.'

'You could have rung me,' said Alice.

Timothy looked at her appealingly.

'Yes; I know I'm not the most social being but—'

'And now you're here . . .'

'It's half term. Oliver's tied up in some big case and couldn't get away and Rosie's looking after the baby. The bank rang about this massive withdrawal of twenty thousand euros and we thought something must have gone wrong. Thought your identity must have been stolen – or worse, you were lying in a gutter somewhere. We tried calling your phone but it just rang; there was no answer. We had to decide what to do. Rosie knew that you'd gone from Paris to Monaco and she knew which hotel you were staying in. She called the Hôtel Hermitage and all they could tell us was that you'd gone to Florence. I was the only one who could get here so I came out to see if I could find you. I knew the chances were slim but I thought that if I wandered about and took in all the major sights I might just bump into you – if you were still alive. It was a chance I had to take.'

Timothy felt a wave of guilt sweep over him. Here she was, the daughter who had always shunned society – not just his, but that of the rest of the world, apart from her beloved Oxford – braving the big wide world to come and look for a father she suspected might have . . . well, it did not bear thinking about. She was the least adventurous, the least sociable of his children and yet she had forsaken her comfort zone to go in search of him.

'I don't know what to say.'

'I'm just glad you're alive,' she said flatly.

He looked at her; it was the first time for many months that he had properly taken in her appearance. She was thin – painfully so – and her dark hair, cut short, emphasised her fine cheekbones and sallow skin. She wore a black jacket over a thin grey sweater and dark grey trousers; on her feet what she would have considered 'sensible shoes' – flat-heeled brogues. Clearly they were regularly polished.

He reached out his hand for hers and squeezed it gently. She managed a brief but genuine smile, before withdrawing her hand on the pretext of picking up her cup and taking a sip of coffee.

'Where are you staying?' he asked.

'In a tiny *pensione* on the other side of the Duomo.'

'You can't be far away from me.'

'Probably not.' She put down her cup and asked 'So did you draw out twenty thousand euros?'

'Yes; I did,' said Timothy, levelly.

'Why? What for? I know you were staying in smart hotels but isn't that excessive even for them?'

'Yes.'

'So?'

'It's a personal matter. I made a loan to someone.'

For the first time, Alice's impassive look was replaced by a more incredulous expression. 'To whom?'

Her couching of the question seemed to exemplify her Oxford life. 'To whom?' rather than 'Who to?' He tried not to sound irritated. 'I told you. It's a personal matter. Private.'

She met his eye with a steady gaze. 'You are quite well, aren't you, Dad? I mean, you don't feel strange or anything? Do you have lapses? Are there times when you can't remember having done things?'

Timothy shook his head vigorously. 'No. Nothing like that. I am sane and level headed and I decided that it was something I needed to do. It is not something I feel I need to explain to my children. It's nothing to do with them.'

'I'm not sure that's strictly true,' retorted Alice. 'If we think that you're not well, that your mental facility is not what it was, then we might have to think of how we can safeguard you.'

Timothy's tone clearly indicated his exasperation. 'Look, I am not going gaga; I am in full possession of my faculties and it will be some time, God willing, before you need to take out a power of attorney over my affairs.'

Alice seemed taken aback. 'Fine. But you can see how it looked to us.'

'Does that include Rosie? Does she think I can no longer be responsible for my actions?'

'Rosie was as worried as Oliver and me that something had happened to you. What do you expect when you go gadding off? You've never done this sort of thing before . . .'

Timothy was becoming rattled. 'I've never been *able* to do this sort of thing before. Your mother and I were bringing up three children for the first twenty years of our marriage and when you'd all flown the nest she had no inclination to travel. What was I meant to do when she died? Stay at home and respect her wishes for the rest of my life?'

Alice looked uneasy. 'That's not what I meant.'

'Well, what did you mean?'

'Look. This conversation is obviously not going anywhere.'

'No. It's not.'

Alice made to rise from her seat. 'I think I'd better go. I've done my bit. I've made sure you're all right, even if I haven't found out what happened to the money.'

'Is that what this is all about?' asked Timothy. 'The money? Your inheritance?' The moment he said it he could have bitten off his tongue.

'Not worthy, Dad. Not worthy.'

'No . . . look . . . I'm sorry. It's just that Oliver wrote me this letter before I left, saying that I was being irresponsible and extravagant and that I wasn't thinking about my children – and my grandchild. I didn't mean—'

Alice was standing up now, her coffee only half drunk and the sandwich untouched on the plate. 'I am not in Oliver's pocket. He happens to be my brother and so there is a degree of sibling empathy, but not much. He's a tactless prat, and his wife is a heartless virago but he's still your son and he was, on this occasion, genuinely worried that something had happened to you. We all three lost our mother less than a year ago; we didn't want to lose our father, too. What you did with the money is none of my business. I couldn't care less if you lost it all at the casino in Monte Carlo. I just wanted to make sure you were all right, that's all.'

She made to leave. Timothy caught her arm. 'Don't go. Please. I'm sorry.'

There was a moment when he thought she would pull away and lose herself in the crowd, but she paused for a moment and said, 'I'll book a flight back tomorrow.' She stared at him as if trying to divine his inner feelings. Then she said, 'We could have supper tonight if you like.'

His relief was palpable. 'Yes. Yes please.'

She pointed across the street from where they stood. 'There's a little restaurant over there on the corner; a bistro. La Riunione, it's called. Rather appropriate in the circumstances. I'll meet you there at eight o'clock.'

'Yes. Fine.' He was in a daze, and hardly noticed as she planted a light kiss on his cheek, turned and was quickly lost in the crowd of tourists. He sat down slowly in his chair, only vaguely hearing the voice of the waiter who enquired of him, 'Coffee, *signor*?'

'No thank you,' he murmured. Then, coming to and looking up, 'Have you got a brandy?'

28

LA RIUNIONE, FLORENCE

MAY

'The knowingness of little girls
Is hidden underneath their curls.'

Phyllis McGinley, *What Every Woman Knows*, 1960

Timothy could not remember being so nervous at the prospect of meeting one of his children. Irritated, yes, in the case of Oliver and Vita, but not nervous; not like this. As the hands of his watch crept towards eight o'clock his stomach began to knot. He told himself it was ridiculous. This was his daughter. All right, so they had had little contact for several years, but she was his daughter nevertheless and as such she hardly posed a threat to his equilibrium. Why then should he be feeling so uneasy?

He took especial care with his appearance, as though that would make a difference to her attitude towards him. It was the highly polished brogues she wore that made him all the more assiduous about his manner of dress – freshly pressed chinos courtesy of the Hôtel Hermitage, along with a clean blue shirt and an olive-green canvas jacket. He checked himself in the mirror before he left his room, and took the stairs rather than the lift to the ground floor, the better to avoid encountering Messrs Winder and Dawes, should they have returned from their early evening repast.

It was to no avail. They met in the small hallway in front of Signor Pollini's desk. 'Oh, Mr Gandy. We missed you at supper,' volunteered the unworldly Mrs Dawes.

'Yes; I'm sorry. Not quite ready.'

'But going out now?' enquired Mrs Winder forcibly.

'Yes.'

'Anywhere special?'

'Oh, just a local restaurant.' He glanced at his watch. 'Must dash. Table booked for eight.'

'Ah, I see. We wondered if—'

But the question came too late. Anxious to avoid either delay or inquisition, Timothy smiled as sweetly as his nervousness would allow and swept past them and out of the door. Clearly, unless he were very calculating about his movements over the next few days, the merry widows would have him in their clutches for the rest of his stay. Right now there was only one person he really wanted to meet and she was somewhere in Paris. He chastised himself for his reluctance to confront his daughter, took a deep breath, and walked down the Via Calzaiuoli towards the restaurant on the banks of the Arno.

She was waiting for him when he arrived. It surprised him that she had changed her clothes. He had somehow imagined that she always wore black and grey and that she took little pride in her appearance. Certainly, he had never noticed it before, but then their infrequent meetings had left him with little real impression of Alice's dress sense, and it was not surprising on their last encounter – at Isobel's funeral – that the daughter of the deceased had been wearing black.

This evening she wore a cotton jacket of royal blue over a cream polo-neck sweater and black trousers. Her cheeks were slightly flushed and her eyes bright. For the first time in his life he realised that his middle child – the one who had seldom enjoyed good health, real or imagined – was blessed with gamine good looks. She had, in the past, always appeared rather sad and wistful, and while on this particular evening she was hardly of a jovial disposition, there was about her a more relaxed demeanour than he could remember. It occurred to him that it might be as a result of the relief at discovering that her father was not dead in a ditch. He felt chastened by the realisation.

He leaned down to kiss her gently on the cheek. She did not pull away. He sat down. She said, 'I didn't order wine. I wasn't sure whether you'd want red or white.'

'What are you having,' he asked, treading carefully.

Alice shrugged.

'Red?' he offered.

'Fine.'

'Silly really,' he said.

'What?'

'I don't really know your drinking habits. Your preferences I mean.'

'It's not surprising. I don't remember us ever drinking together; except at Christmas once I'd reached the venerable age of sixteen. Do you remember what we used to have?'

Timothy was surprised by the enquiry and shook his head.

'Mateus Rosé.'

'No!'

'Yes we did. So Mum could make lamps out of the bottles afterwards and sell them at Liberal Party bring-and-buy sales.'

'I think the Liberal Party owes its existence to your mother.'

'I think the Liberal Party was the only reason she drank.'

The conversation dried up after the initial sally, each of them clearly trying to adjust to the other's proximity.

A waiter broke in on the silence. *'Vino, signor, signorina?'*

'Si. Grazie,' said Alice. *'Una bottiglia di Brunello per favore.'* The waiter nodded, said, *'Certamente, signorina,'* and disappeared.

Timothy tried, not altogether successfully, to conceal his surprise at her knowledge of Italian.

'Evening classes,' said Alice, by way of explanation.

'I didn't know.'

'There's a lot you don't know, Dad,' she said.

Timothy did not answer his daughter. Instead he waited for the expected tirade. It did not come. Another waiter brought a basket of bread and a small dish of olive oil, placing it down between them and adding two new glasses before retreating. The uneasy silence prevailed as the original waiter returned with the requested bottle of Brunello di Montalcino, showing the label to Alice, who nodded. Father and daughter watched as he withdrew the cork and poured a little wine into Alice's glass. She sipped it, signified her approval and waited as the waiter poured wine into both their glasses before depositing the bottle on a small table next to theirs and heading back towards the kitchen.

Alice raised her glass, met her father's eyes and said, *'Saluti.'*

'Saluti,' said her father in reply.

They both drank, then silence reigned once more until, as is the time-honoured custom, they both spoke at once.

'We just,' said Alice, as her father said, 'I only . . .' Then they both stopped.

'How's Oxford?' asked Timothy, thinking to break the ice with an anodyne question.

'Pretty much as it always has been,' replied Alice. 'The students come and go but the place remains the same.'

'And you? Do you remain the same?'

Alice looked him in the eye. 'What does that mean? The same as what?'

'Ah, I see,' said Timothy. 'No small talk in Oxford.'

It was, in itself, a relatively mild reproach, but it unleashed the cataract of feelings that Timothy had expected of the evening.

'I know what you must think,' said Alice quietly. 'What you have always thought. That I'm an unsociable sort who only thinks about herself and cares little for her family.'

Her father made to interrupt. He failed.

'Well, you're wrong. I knew very early on that you and mum weren't suited. I could see it even if you couldn't. Oliver didn't care and Rosie's way of coping with it was to jolly us all along. Well, I felt it deeply. Oh, I know you both thought I was a weak soul with no real get-up-and-go, but the truth of the matter was that the atmosphere at home completely undermined my self-confidence.'

Timothy butted in. 'But there was no atmosphere. I made sure of that. Your mother and I never argued; never had shouting matches . . .'

'Exactly. And that's what I knew. I watched you getting more and more subdued until you almost weren't there. Did you think that I didn't notice? Did you think that I was comfortable with it? Rosie was younger than me and Oliver was older – one was blissfully unaware when it started to go wrong and the other on the verge of leaving home. I'm not being selfish but I was the one at the epicentre of this unhappy marriage . . .'

'It wasn't unhappy!'

'Oh Dad! Who are you kidding? You were miserable. You just found a way of sublimating it, that's all.'

'But . . . if I did it was because I didn't want to . . .'

'Because you didn't want to upset your children.' Alice sighed and shook her head. 'You'd be surprised what children notice, Dad. They pick up on the slightest of atmospheres. Especially in their early teens, which is when I began to realise that things were not as they should be between you and mum. Not as you'd like them to be. Believe me, I took no pleasure in watching you retreat into your shell; especially since I knew what you *could* be like. I remember you, when I was very young, reading me stories at bedtime. Doing all the characters. Then, gradually, the bedtime stories stopped and you seemed distant; locked up in your own world. It wasn't just Mum you were finding a way of coping with, it was us as well.'

'But Rosie never . . .'

'Rosie is a saint. I watched her trying to keep us all together. All right, so even she gave up with Oliver in the end – anyone would have; he has the hide of a rhinoceros and the sensitivity of a bull in a china shop – but she battled on trying to keep things going. I don't have her stamina when it comes to social work. I found the only way to get through it was to do what you were doing, I suppose; go into myself and find some sort of solace there. It was a stupid way of coping, I know that now. Taking to my bed. But there at least I had some respite from what I knew was going on downstairs. I could read, disappear into another world. Like you. And then, when I got to Oxford I found a world that suited me. There are lots of people in academia who use it as an escape. I freely admit to it. I'm ashamed of it in a way. But it was my salvation. I found myself there. I don't always like who I am, what I've become, but it was preferable to . . . well . . . who knows what.'

Alice stopped speaking and picked up her glass of wine. 'So there you are. I've unburdened myself. The unsociable daughter has spoken.'

Timothy sat quite still as Alice's words sank in. Then he said, 'I'm so sorry.'

'Water under the bridge now, Dad. Water under the bridge. Time to move on.'

'But I only did what I did . . .'

'Oh, I know you did it with the best intentions. It's just that kids are more astute than you give them credit for. I work with hundreds of them at Oxford; from all walks of life, with all sorts of hang-ups and all sorts of backgrounds. Most of them are bruised in one way or another. But they survive. As I did.'

Her father said quite slowly, 'I feel so ashamed.'

'No. You mustn't. You did what you thought was right; took what you considered was the best course of action. But sometimes broken marriages don't fall apart, they just limp on covered in plasters. I suppose I was just more aware than my siblings of the plasters.'

Timothy put his hand to his mouth, then said slowly, 'What a revelation. I'm surprised you're still speaking to me. Surprised that you bothered to come out here.'

'I came out here because you're my dad. And I haven't got a mum any more.'

'No.'

'I'm not criticising you, Dad. Or blaming you. Just explaining my own course of action.'

'Yes. It's just that it's rather a lot to take in after all these years. I'd sort of . . . well, to be honest . . .'

'You'd given up on me?'

'No. Not exactly. Well . . .'

'You thought I'd given up on you? On the family?'

'I suppose.'

They were interrupted by the waiter who came to take their order. Timothy hovered over the menu, his eyes darting to left and right, unable to concentrate or make any kind of decision in the wake of their conversation.

'*Due prosciutto e melone et due spaghetti carbonara per favore,*' said Alice, folding up the menu and handing it back to the waiter.

'I'm not sure I have any appetite,' murmured Timothy.

'Well I have' said Alice. 'I haven't had pasta in years. I feel strangely liberated.'

The Parma ham and melon arrived, and the revelations subsided for a while as father and daughter ate – the one avidly and the other distractedly. The wine did at least help Timothy to unwind. A little. He suspected that the flush in Alice's cheeks had been due to a fortifying glass before she had arrived at the restaurant, the better to confront her father. It cannot have been easy for her after all this time, he realised, to unburden herself and tell him her innermost feelings – territory he had not been privy to before. He doubted if anyone had.

They had begun to eat the spaghetti carbonara when Timothy said, 'About the money; the twenty-thousand euros . . .'

Alice paused, her fork on its way to her mouth, and said, 'I don't need to know, Dad. You're quite right. It's your business.'

'I know. But I want you to know. I don't know why, but I do. It's a loan I've made to somebody. Somebody I've only just met. It may be a foolish risk to take but it's something I wanted to do.'

Alice swallowed her pasta and took a sip of wine. Then she said, almost casually, 'Is it a woman?'

Timothy paused, then said 'Yes.'

Alice took another sip at her glass. 'You must think very highly of her.'

'I do.'

'Well then . . .'

'You don't think I'm stupid?'

'We're all stupid where love is concerned.'

Her candour caught him unawares.

'Well, I don't know that it's love.'

Alice frowned at him disbelievingly.

'I mean . . . I wouldn't want you to think that I was rushing to replace—'

Alice laid down her fork and spoon and leaned towards him. 'You've been alone for long enough Dad; and I don't mean just since mum died. If you've found someone else then I don't blame you.'

Words failed him. It seemed that revelation followed upon revelation. He drained his glass of wine and lowered it gently to the table.

Alice picked up her own glass and took a large gulp, then said, 'You've never asked about my own relationship. Don't you want to know?'

'Is it any of my business?' he asked with a note of wariness in his voice, hoping that his tone did not imply disinterest.

'You're my father. You should know, at least.'

Timothy sought to ease what he imagined would be an uncomfortable admission for her. In the moments before she spoke all manner of things crossed his mind.

'There is somebody. A woman. A work colleague.'

Her father said nothing but continued to listen, his face betraying little of his inner feelings.

'Are you shocked?'

'No,' he said, as evenly as he could.

'We've known each other for a year. We're thinking of moving in together.' She looked at her father enquiringly. 'Are you sure you're not shocked? Surprised even?'

'I don't know what I am,' he murmured. He thought for a moment, laid down his fork and spoon and then said, 'Yes; I do know what I feel. Relief. Relief that you've found someone. Until yesterday you'd been so far distant that it was almost . . .'

'As if I didn't exist?'

'Never that. Never. You're my daughter. But I'd learned to live with you on your own terms, and if that meant living at a distance then I had to respect your wishes. I can't say that I was comfortable with it but . . . well . . . as you say, I had to find a way within myself of coping with it. I'd tried to reach you, in the early days but . . . I suppose I'd resigned myself to you being reclusive; preferring your life in Oxford to anything we – your mum and I – had to offer.'

'I'm sorry,' said Alice.

'But to learn that you've found happiness – your kind of happiness – how could that shock me? What sort of person would it make me if my own daughter's happiness made me *un*happy?'

'But you'd no idea that—' Alice shrugged, reluctant to say the words in front of her own father.

'You'd fall in love with another woman?'

Alice nodded. Her eyes filled with tears and Timothy watched as one of them tumbled down her cheek.

'Oh, Alice! What have we done? What have we come to?' he asked, his voice brimming with the warmth she remembered from being a small child.

She brushed away the tear impatiently as her father, in his usual reflex action, reached into his pocket for the handkerchief. It was not there. He reached across and lifted her chin with his right hand, deftly wiping away another tear with the index finger of his left. 'No hanky,' he said. 'What's the world coming to?'

She smiled bravely through the tears and sniffed. 'Stupid. I'm supposed to be strong about things like this.'

'I'm rather glad you're not,' he said, meaningfully. 'So tell me about her.' Then, anxious that she should not think him prying, 'If you want to.'

Alice pulled a tissue from her own pocket and wiped her eyes. 'She's a lecturer at St Cat's. Maths. A year younger than me. Her name is Pippa and we . . .' she hesitated . . . 'seem to like the same things. Same values. We don't like the same music – she's into country stuff and I prefer Monteverdi but I . . . we . . . can live with that.'

'And you're happy?'

'Happier than I've ever been.'

'Then so am I. Delighted.' He refilled their glasses, causing the waiter advancing on their table to turn on his heel having seen that his job had been usurped.

Timothy raised his glass and said, 'Here's to you and Pippa.'

'Thank you,' she spoke softly, diffidently, her eyes fearful of meeting his.

'I don't think I can eat any more,' said Timothy.

'Nor me,' said Alice. She put down her fork and spoon and dabbed at her mouth with the corner of the napkin. Then something happened that caused the years to fall away. It was a simple thing; a thing that no one else would have remarked upon or even noticed. She bit her bottom lip with her teeth and looked sideways. Instantly he was the father of a small child once more; the child he read stories to at bedtime, the child who always seemed tentative and nervous, and who would bite her lip in moments of stress and anxiety. All he wanted to do now was enfold her in his arms. Instead, divided as they were by a table, he contented himself with murmuring, 'I've missed you.'

'You too, Dad,' she said, meeting his eye at last.

'What a day.'

'Yes. A day of revelations.'

'But good ones.'

'You think?'

'I've learned a lot over the past few hours. About myself . . . and about you. And most importantly I've got my daughter back.' He worried, suddenly, that he might have overstepped the mark; that he might be taking too much for granted.

'I think . . . I hope,' he added.

Alice nodded her acquiescence. 'Even though I'm still in Oxford?'

'Even though. At least I know that you're happy there.'

'Content,' she corrected.

'Content, yes. More lasting than happiness. Less evanescent.'

'And you?' she asked.

'Me? Oh, I wouldn't worry about me if I were you. I'm old enough and wise enough to battle my way through.' He grinned at her and rubbed the top of her hand with his. She looked at him with a daughter's eyes and he knew, at that moment, that she was not remotely convinced.

29

FIESOLE, FLORENCE

MAY

'Your son is your son till he gets him a wife;
Your daughter's your daughter for all of her life.'

Old proverb

Alice had booked a late afternoon flight from Florence to Heathrow on the day following their meeting. Her father suggested they spend the morning together – if she could bear it. She raised her eyes heavenward and asked what he would like to do. 'I'd like to go to Fiesole – up on the hillside – and look down on Florence.'

They took an orange number seven bus from Florence and, as the sun rose higher in the sky, at around 11.30am, they found themselves sitting on a low wall below the monastery at Fiesole, gazing out over the roofs of the city below.

'What do you think?' asked Timothy.

'I think it's amazing. And beautiful.'

'Here you are then, librarian,' said her father, handing her his ancient Baedeker. 'Tell us all about it.'

'Where did you get this?'

'On line. I went on a site for old books. I wanted a guidebook that was contemporary with the one Lucy Honeychurch used in *A Room with a View*.'

'How . . . romantic,' said Alice, with a note of surprise in her voice. 'I never thought of you as being . . .'

'Interested in literature?'

'Romantic literature.'

'Well, it's a story really, isn't it? A good story. Of different people and how they can misunderstand one another.'

His daughter regarded him suspiciously. 'Y-e-s. But a romantic story.'

'Is that so terrible?'

'Not at all.' She shrugged, with the intention of moving the conversation on. Her father did not prevent her. She looked at the date printed at the bottom of the title page. 'Nineteen-o-four. Contemporary, then . . . with Forster, and the book.'

'What does it say about Fiesole?'

Alice read out various snippets of information about the cathedral, the numerous paintings by Fra Angelico that were to be found there, the shrine of St Romulus, the monastery and the population of the town at that time – 4,951. 'Oh; and this is fun: the residents "are engaged in straw-plaiting (for fans about ½ fr., little baskets 1fr.)".'

He had never really thought of Alice as having a sense of humour. The fact that she had picked out an amusing passage as well as dry facts surprised him. 'Francs rather than lire? Odd. Still, we must see if we can find a fan for you to take home.'

'Not a lot of call for them in Oxford.'

'No. But a souvenir of a visit that neither of us will forget.'

Alice closed the book and turned to meet his eye. 'He was an interesting character.'

'Who?'

'Forster.'

'Cambridge rather than Oxford wasn't he?' asked Timothy.

'Yes but we don't hold that against him.'

Again she made him smile; her voice was serious but her sentiment wry.

'His father died when he was a baby. He was brought up by his mother and his father's sisters. A house full of women.'

'Poor man,' said Timothy, hoping that his remark would be interpreted as sardonic rather than in earnest.

Alice affected not to hear. 'He was ahead of his time really; in terms of the rights of women to forge their own identities and have their own opinions – opinions that should be taken note of and not just disregarded.'

'A feminist then?'

'Yes.' She looked out across Florence now, her mind seemingly elsewhere. He followed her gaze and the two of them stood silently for what amounted to several minutes. The sun was at its height and caused them to shield their eyes from its glare. Neither of them had thought to bring sunglasses. Timothy was glad of that; it meant that he could see clearly his daughter's expression as she spoke and as she listened. Birds sang; bells began to chime, first in the *campanile* behind them, then in the valley below. It was noon.

He wondered what she really thought about him; whether she regarded him with sympathy or pity. She was still hard to fathom, hard to read. The years of withdrawing into herself had made her adept at being opaque, but he had seen in her over the past twenty-four hours far more than he had been able to divine over the past twenty-four years. He looked at her, gazing out over the Italian landscape, her slender frame contrasting with the rugged cypress-studded hills and sturdy stuccoed villas, and wondered how such a fragile being had accrued so much inner reserve. Was it all his fault? His and Isobel's? How much of her resilience was due to nurture and how much nature? He suspected that in Alice's case that nurture was responsible for the lion's share. Had his attitude towards Isobel affected Alice's own attitude towards men? Was he to blame for the fact that she now chose to have a relationship with another woman?

Mixed with a father's guilt at such a possibility was relief; relief at her feeling able to level with him the night before; to some degree at least. Relief, too, at the fact that his elder daughter had found happiness or, as she preferred to call it, contentment. He must take care not to push too hard, not to expect the barriers that had been erected over most of her life to be lowered and dismantled within the space of a day or two. He would be patient. He would keep the door open. He would keep in contact; make sure that she knew he would like her to do the same. He must also make her aware that it mattered not a jot to him where she found love; what did matter was that she should find some kind of ease, some kind of serenity in a life which, it seemed, was only just beginning to be lived to the full.

The bells had stopped now. They walked down the hillside and found a small café. They ordered coffees and crusty rolls filled with Italian cheese. He noticed that Alice barely touched hers, but he resisted the temptation to chide her as though she were still a small child.

In the bus on the way back to Florence they spoke little; each of them lost in their thoughts. He waited for her to enquire further about his own situation; to ask who it was that had ensnared him, for that is, no doubt, what she thought had happened; that some woman had worked her charms on a rather sad old man who was clearly starved of affection.

But Alice made no further enquiries, and he was grateful for that.

They said goodbye outside the famous doors of the baptistery, Timothy making sure she saw them before she departed. He really wanted to ask her to stay a little longer, but she did not offer and he did not want to press her. They hugged, briefly, he kissed her on both cheeks and then she turned to go. He watched her walk away, then saw her hesitate. She turned and came back to him. Timothy was a good six inches taller than she was. She stood in front of him and looked up into his eyes.

'You must think I'm a bit weird I suppose.'

He shook his head. 'No. Not at all. I'm just glad for you . . .'

Alice smiled. 'It's funny you should have read the Forster.'

'Funny? Why?'

'I've read everything he wrote. He struck a chord, I suppose.' She hesitated. 'I've always remembered one thing he said.'

Her father looked at her enquiringly.

'We must be willing to let go of the life we have planned, so as to have the life that is waiting for us.'

Then she squeezed his arm, smiled at him, turned and disappeared into the crowd.

30

FLORENCE

MAY

'For whatsoever from one place doth fall,
Is with the tide unto another brought:
For there is nothing lost, that may be found, if sought.'

Edmund Spenser, *The Faerie Queen*, 1596

There was a kind of void when she had left. A sort of hollow echo. There were things he wished he had said, but then again maybe he had got the balance right – solicitous without being prying. At least, he hoped that was the way she saw it.

The first thing he did when she had left was to take his mobile phone into a shop that offered repairs. In fractured Italian he managed to make it clear to the man behind the counter (a youth of little more than fifteen who had the back off and the battery and sim card out before he could say knife, or even *coltello*) that it was not working. He was not sure, from the rapid-fire comments from the youth – something about '*batteria scarica*' quite what had been the matter, but judging by the expression on his face and the use of the word *'riparato'* he assumed that, when his ministrations were complete, all was now well and the phone was functioning normally.

Twenty euros the poorer, and armed with a new – and unbroken – lead which the youth had waved at him accusingly, he parked himself outside a café and sent a brief text to Rosie apologising that his phone had been out of order but that it was now sorted and he was perfectly well and having a good time. He longed to speak to her but felt it better that he left it for a day or so in the hope that Alice would have done the groundwork and informed her brother and sister that their father had not entirely lost the plot and was in full possession of his faculties – or what passed for them at the age of fifty-five. He also rang his bank to reassure them that the transaction he had initiated was perfectly in order and that his credit card was still in his possession. He apologised for not informing them of his intended peregrinations and explained that he would be touring Europe for the next few weeks. When the voice at the other end of the line asked just how long that would be, he was unable to be categorical. They seemed satisfied with his vagueness and wished him a pleasant trip.

There. Done. Sorted. For now. Then his phone flashed to tell him that the battery was low. Obvious really. Stupid of him. He turned it off and made a mental note to plug it in and charge it that evening. Maybe Alice was right; maybe he wasn't fit to be let out.

He went to the Accademia in the afternoon and finally set eyes on Michelangelo's David. The statue impressed him every bit as much as it had done the Yorkshire Women's Institute, and he smiled at the memory. He thought about sketching it but decided that when it came to sculpture, such creativity was probably best left to the Master. Anyway, he was bound to get the feet wrong. He'd never been good at feet.

The widows, determined not to be shaken off, were lying in wait for him when he returned to the Hotel Gandolfo later that afternoon.

'Mr Gandy, we have booked a table for seven-thirty this evening,' said the forceful Mrs Winder. 'We realise that six pm was probably too early for you and so we made our reservation at a slightly later hour which we hope will be more congenial for you. Is that all right?'

Quite untypically his reply was curt. 'No; I'm sorry. I have other plans this evening. Thanks all the same.' He managed a brief but hardly apologetic smile as he mounted the stairs to his room, leaving the two ladies staring after him, their faces a picture of bewilderment and dejection.

As he showered the events of the day played over in his mind. For the first time since he left Paris, Francine was not the only woman uppermost in his thoughts. He could still hardly believe that his elder daughter had put in an appearance; added to which, she had shown up because she was concerned about him. Alice: the sickly child that he had assumed had turned into nothing more than a cypher, had shown grit, determination and compassion. He had become so used to feeling that, although he was the father of three, there was really only one daughter who impinged on his life and with whom he had any day-to-day involvement. Rosie had become his focus; Oliver his Achilles heel. Alice hardly ever intruded upon his thoughts, and now she had reappeared he felt a mixture of relief and guilt at having all but expunged her from his memory.

He sat down on the bed, his towel wrapped around him, as

his mind whirled. Deep inside he felt a sense of profound joy at the return of 'the prodigal daughter', except that prodigal was not a word that could be applied in any way to Alice – a woman of measured emotions and fragile sensibilities. When he returned home he would go and see her, in Oxford, if that was acceptable to her. He could not imagine that she would demur. Not after a reunion which, he hoped, had meant as much to her as it did to him.

He towelled himself dry and whistled softly to himself as he dressed, then took the stairs two at a time and swept out into the street with a spring in his step as Florence enfolded him in her eventide embrace.

He glanced at his watch as he crossed the Piazza della Signoria. It was seven thirty. He felt a pang of guilt at having dealt with the two widows so peremptorily, but consoled himself with the fact that they had no right to assume that he would fall in with their plans. They were on their holiday; he was on his. He would dine with them tomorrow or the next day – out of politeness – but they could not assume that he was there for their convenience. That wasn't being unreasonable was it? It was just that tonight he needed to be alone; in his own company, to think, to decide what to do – where to go – next. There were still three places on his original list: Rome, Naples and Venice. That was his intended itinerary and it still held good didn't it? Or was there, at the back of his mind, the feeling that he might cut short his planned trip and head back to Paris?

But that would be a waste. Francine had sent him on his way, insisting that he undertake his planned Grand Tour – to do otherwise would leave him feeling that the whole enterprise had been a waste; there would be no sense of achievement and, anyway, he wanted to see Rome and Naples and Venice didn't he?

He passed a shop selling all kinds of paper: marbled and

finely figured, along with coloured inks and artisan stationery. It was still open and one or two tourists were buying tasteful souvenirs. He saw, in the window, a sturdy cardboard folder covered in paper that was marbled in shades of pink and blue; the corners reinforced with dark blue leather. It seemed so Italian, so Florentine, so of the place and of the moment that before he had consciously made any decision he found himself paying for it and having it wrapped in brown paper, along with a couple of art pens. It would make the perfect place to keep his sketches and watercolours, rather than leaving them in the pad where, each time he took it out, there was a danger of them being damaged, smudged or defaced by a passing shower.

He exited the shop and walked through the narrow streets towards the Arno, intent on having a light supper by the river and watching the Florentines come and go. As he neared the embankment he came upon a small group of people. They were clustered around someone who had obviously come to grief. A passer-by who had fallen, it appeared. He made to walk by, rather than joining the group and gawping, but as he did so he heard a woman's voice saying tremulously, 'But I am the weak one. I can't understand it.' It was Vera Dawes.

Swiftly he pushed his way through the edge of the small group and found Mrs Dawes standing over the crumpled body of her companion. No one appeared to be doing anything. Clearly the incident had happened just a few seconds before. Timothy looked down at the figure on the pavement. Sylvia Winder lay in the foetal position, a pool of blood by her head; a pool of blood that was growing wider as he gazed. Timothy knelt down and felt for the old woman's pulse. It was faint. '*Ambulanza!*' he shouted at one of the onlookers. Then, seeing no sign of action, he cried again, '*Ambulanza! Immediato!*' At this injunction, two of the younger onlookers sped off and Timothy spoke gently into the ear of the supine woman. 'It's all right, Mrs Winder. Help is on its way. It won't be long now.' He looked up at Vera Dawes and saw that she was sobbing disconsolately, her body shaking. 'Can someone look after this lady?' he asked, his Italian failing him at this point.

'Come on, dear,' said an English voice. A middle-aged man – a tourist – put his arm round Vera Dawes and shepherded her over to a bench where, along with his wife, he murmured the customary platitudes about everything 'going to be all right'. Timothy stroked Sylvia Winder's hand. It seemed alarmingly cold.

Within ten minutes two paramedics were carefully lifting the limp body onto a stretcher and loading it into the ambulance. They wrapped a blanket around Vera and helped her up the steps of the vehicle, closing the doors behind her with a hollow slam. Having been told he must remain behind, Timothy watched as the vehicle snaked its way through the gathering of tourists; a strangely anachronistic sight among the elegant ancient buildings of Florence.

He could do nothing but watch helplessly as it disappeared from view, and think that if he had not been so churlish – so selfish – and gone with them to supper, the accident might never have happened. The crowd swiftly dispersed and he found himself alone except for passers-by skirting the pool of blood that lay on the time-worn pavement.

He bent down and picked up the folder he had placed on the ground while attending to the old lady; the corner of the package was stained with blood. Carefully he removed the brown paper and deposited it in a nearby waste bin. The folder inside was unaffected; its swirling pattern of pink and blue highlighted by the last rays of the sun that were, within a few moments, obliterated by a large deep grey cloud. He looked around for a shopkeeper who might be able to mop up the blood, but none was forthcoming. Then he felt the first spot of rain. It landed with a spat on his new purchase. Swiftly he slipped the folder underneath his jacket. By the time he reached the shelter of a shop awning the squall was in full swing; great cracks of thunder rent the warm air, flashes of lightning came in rapid succession and torrential rain hammered down on the ancient city. He doubted that there would be any need to mop up the blood now; it would be washed away by the downpour. In half an hour there would be no trace of the accident.

He folded his arms and shrank against the shop window as the rain pounded the *piazza*, wincing at the thunder-claps which shook the plate glass behind him. There was little he could do but wait, and brood, on what might have been, on the status quo, and on the future – for himself, Mrs Dawes and Mrs Winder. After twenty minutes the rain slackened and gradually abated. What was left of the sun made a farewell gesture before being obliterated by kinder, paler clouds.

Timothy stepped out from under the awning and walked down towards the Arno. His appetite had left him. He no longer felt in need of food, though a drink would be more than welcome. He went into a bar, ordered a brandy and sipped it gently before making his way back to the Hotel Gandolfo.

In the reception area, Signor Pollini was speaking on the telephone. '*Com e lei? E morta? Molto triste,*' he said. He glanced up at Timothy and shook his head. '*Si. Grazie.*' He said softly, before putting down the telephone.

'I am afraid it is not good news, *signor*. The lady Winder. She 'as died.'

Timothy did not expect to see Vera Dawes at breakfast the following morning, so he was surprised when she appeared half an hour after he had taken his own seat at the table in the corner. He stood up as she entered. 'I'm so sorry,' he said.

The old lady smiled weakly, her eyes brimful of tears as she walked slowly to the table in the window and lowered herself into her chair. She glanced across the table to where Mrs Winder was normally seated and Timothy could see her lower lip trembling.

'Would you mind?' she asked him, indicating the empty chair opposite.

'Sorry?'

'Would you mind coming and sitting at my table?'

Swiftly, Timothy stood up and moved across to take the place normally occupied by Mrs Winder. 'Not at all,' he said. He could not stop himself asking the obvious question, 'How are you?'

'A bit shaken. It was all so sudden.'

Timothy was unsure whether to ask her what had happened, but his uncertainty was short lived since Vera Dawes launched into a full description of the events of the previous evening.

'It was a silly, simple thing. We were walking across the square – the *piazza* – and looking about us at the buildings. The sort of thing we've been doing every day. Sylvia tripped, that was all. She must have caught her foot on an uneven paving stone. She fell so quickly. I heard her head hit the pavement. It was such a dreadful sound. A sort of crack. She didn't say anything; just groaned. A soft, low groan . . . And then people came, and you came and . . . well, you know the rest. She had gone by the time we got to the hospital.'

At this point emotion overtook her and she reached up the sleeve of her cardigan for a lace-edged handkerchief that was already damp.

'Oh dear,' she murmured. 'Oh dear, oh dear. It should have been me. I am the weak one – not Sylvia.'

'What will you do?' asked Timothy. And then, swiftly, 'Is there anything I can do to help?'

Vera Dawes clutched at her handkerchief and shook her head. 'I don't think so, thank you. Signor Pollini has very kindly offered to help me. There is no British Consulate in Florence any more, you see. It closed a few years ago. But he knows what to do. He is being very kind.'

'As long as you are sure.'

Mrs Dawes nodded her thanks.

'Coffee?' he asked, reaching over for the pot on his own table.

'Oh yes please.'

'Will you go home now?'

'Yes. Once I've sorted things out. I think that will be the end of my gallivanting. I can't really do it alone. Not like you.'

For a moment he felt guilty at the advantage of his independence and relative youth, but then Mrs Dawes said, 'I suppose you feel a bit awkward about last night?'

'A little. If I had come with you—'

'Oh, Mr Gandy, you must not think that. Not at all. Sylvia could be very bossy, and I told her that you have your own life to lead.'

'You weren't offended?'

'Not in the least. I thought it was an imposition asking you, but Sylvia is . . . was . . . a very forceful personality. I suppose that's why I holidayed with her really; she was a very good organiser and I am a bit . . . feeble when it comes to that sort of thing. It suited her to lead and it suited me to be led.'

'So when will you leave?'

'Signor Pollini is sorting out my flight.' She hesitated for a moment, holding back another rush of tears. Having reined in her emotions she continued. 'We shouldn't be too sad, should we? Sylvia had a long and happy life. She was eighty-two you know. And at least she went quickly.'

'Yes but . . .'

'It doesn't do to dwell on things does it, Mr Gandy? One has to move on. I shall be back home tomorrow and Sylvia's son is taking charge of things. He's flying out to Florence today so I really only have to get myself home now and I can just about manage that.'

The proprietor came with another pot of coffee and left it on the table, along with a basket of pastries and a bowl of fruit. 'Thank you, Signor Pollini,' said Vera. 'You've been very kind.' Then she turned to Timothy, trying to lighten the mood. 'What about you, Mr Gandy. What's next for you? Where will you go?'

Timothy was caught unawares by the enquiry. 'I'm not sure,' he said. 'I have one more night booked here, then I had planned to go on to Rome, Naples and Venice but . . .'

'You're not certain?'

'No. I might go straight to Venice. Leave Rome and Naples for another day.'

'Yes. There's such a lot to see isn't there? Such a lot to take in. One can get rather dizzy with it all.'

Timothy nodded understandingly, and again it crossed his mind that he could go back to Paris. He banished the thought from his head and said, 'I had a surprise visit yesterday; from my daughter.'

Mrs Dawes looked puzzled.

'My elder daughter. I haven't seen her for a while. Not since my wife died. She came out to check that I was all right.' He was speaking as though thinking out loud. Turning over things in his mind, but audibly.

'That's nice,' said the old lady. 'It's important to keep in touch isn't it? So easy to let things slide.'

'Yes,' he said absently.

'That's what happened to me. I have two children. Two boys. I see them now and again. Well, not very often actually. Sometimes at Christmas, sometimes not. But they have wives and children, and that's what takes up their time now. It's as it should be really I suppose. But I do wish I saw more of them.'

Tears flowed down her cheeks once more, and Timothy took the old lady's hand and squeezed it. He tried to think of something comforting to say, but no suitable words were forthcoming. He managed an encouraging smile; that was all. It seemed a pathetic offering to a woman whose life appeared to be diminishing by the minute.

Children: they were at the heart of your life for the first twenty years, and then what? He hoped that in a few years' time he would not find himself in the same position as Vera Dawes. But he knew that the only way such a set of circumstances could be avoided was by dint of his own efforts. It was a salutary thought, and one that he knew for the rest of his Grand Tour would steadily chip away at him, gnawing its way into his consciousness. His future happiness was in nobody's hands but his own, but insularity – the kind of isolation within marriage that he had become accustomed to – must not be a part of it. He had responsibilities towards his children. If he did not fulfill those responsibilities then how could he expect anything from his children in return? Would it be possible to enjoy a comfortable relationship with them, and also with another woman? A woman nearer their age than his own? If only he knew.

31

SANTA CROCE, FLORENCE

MAY

'The chapel of the Medici, the Good and Bad Angels of
Florence; the church of Santa Croce where Michael
Angelo lies buried, and where every stone in the cloisters
is eloquent on great men's deaths; innumerable churches,
often masses of unfinished brickwork externally, but
solemn and serene within; arrest our lingering steps, in
strolling through the city.'

Charles Dickens, *Pictures from Italy*, 1846

Until the previous day he had been considering extending his stay
in Florence; there was so much he had not seen: the Boboli Gardens,
the Bargello, the Medici Chapel. But the events of the last twenty-
four hours had unsettled him – the one celebratory, revelatory
even, and the other tragic. Somehow the atmosphere of the place
was tainted, but he could not leave without a visit to the one place
that bore a name which held a powerful resonance for him; the
oldest Franciscan church in the world, reputedly founded by St
Francis himself: the Temple of the Italian Glories – the place that

Lucy Honeychurch had been looking up in her Baedeker when she was reprimanded by the overbearing Miss Lavish.

The façade of Santa Croce towered above him as he stood in the *piazza* below. It presented a strangely formal neo-Gothic façade – like an elaborately decorated house of cards – and had, towards its central apex, the Star of David. Suddenly aware of life mirroring art, he remembered the scene conjured up in *A Room with a View*, of the fight, and of the mortally wounded man falling at Lucy's feet as blood ran from his mouth. The fictional image in his mind coalesced with the vivid memory of the day before, of Sylvia Winder lying at his feet in an ever-widening pool of blood. It was at this moment that he decided it was, indeed, time to move on, but not before he had taken in the elaborate tombs of Michelangelo and Galileo, of Machiavelli and Rossini.

On leaving the church, his head swimming with images of elaborate funerary monuments, of sienna-dappled sarcophagi and heavenward-looking saints draped in folds of marble, he sat down on a vacant seat and breathed deeply for a few minutes. Soon the incense-laden atmosphere of Santa Croce that seemed to fill his lungs and cause his head to swim was replaced with purer air, laced with the merest hint of carbon monoxide. Florence, he decided, was a rich diet to be taken in several small doses rather than in one gargantuan helping.

He took out his sketchbook and began to outline the façade of Santa Croce, deciding that this would be a pen-and-wash creation to add to his growing clutch of hand-crafted memories. The newly acquired pen soon began to work its magic, and he produced a passable image of the towering façade. He was, he thought, getting better – his penmanship was not yet on a par with the likes of Ptolemy Dean or Matthew Rice but the old skills had not deserted him altogether. After an hour and a half he folded up the pad, satisfied that he had made another contribution to the Florentine folder that would hold his modest art collection.

He looked at his watch. One o'clock. He was not yet hungry, and walked to Santa Maria Novella station to check on train times. But where to go? Rome was next on his itinerary, but he was not at all sure that he was ready to be assaulted by even more ancient history. Why had it never occurred to him that the Grand Tour taken by gentlemen of the 18th century had been taken at a slow pace for a very good reason?

What he would have loved more than anything now would be to flop down on Rosamund Hawksmoor's terrace and breathe in the soft sweet air of St Jean Cap Ferrat – air fragranced by orange blossom and lavender. That episode of his life all seemed a million miles away from Florence – the world of Archie and Serena, Rosamund and her dipsomaniac butler. Another place, another life almost. And Francine seemed even more distant. Did he still feel the same about her? Yes. There was no doubt in his mind about that. He had simply disciplined himself to move on in order to make the most of his trip; to avoid pining for her and dreaming away the next few weeks. On that count he had been only partially successful.

He felt embarrassed by his lack of decisiveness. When he had begun his trip, the itinerary was clearly set out in his mind: Paris, Monaco, Pisa, Florence, Rome, Naples and Venice. Pisa had been bypassed thanks to Rosamund's intervention, and St Jean Cap Ferrat, via Nice, had been added. Surely it was a good thing to be flexible? And he had most certainly enjoyed the diversion. Benefitted from it in a funny kind of way. Rosamund had set him thinking – about all kinds of things; issues he had previously either ignored or taken for granted.

It occurred to him that he was like a student on a gap year, except that his trip would stretch into weeks, not months. He must get a grip; must marshal his thoughts. He was just being feeble wasn't he? What was the sense in missing out Rome, for goodness sake? The cradle of history. The more he thought about it the more resolute he became that he would go there. Naples; he would miss out Naples. If he had . . . what . . . four nights in Rome . . . five? And then went on to Venice to round off his trip? Yes; that made sense.

He scanned the rail timetable at Santa Maria Novella station and was surprised at the shortness of the journey. He could be in Rome in little over an hour; three hours on the slow, stopping train. He would walk across the Ponte Vecchio to the Pitti Palace and the Boboli Gardens this afternoon, take in the Uffizi tomorrow morning and then set off for the Eternal City on the slower of the trains, the better to get his breath back.

The Boboli Gardens were the first disappointment on his Grand Tour. Unlike the gardens of Versailles, where it appeared likely that at any moment the court of Louis XIV might sweep into view and alight from their gilded carriages, the Boboli Gardens seemed long abandoned by the Medicis. It was not that they were poorly maintained, but that they were so lacking in the rich atmosphere that had pervaded the royal gardens in France and given them so much vitality. These gardens and grounds seemed weary; tired, dusty and somehow forsaken, in spite of their formality and the plentiful provision of statuary at the angle of every junction and the termination of every vista. Maybe it was just him; maybe his mood had been broken by the previous day's tragedy. He looked in his 1904 Baedeker and read, 'The charming grounds, adorned with numerous vases and statues, were laid out in 1550 under Cosimo I, and attract crowds of pleasure seekers on Sundays.' He found himself relieved that it was not a Sunday, if the pleasure seekers were still sticking to their century-old tradition. Today there was a reasonable scattering of visitors, but not so many as to jostle you at every turn.

He found a bench in a quiet corner where the sun warmed
his back, and took out his phone to make the call he had been
avoiding. He dialled Rosie's number, and found his heart leaping
at the sound of her voice as she answered.

'Hello,' he said. 'It's Dad.'

There was a hollow silence, then Rosie said softly, 'Oh, Dad.'
Just that. Nothing more. He found himself unable to speak for
a few moments. Then he heard her voice again. 'Are you there?'

He took a deep breath and cleared his throat. 'Yes; I'm here.'

'Oh, I'm so relieved. We were so worried.'

'I know. I'm so sorry. I tried to phone but . . .'

'Never mind. You're OK, that's the most important thing.'
There was another pause before she asked, 'Where are you now?'

'I'm sitting in the sunshine in the Boboli Gardens in Florence
and tomorrow I move on to Rome.'

'And are you having a good time? Is it as interesting – as
exciting – as you hoped it would be?'

'Oh yes. It's every bit as exciting as I hoped it would be . . .
and probably a bit more.'

'Alice rang,' she said. 'She told us you were fine and that
you'd just had a problem with your phone. We were worried
about the money – I mean in case something had happened to
you – but Alice said it was all sorted and there was nothing to
worry about. Is that right?'

He hesitated for a moment, taken by surprise and heartened
by the generosity of spirit evinced by his elder daughter. 'Yes;
it's all perfectly straightforward.' He felt a little nervous at his
economy with the truth but salved his conscience by saying,
'I'll tell you all about it when I come home, but don't worry
– that's the most important thing. I'm absolutely fine.'

'And happy?'

'Yes.' He thought for a moment. 'Very happy.' There was so much he wanted to tell her, so much he wanted to share with her. He longed to take her into his confidence – the daughter to whom he had always felt closest – but he did not want to do so at arm's length, on the telephone, from a foreign country, without the benefit of her being there in front of him so that she could read his expression and detect the nuances in his voice. She was sensitive and he did not want to blunt those sensitivities by blurting it all out from several hundred miles away.

'Oh, I'm so pleased,' she said, with that genuine ring in her voice that he had so missed. 'We're missing you. Elsie's cut another tooth – her cheeks are as red as apples.'

In all the excitement of the past few days he had rather forgotten his granddaughter. He felt a pang of remorse. 'I'm missing you all, too. It's so good to hear you. Give Elsie my love and tell her to be as good as her mother was when she was little.'

'I will. Oh Dad! I'm so glad you rang. Look, I can't stop; we're just about to go out of the door and Elsie is in her buggy. Will you ring again? I mean, in a few days' time? I don't want to pester or be a nuisance, it's just that we were so worried.'

'I will. And stop worrying. I'm grown up and very capable of looking after myself.' His conscience raised an eyebrow at this remark. 'But I'll ring from Rome or Venice in a few days' time.'

'Great! Be careful, Dad. Love you.'

'Love you too, sweetheart.'

'Bye.'

'Bye.'

And there the conversation ended. He sat back on the bench and reached for the handkerchief in his pocket as the tensions of the previous few days were released in heaving sobs. How ridiculous, he thought, a man in his fifties weeping like a baby.

32

FLORENCE TO ROME

MAY

'Railways and the Church have their critics, but both are the best ways of getting a man to his ultimate destination.'

Rev W. Awdry, author of *Thomas the Tank Engine*
(1911-97)

Calming was perhaps not the right word, but rail travel always comforted him, and in Italy the trains did seem to run on time. Perhaps Mussolini's alleged legacy lived on. Having upbraided himself for his feebleness and lack of stamina when it came to sightseeing, he felt a growing sense of anticipation at the prospect of exploring Rome – the ancient sites of the Forum and the Colosseum; the more modern and romantic-sounding Spanish Steps and Trevi Fountain.

For now, though, he contented himself with gazing out of the window at the passing countryside – a varied mixture of rural delights and industrial incursions – and occasionally dipping into his battered Baedeker which promised a host of delights, from tramways and omnibuses to cabs both open and closed, carriage hirers and shops selling engravings. He doubted that any of them would still exist, and when he turned the page and saw the heading 'A Fortnight's Visit', he felt temporarily overwhelmed and closed the covers of the small red book.

They were stopping at Orvieto, a name he recognised from the wine he had sampled in Italian restaurants. It was never very expensive but seemed always a refreshing accompaniment to fish in Italian restaurants. He wondered if it would taste any different in the land of its birth. His idle thoughts were interrupted by the arrival of an embarking passenger; a nun. She was struggling with a small but bulging suitcase, and Timothy got up from his seat to help her deposit it in the overhead luggage rack.

'Thank you, THANK YOU!' she said, her strong Irish accent giving away the country of her birth.

'My pleasure,' said Timothy, returning to his seat.

In spite of the fact that there were few passengers, and that the nun could have chosen to place herself almost anywhere in the carriage, she sat opposite him and began to smooth the folds of her habit. It was not long and black, as Timothy remembered from his childhood, but a shade of rich burgundy, topped with a white collar and finishing just below the knee. Where once only a circle of the face would have been on view, encased in a tight white coif and whimple, Timothy could see a froth of chestnut hair above the forehead, topped by a white band and a much reduced veil of black cloth. Clearly, nuns' habits were not what they were.

The nun was breathing heavily, as though she had been running. She was, he guessed, in her forties or fifties. Her cheeks were flushed from the exertion of catching the train, and her pale blue eyes gleamed as she glanced out of the window at the now receding station. Her right hand fingered the large silver cross that dangled from a chain round her neck, and her lips moved slightly as though she were running through some murmured litany – perhaps in thanks for catching the train which she must clearly have been in danger of missing.

Timothy went back to his book. To no avail. Her brief prayer completed, this was a nun intent on making good use of her temporary freedom from the constraints of the convent.

'You're English?' asked the nun.

'Yes,' said Timothy politely, smiling at her and then attempting to resume his reading. He was checking out the location of the small hotel he had marked in his up-to-date travel guide. It would be a good idea, he decided, to plump for something rather larger than his two previous places of residence in the hope of having a quieter life. Clearly that state of affairs was to be postponed a little longer.

'Isn't it a wonderful part of the world?' asked the nun.

'It is. Yes. Lovely.' He went back to his book.

'Are you on your way to Rome?'

'I am, yes.'

'Wonderful. Me, too. I'm going to see the Holy Father.'

Timothy was finding it difficult to keep himself to himself without appearing rude. He felt obliged to remark, 'That's exciting then.'

'Oh, it is! I'm having such an amazing time. I can't wait to tell the sisters all about it.'

He tried his best to avoid prolonging the conversation, but the nun's naïve enthusiasm was impossible to ignore. To do so would have been churlish. He lowered the travel guide to his lap and smiled at her. 'Have you escaped for long?' he asked.

'Oh, that's dreadful! I'm not escaping; I've just been given remission for good behaviour!' The nun winked.

Timothy laughed. 'So where is your order?'

'In Dublin. The Sisters of Bethlehem.' She stretched out her hand in greeting. 'I'm Sister Mary Agnes.'

Timothy shook it and beamed at her: 'Tim Gandy.'

'And where are you from Timothy?' She used his full name, perhaps in saintly reference.

'Sussex. Chichester.'

'Oh yes. Lovely cathedral. Enormous spire!' Her eyes lit up even more. Then she added, with a mock frown, 'Anglican of course.'

'Yes.'

She was beginning to breathe more normally now, but the eyes still sparkled. It was as if she was bursting to communicate, but then, Timothy conceded, this was probably her only chance before she returned to the seclusion of her order; if, indeed, it was that sort of order. He could not imagine a person of such an outgoing nature as Sister Mary Agnes taking kindly to a vow of silence. Hers was probably an order that worked out in the community. Not that he was given much of an opportunity of asking, for the nun rattled away ten to the dozen.

'Out here they're all Catholic, of course. Well, almost all. Like the cathedral at Orvieto,' she explained.

'There's a cathedral there?'

'Heavens yes! Thanks to the Miracle of Bolsena.'

'I'm sorry?'

'The drops of blood. Don't tell me you've never heard of it!'

'Well, I can't say I have . . .'

'It was a long time ago, of course, but it's still a famous miracle.'

Timothy found himself leaning forward in his seat as the nun related the tale. It was almost as if she were presenting *Jackanory*; the wonder and excitement in her voice was palpable.

'There was this priest, you see. Peter of Prague he was called. German he was.' She paused for a split second of reflection, then muttered, 'I'm not sure why, then, he was called Peter of Prague, because Prague is in Czechoslovakia isn't it? Or has it moved? Perhaps back then it was all a part of Germany. Anyway, no matter. That was his name and who am I to argue? He was a bit of a doubter – like Thomas. You remember him? Only Peter was travelling to Rome – on a pilgrimage – and on the way he was ministering in Bolsena – near the coast – and as he put the Host on the plate (and he was never totally convinced that the Host was, indeed, the body of Our Lord, which, as you know, is at the very heart of our Catholic faith) so he noticed that blood was beginning to flow from it.'

She observed Timothy's raised eyebrows and continued: 'It's true! It even dripped on to the floor, and on to the corporal – the linen cloth.'

She was warming to her story now, her eyes shining even more than previously. She continued at breakneck speed: 'Well, Peter knew that Pope Urban the Fourth was staying in Orvieto at that time – it's less than twenty miles away, though I suppose in 1263 it took half a day to get there – so he gets on his horse (well, he might have got in a carriage; no, a cart back in the thirteenth century; or he might have walked, I'm not sure) and he goes to His Holiness and tells him what has happened. Well, His Holiness is delighted – he absolves Peter and has the holy corporal brought to Orvieto where it's paraded through the streets. Now it's in a golden shrine in the cathedral and Pope Paul came to visit it in 1964 – the first time a pope ever flew in a helicopter.' She paused for breath; her face positively glowing. 'So what do you think of that? Isn't it amazing?'

'It is,' said Timothy, genuinely. 'And did you see the shrine?'

'Oh I did.'

'And do you believe in miracles?'

'Timothy! Of *course* I believe in miracles. I'm a nun – and that's a miracle in itself.' She winked at him again.

'It's a wonderful story.'

'Oh dear! I sense a note of doubt in your voice.'

'No. I mean . . . it's just remarkable.'

'That it is! And it's remarkable that I'm here and on my way to the Vatican to see His Holiness.'

'You've got an audience with him?'

'That I have.'

'I'm very impressed.'

'Oh, I wouldn't be. It's me and twenty thousand other people from all over the world. I shall be down there in St Peter's Square looking up at him along with all the others; I just hope I don't get a tall priest in front of me, 'cos if I do I'm scuppered. I'm only five-foot-four you see. But it will be a special moment. And then I shall get on a plane and fly back to Dublin and the sisters and my life of prayer.' She flopped back in her seat, seemingly exhausted from the effort of telling her story, and looked out of the window for a moment before turning back and saying, 'But listen to me. Rabbiting on and not asking after you.'

'Oh, don't worry about that.'

'But I do, I do. Where are you going? I mean, to Rome obviously but are you on holiday or what? Do you have a family? Are they not with you?'

Timothy explained as briefly as he could about the Grand Tour and how it had come about. Sister Mary Agnes listened attentively and without interrupting as he told her the bare essentials – of Isobel's death, of his desire to travel now that he was alone, of his children (carefully avoiding any mention of their respective characters) and his grandchild.

'Oh what a blessing! You must be missing them.'

'Yes,' he said, softly. 'I think I am.'

'And how long do you think you'll stay in Rome?'

'Five nights. That's the plan. Then I'll go on to Venice and finally home.'

She nodded understandingly. 'Travel is a wonderful thing.'

'Yes.'

'It must have helped with your sadness.'

'In a way.'

'But not altogether?'

'No. Not altogether,' he confessed.

'There is that saying, isn't there?'

'I'm sorry?'

'You know; that when God closes a door he opens a window.'

'Yes,' admitted Timothy, though with less than complete conviction.

'The trouble is, Timothy, don't you find that sometimes He opens more than one window at once, and then you have to choose which one to go through?'

He looked at her inquisitively. What was it about this woman? Was it just that she was a nun and therefore had an aura, real or imagined, that came with the vocation? No; he knew enough about nuns to understand that not all of them had the vitality and the *joie de vivre* of Sister Mary Agnes nor, he doubted, the perspicacity. It could be just his imagination, a question of attribution when it came to her somewhat clichéd remarks, but their appositeness was, all the same, a little unnerving.

'Am I right?' she asked, her pale blue eyes probing into his very soul.

Timothy tried not to look taken aback. 'Yes,' he said levelly.

'There was a Saint Timothy, you know.'

'Good heavens!' he said, shaken out of his reverie and wondering what was coming.

'He was a disciple of St Paul. A martyr to stomach trouble. A quiet and timid man by all accounts.'

'Probably on account of the indigestion.'

She ignored his feeble intervention. 'But he turned out to be something of a star. "A good man", St Paul called him. He was the first Christian Bishop of Ephesus in the first century AD, you know.'

'I didn't. But I don't think there's any danger of that happening to me,' said Timothy, making a second attempt to lighten the atmosphere.

'Oh, you'd be surprised at what can happen to mere mortals. Who'd have thought that I would have become a nun?'

'Didn't you always want to be?'

'Good gracious, no! I thought they were all women who were disappointed in love. But I soon learned.'

'So why did you?'

'Oh, bless you! It's a long story . . . and here we are.'

The train was slowing. They were arriving in Rome and Sister Mary Agnes rose from her seat and smoothed down her habit. 'Would you mind handing me down my case? I don't think I can quite reach.'

'Not at all.' Timothy stood up and took the handle of the nun's luggage, lowering it safely and handing it to its owner.

'You're very kind, Timothy.'

'It's been a pleasure.' He took down his own holdall and checked that his suitcase was still safely deposited in the bay at the end of the carriage. 'Can I help you off the train?' he asked.

'That would be very kind.'

The doors were opening now, and Timothy followed behind Sister Mary Agnes, carrying his own holdall and pulling her wheeled case behind him. He handed it down to her as she reached the platform and went back for his own suitcase before joining her and walking with her down the long platform. As they got to the barrier she turned to him. 'You should go to St Peter's for a service, Timothy. I know you're not a Catholic but I think you'll find something there. In the music, if nothing else.'

'I'll do my best.'

'Yes,' she said, thoughtfully. 'I think you will. God bless you.'

They began to walk to the exit. As they did so, he asked, 'What happened to St Timothy?'

'Oh . . . well . . . it was not a happy end, but I would not want you to get upset about that. He lived to be eighty or so.'

'And?'

Sister Mary Agnes could see that she was not to be allowed to leave until she had answered his question. 'He was stoned to death.'

Timothy said nothing, but the nun could see that he was not thrilled at the news.

'Now then, Timothy, you must remember one thing: life is full of ups and downs and much of it we have little or no control over. But there are some things we can avoid if we are careful. I think it highly unlikely that you will suffer the same fate as your namesake. Now run along and be a good boy.'

Timothy chuckled. Then he reached out and shook the nun's hand. 'Thank you for your company,' he said. 'Good luck at St Peter's. I hope you get a good view of His Holiness.'

'And God speed to you, Timothy. And when you have to make that big decision, may God be with you and guide your heart.'

'Big decision?'

She nodded and gave a parting wink.

A black car drew up, the rear door opened and Sister Mary

Agnes lifted up her case as though it were a featherweight, threw it across the back seat and slipped inside with all the agility of an Olympian athlete. The door closed and the car sped away.

Timothy looked after her, as the slipstream of the car ruffled his hair. One whirlwind leaving behind another in its wake. He joined the queue for taxis and slipped his hand into his jacket pocket for his handkerchief. He withdrew it and found that sitting neatly within its folds was a small and delicate rosary composed of chestnut brown beads and a tiny silvered cross.

33

ROME

MAY

'Fumum et opes strepitumque Romae'
(The smoke and wealth and din of Rome)

Horace (65–8BC) *Odes*, Book 3, No. 29

The taxi ride to his hotel was a test of nerves. He had thought that the traffic and the standard of driving in Florence left something to be desired, but he had not at that point encountered the devil-may-care motorists and taxi drivers of Rome who clearly had one hand on the wheel and the other on their own rosary. Down the Via Cavour tore his white taxi, when the stop-start traffic would allow, and around the stupendous memorial to Victor Emmanuel II; then a right turn up the Via del Corso and past the church of St Ignazio di Loyola to the small street where the red, white and green flag dangled over the elegant portico of the Hotel Libellula. It might as well have been a chequered flag, bearing in mind the frantic nature of the journey. Swerving between cars and bicycles and motor scooters, occasionally mounting the pavement and frequently sounding the horn, his youthful driver, whose face was partially hidden by a large pair of Ray-Bans, chewed gum remorselessly.

As he stumbled out of the cab, Timothy handed over the requested 48 euros without a word, his face ashen. The hotel porter relieved him of the burden of his cases and led the way into the welcome calm of the marble-floored lobby where, among palm fronds and to the muted strains of Vivaldi's 'Gloria', he checked in and was shown up to a good-sized and brightly lit cream-painted room on the third floor. He tipped the porter, closed the door and flopped down on the large double bed to get his breath back. He woke half an hour later, surprised at the fact that he had dozed off, and opened the window to let in the fresh air. It was six o'clock; a fact confirmed by the striking of church bells in the vicinity.

He washed, changed his shirt and took the lift to the ground floor where, with a nod to the porter behind the desk, he left the hotel and, to the accompaniment of a million car horns and internal combustion engines, set out to discover the evening delights of Rome.

For the first two days of his visit, Timothy was lucky enough to get what he most desired – solitude. Not the solitude of a hermit but the self-containment of the tourist who wishes to travel alone and who is happy in his own company. Once he had become accustomed to the clamour and hectic energy of Roman street life he began to enjoy it, finding in the daily activity of the Eternal City a likeable vitality that lifted his spirits.

There was plenty to sketch and paint, and his Florentine folder began to fatten. The Forum was larger and more extensive than he had ever imagined. On the days when the traffic was unrestricted, the Colosseum became the centre of a vast roundabout, but its heart was pervaded by an atmospheric calm that sent a shiver down his spine at the prospect of gladiators and lions in combat. To gaze upon the very tunnels down which the animals had entered the arena made his blood run cold.

The soaring Spanish Steps made him smile; not that they were intrinsically humorous, but that a newly married couple – she in a vast froth of white tulle with crimson roses holding her veil in place, he in a tightly tailored Italian suit, his thick black hair slicked back and his even white teeth shining in the sunlight – were standing halfway up the precipitous flight having their photograph taken. To one side stood the families – men and women of all shapes, sizes and ages dressed in their smartest clothes, with tulle-bedecked toddlers and miniature versions of the groom running in and out of their legs. It was clearly a day of jubilation for the two families, and he found himself wishing them all happiness in the best Italian he could summon up, to their obvious surprise and delight. The young couple looked relaxed and carefree, entering into the marriage lottery with hope in their hearts and never a backward glance. He sighed to himself and walked away.

On the third day he walked to the Vatican – across one of the bridges that spanned the wide and sluggish River Tiber and into St Peter's Square, where tourists beetled about like ants, many of them posing with selfie-sticks, their backs to the great dome of the cathedral. It crossed his mind that they might not actually see the sights of Rome until they returned home and showed their friends and families the snaps on their mobile phones.

The Sistine Chapel he found a little too strident for his taste – it had much in common with the Chagall ceiling in the Paris Opera, though the two were separated by four hundred and fifty years. St Peter's itself was cavernous – towering convoluted pillars at its centre – but it still possessed an air of calm that he found welcome after two days of sightseeing. From some-where distant came the sound of a choir practising. At first he did not recognise the music; the strains were of some unfamiliar liturgy – probably modern. And then he heard the notes of one piece of music that he had always associated with Rome and the Vatican – the soaring treble of Allegri's *Miserere*. How odd that they should be singing it now. He had wondered, in a fanciful moment, if it would happen, but had told himself that the stuff of dreams seldom translated into reality. He knew the legend – that this piece of Allegri's music, written in 1638, was performed only in the Sistine Chapel and that transcription of the closely guarded score was forbidden, even by those who performed it. Then in 1770, the fourteen-year-old Mozart heard it as part of the congregation, went home and wrote down the music with astonishing accuracy – thus releasing it from more than a century of Sistine captivity.

He sat quite still and closed his eyes. The footsteps of tour-ists echoed on the marble floor of the gigantic building, but his mind took flight with the cascade of angelic notes that fell like rain from the lofty heights of the dome of St Peter's. And then the music stopped and the soft chatter of a hundred nations filled the air once more.

Timothy reached into his pocket and withdrew the rosary, running his fingers over the tiny beads. His mother had instilled in him a lifelong wariness of Catholicism. He had been brought up 'low Church of England', but regular worship had fallen away when he had left home for college. He retained a fondness for the language of *The Book of Common Prayer*, and every now and then felt the need to send up a supplication to some unseen deity. But that was as far as it went. It was not that he did not believe; it was simply that he was not sure of what he believed in, aside from the power of goodness, honesty and loyalty. He was, he supposed, not quite agnostic, but as with so many things in his life, those that presented seemingly insuperable challenges were put on the back burner to be attended to later. There were a lot of pots and pans on that particular part of the stove.

It was the best part of an hour before he walked out of St Peter's and made his way back across the river. Having allowed himself to be awed by its ecclesiastical grandeur he felt in need of refreshment. Fortified by a cappuccino and a pastry on a pavement café, he wove through side streets and thoroughfares, past baroque churches and glittering modern shopfronts with his guidebook in his hand and his canvas bag containing pad and paints, heading for the Trevi Fountain. Soon the strains of Allegri were erased from his mind, to be replaced by the voice of Frank Sinatra singing 'Three Coins in the Fountain.'

The sight of it was simply breathtaking: a gigantic confection of sea god and horses – Oceanus and his hippocamps said his Baedeker – the horses leaping from the foam between rugged rocks over which spewed glittering cascades of water. Rainbows arched through the spray in the afternoon sunlight. Backed by the towering façade of the Palazzo Poli and its Corinthian pilasters, it was the ultimate in Baroque grandeur. He could see why it had become a magnet for lovers; not lovers of minimalist architecture, that was for certain, but any lover with a truly old-fashioned romantic streak. Lovers, he supposed, like himself.

He reached into his pocket. It had to be done. He found three one-euro coins and, sitting on the raised rim of the fountain, he tossed them over his shoulder one by one into the frothing waters of the Trevi. Who were they for? Perhaps the three women in his life: Rosie and Alice and Francine. Which one would the fountain bless? Well, who knew the answer to that one?

And then the phone in his pocket vibrated. He pulled it out and looked at the screen. A text. From Archie Bedlington. It was brief. 'Thought you'd like to know. Serena and I are engaged. Archie x'

34

ROME

JUNE

'I tossed three coins into the Trevi Fountain, as is the custom. Two of them fluttered to the depths, but one of them seemed to hover for a moment on its way down. I could not but wonder at the significance.'

Nancy Hart, *In My Dreams*, 1963

The following day several things occurred to him: First, he needed to decide when he was to leave for Venice (the Hotel Libellula had been pleasantly flexible regarding the duration of his occupancy; half term was over and they were not so full as they had been the previous week). He also needed to arrange accommodation. Second, he ought to ring Rosie and put her mind properly at rest, and third, he wanted more than anything to talk to Francine. It also occurred to him that he had done very little shopping. Joseph Addison, whom he felt he had rather unjustly neglected on the trip, bearing in mind that it was he who had given him the idea of a Grand Tour in the first place, had recommended marble pillars and busts. Timothy Gandy, on the other hand, had settled, so far, for a marbled paper folder from a Florentine art shop; pillars and busts of any material being neither a realistic nor a desired option.

His new guidebook recommended the Via Condotti as a suitable place to find quality goods, a fact borne out by his perusal of the varied boutiques on this street just across from the Spanish Steps which proved to be a treasure trove of Italian merchandise, if not from A to Z then certainly from Prada to Versace.

He gazed in the windows at the shimmering gowns and sparkling jewellery, at the leather handbags and jackets, at footwear seemingly crafted by shoemakers with endless imagination and bought by customers with bottomless pockets. He chastised himself for being mean-spirited and came away with a large brown leather shoulder bag for Rosie, the better to carry around all the paraphernalia needed for little Elsie, and a smart black wallet for Alice, having noticed that the one she produced after trying to pay her way in the Florentine restaurant was, untypically for her, falling to bits. He hoped they would both appreciate what was intended as a helpful gesture rather than regarding it as a criticism of the status quo.

And for Oliver? Could he really return home without a present for his son? Yes; he most certainly could, but he bought a small glittery clutch bag for Vita which, he hoped, might be a satisfactory peace offering – not that he felt there was any real need for it on his part. With any luck things would settle down on his return and he could carry on as normal.

And what did that mean? What was normal, now that he had met Francine? If his apparently profligate attitude to money had raised Oliver and Vita's hackles, how would they react when they discovered her existence?

Then he checked himself. His mind was racing; racing away

with assumptions about the future when he hardly knew what it held himself. He certainly had no idea what Francine imagined would be the likely outcome of their liaison. It was all so uncertain, so nebulous. It was time to bite the bullet. He would be home within a couple of weeks and there were things he must sort out before then. How could he return with so many things unresolved?

Late that evening, in the seclusion of his room, he wrote down on a sheet of paper, as he so often did at home, the things that needed to be attended to. The list read as follows:

- Call Archie to congratulate (or text?)
- Book Venice hotel – last hurrah – a good one. Cipriani too expensive? Gritti Palace?
- Book train ticket home
- Laundry
- Francine. Call? See?

It was the final entry on the list that gave him most heartache and which he found himself agonising over.

He sat down on the bed and dialled Francine's number, his heart palpitating as the ringing tone sounded at the other end of the line. There was no answer. He pressed the disconnect button and thought for a moment. It was probably too late; she would be in bed. Or out. There was no reason to worry.

He tried to put it out of his mind. He got up and walked to the window, opening it wider and listening to the sounds of the traffic below, then he walked back to the bed, picked up the phone and texted Archie: 'So pleased for you. Give my love to Serena and tell her she's a lucky girl. But then you're lucky, too! Have you told Rosamund?' Then, aware that he might be sounding like an interfering father (something with which Archie was all too familiar) he erased the last sentence and retyped: 'Rosamund will be thrilled. As am I. All best, Tim x'

He erased the 'x' and then reinserted it. It displayed fondness, after all – a kind of father/son fondness. Rosie used lots of them. One would not be misconstrued. He smiled and shook his head at the fact that he was over-thinking it all. He pressed the send button and laid the phone down once more.

The other items on his list he would attend to in the morning, but having rung Francine and received no reply he worried that he had not only left it too late in the day to call, but that she might have been hoping for a call days ago. What if she had given up on him? He had wrestled with his thoughts constantly as to whether he should ring her. He even thought of calling her every day to tell her what he had been doing, what he had seen, whom he had met. But she had sent him off with the valediction to enjoy himself on his grand tour and to tell her everything that had happened on his return. But when would that be? Did either of them know?

Rational thoughts began to be replaced by irrational fears: that something had happened to her; that she would not need him now she had his money; that she had been reunited with her ex-husband . . . all these possible explanations for her absence from home swam in his head as he prepared for bed. It was two hours before he finally fell asleep; his slumbers disturbed by random notions that bore little consolation and no interpretation.

He woke early – the watch on his bedside table showed that it was 7.15am. Too early to ring her? No. She would be in at least, even if he woke her. Rather that than leaving it until a respectable hour when she might well be out and about and uncontactable. He had only her home number – not her mobile, nor the number of the gallery. He wanted to see her more than anything. Wanted to be with her. Wanted to sense her nearness and to feel her touch. He dialled the number. There was no reply. Perhaps she was in the shower. He waited until 8am and then dialled again. Still no answer.

He would change his plans. Venice would have to wait. He would travel from Rome to Paris. It was weeks since he had seen her. He needed reassurance that he still mattered to her. He knew that she mattered to him. An inner voice told him he was being irrational and that he should continue his tour and see her on his way home. But rational thoughts gave him little comfort. He had probably waited too long as it was.

He breakfasted hurriedly and warned the hotel concierge that he would be leaving later that day. He would confirm his arrangements within the next couple of hours. The prosaic thought that there would be no time to sort out his laundry he dismissed from his mind. He took a taxi to the station and checked train times. The concourse was bustling with commuters, but he managed to discover from a somewhat impatient clerk at the ticket office that there were three trains leaving for Paris that day: the 9am train would arrive in Paris at 7.49pm, the 1pm train would arrive at 11.19pm and the overnight sleeper left at 7.20pm to arrive in Paris at 9.30 the following morning. He knew he was too late for the first train – he had not even packed before he left the hotel – and that the second would arrive in Paris at too late an hour. He decided on the sleeper. He would leave Rome that evening and call on Francine early the following day.

Back at the hotel he packed his bags and left them with the concierge while he spent his last day seeing the sights of Rome. His mind was too distracted to allow him to sketch or paint;

instead he contented himself with visiting the Appian Way and the Baths of Caracalla.

He lunched in a streetside café warmed by the Roman sun and on his way back to the hotel late in the afternoon he passed the church of St Ignazio di Loyola. He had not intended to go in, but he did not need to be at the station for a couple of hours yet, and something drew him towards the majestic doorway. Perhaps it was a need for calm, or reassurance; perhaps the sound of the choir singing. It occurred to him that he had visited more churches in the last two weeks than he had in the previous two years. He slipped into a pew and looked up at the depiction of heaven and the saints above; a scene so beautiful and so overwhelming that he found himself shaking his head in wonder. He suspected that it was his love of drawing and painting that made him so sensitive to the frescos in Italian churches, though their grandeur and elaborate appearance was not necessarily to his taste. Yet here, in Rome, they seemed the perfect complement to the rococo architecture, and to perfectly sum up his current feelings about life: that it was richly varied, transient in nature and overwhelming in its complexity.

He would miss Rome. He would miss Italy. But at the end of his next train journey he would at least have a clearer view of his immediate future. The prospect was almost as uplifting as the angelic scene above his head. But it also scared him half to death.

35

ROME TO PARIS

JUNE

'Love is like the measles – all the worse when it comes
late in life.'

Douglas Jerrold, *The Wit and Opinions of Douglas
Jerrold*, 1859

Sleep seemed impossible. The train rattled and jolted and the
other three souls in his compartment of four couchettes were
French football fans returning from a European Cup match they
had lost. They were not in the mood for sleep and, as a result,
the journey was one of the worst he had ever endured. He had
tried to book a single sleeping compartment, but the booking
clerk explained that they were full and at this late juncture he
was lucky to find even a single berth in a couchette.

At least the football fans paid little attention to him and
eventually, having drunk their fill of Peroni – as witnessed by
the collection of empty bottles at their feet, they collapsed on
their bunks and snored loudly. At first he felt angry, but then
began to see the funny side of the situation – and its absurdity.

Here he was, a widower in his fifties, confined to a sleeping compartment in an Italian train with three French football fans on his way to see if a woman he had met in Paris less than a month ago was as desperate to see him as he was to see her. It was not so much funny as ridiculous. It occurred to him that his barrister son would have little difficulty in persuading a judge and jury that his father had completely lost his reason.

As daylight began to sneak its way between the blinds on the windows, he eased his aching body from the bunk and went in search of refreshment. He found a seat where he could perch and drink a cup of strong coffee; the stale baguette he purchased remained only half eaten, but it at least helped to assuage the hollow feeling he felt in his stomach.

They were only half an hour from Paris. He would make one final attempt at contacting her. He dialled the number, half expecting it to ring and ring. But after only a few moments his call was answered. It was Francine. His heart leaped. It really was her. 'It's Tom,' he said, trying to control the excitement in his voice. 'How are you?' he asked, the sense of elation clearly audible.

There was a pause before the answer came. 'I am fine, Tom. 'Ow are you?' Another pause, then, 'Ow 'as your trip been? Where are you?'

'If I told you I was on a train from Rome to Paris and could be with you in an hour what would you say?'

There was silence at the other end of the phone. For one dreadful moment he thought she was going to tell him not to come. That it had all been a terrible mistake. But she did not. Having got over the surprise she said, 'Will you come to the *appartement*?'

'If that's where you are, yes. I'll get a taxi from the station.'

'Zen I shall see you in an hour, yes?'

'Yes. I'm looking forward to it. I've lots to tell you.'

'Wonderful,' she said. 'I will see you zen. Bye.'

It was all so brief; after so many weeks the conversation seemed somehow peremptory. Perhaps it was the rattling of the train, the noise of the rails that had precluded a more intimate conversation. Perhaps it was just that he was tired and that the football fans were now pushing past him having woken and decided they needed to eat. Under such circumstances any kind of phone conversation was fraught with difficulty.

He slipped the phone into his pocket, but before he had let go of it, it rang again. She was obviously feeling the same as him; that they needed to share a few more words of affection. But it was not Francine this time. It was another number that was unfamiliar to him.

'Hello?'

'Dad?'

'Yes?'

'It's Rosie.'

'Hi! Where are you? I didn't recognise the number.'

'I'm at the hospital. With Elsie.'

The elation he had felt at hearing Francine's voice was replaced with a sinking feeling in the pit of his stomach. 'What's wrong?' he asked.

'They don't know. She wasn't well during the night and I brought her in here. There's a chance it could be meningitis.'

'Oh God!' he heard himself say, and then he could have bitten off his tongue. 'I mean, are they sure?'

'Not yet. They've done a lumbar puncture and they won't know for some time whether it's bacterial or viral.'

'Well, at least you're in the right place,' he offered, attempting to console his daughter. He could detect in her voice the tremor of fear. Rosie, the capable one, was at the mercy of the fates, and his only grandchild was lying in a hospital cot awaiting . . . what?

'Yes,' she said. Then she started to speak again, but as she did so, her voice cracked and he could hear that she was crying.

'Is Ace with you?' he asked.

'No.'

'Why not?'

'He's up in Scotland doing a survey.'

'Can't he come back?'

'He's trying to. He's on Taransay taking part in a wildlife survey and they can't get a boat to him because the sea's too rough. I'd call Oliver but . . . oh Dad . . .'

Hearing the note in his daughter's voice tore at his heart. She was his little girl; always had been, always would be. There was nothing more important in the world. Nothing. He did not hesitate. 'I can be with you in . . .' he glanced at his watch, ' . . . in as long as it takes me to get to you from Paris. Some time after lunch.'

Rosie choked back the tears. 'But I thought you were in Rome?'

'I was, but I'm about to arrive in Paris. I'll catch the Eurostar and if there's no room on that I'll fly home. I'll be with you as soon as I can.'

'Oh Dad, thank you. You are kind. I don't want you to end your trip but . . .'

'Don't even think about it. This is far more important. You get back to Elsie and I'll be with you as soon as I can. I'll keep you posted as to where I am. All right?'

'Yes.' There was a note of calm seeping into her voice now. She had been trying to hold it together on her own in the absence of Ace but there was a limit even to Rosie's fortitude. 'I don't know what I'd do without you, Dad.'

'Just hang on sweetheart. I'm on my way.'

'Bye Dad. And thank you.' The conversation was replaced by the dialling tone.

He looked out of the window, only half seeing the countryside fly by. Then he dialled Francine's number to explain what had happened. There was no reply.

36

PARIS TO CHICHESTER

JUNE

'He has not seen speed, who has not seen a father run to
the aid of his daughter.'

Richard Arncliffe, *Pater Familias*, 1949

All other thoughts were banished from his mind on the journey
from France to England. His jaw ached from being clenched
with anxiety; his fingers tapped impatiently on the train
windowsill; the Channel Tunnel seemed endless. His appetite
vanished. Then there was London to be crossed and the hour-
and-a-half journey from Victoria Station to Chichester. Twice
he tried calling Francine, and on neither occasion was there any
reply. She would ring him; of that he was sure. After all, she
had his number. But during the course of his journey, no call
came; the watched phone became the watched pot and sat
silently on the drop-down table of the railway carriage, steadfastly refusing to boil.

Now there were greater worries. His perspective had changed
in that brief time between talking to Francine and then to Rosie.

There was no question, at this moment, where his priorities lay. And this was not an onerous responsibility; not a burden to be regretted and swept aside, even though its load might be heavy. This was not a problem that had to be considered and evaluated; it was an instinctive reaction, a desire to be a father to his daughter and a grandfather to her child. Ace's parents had died when he was young; Timothy was Elsie's only grandparent – something which had not really registered with him until now.

The train rumbled across the level crossing and into Chichester railway station just after half past three in the afternoon. He piled his luggage into the taxi and said, briefly, to the driver, 'St Richard's Hospital please.'

He found Rosie sitting beside a cot in which Elsie was sleeping soundly. At the approach of footsteps his daughter turned round. Her eyes were red and he could see that the tears had been recently flowing. She had a hunted look; the kind of look engendered by denial, overlaid with the harsh iron grip of reality. She slid her arms around her father's waist, laid her head on his chest and sobbed.

Timothy said nothing for a few moments; he simply stroked the back of her head and swayed her gently from side to side, as if rocking her to sleep. Gradually, the tears subsided and Rosie eased away from him and looked up into his eyes. 'Thank you for coming.'

Timothy shook his head. 'Don't be silly. This is where I need to be.'

'Yes,' she said softly.

'What's the news?' he asked.

'We won't know for a couple of days whether it's bacterial or viral meningitis.'

'There's a difference?'

'Yes.'

He looked at her enquiringly.

'Bacterial is the serious one. It can lead to permanent brain damage. She's on antibiotics just in case . . .' her words tailed off.

'And viral?' he asked.

'Not quite so serious. If it's viral she should get over it. All we can do is wait and see what happens.'

Timothy peered into the cot. 'She seems to be sleeping peacefully.'

'Yes. It's just a matter of wait-and-see now.' There was a note of futility in her voice. Of helplessness.

'But you've done all you can. You got her here quickly.'

'That's what the doctor said. He said I was right to bring her in and not wait.'

Timothy motioned his daughter to sit down. He pulled up another chair and sat beside her. 'Well then, we'll all have to do our bit. Why don't you go and get a cup of tea and a sandwich?'

Rosie shook her head. 'Not hungry. They bring me cups of tea every now and then . . .'

'But we need to look after you as well. If you keel over, what's Elsie going to do?'

'I know, Dad. But I'm fine really. I can cope. Better now you're here.' She brightened a little. 'But why were you in Paris and not in Rome? I'm not complaining, it was lucky that you managed to get here so quickly.'

'It's a long story.' He made to change the subject. 'What news of Ace?'

'He's on his way. They managed to get a boat to him. He should be back by tonight. I feel guilty at calling you all home really.'

'Hey! That's what we're here for. That's what families do. Good families.'

'Yes.' She looked thoughtful and Timothy was pleased to see that her anxiety seemed to have been relieved ever so slightly.

He looked at Elsie sleeping; her tiny body rising and falling with every breath. 'So she has to stay here for a while?'

'Until we know, yes. Then, if it's viral we can take her home. At least they got the antibiotics into her quickly. They don't do anything for viral meningitis but if it is bacterial they will be making a difference. I hope.'

Her eyes began to fill with tears once more. She pulled a wad of tissues from the sleeve of her baggy cardigan and blew hard into them. 'Whatever happened to me, Dad? I'm supposed to be the capable one.'

'The one who holds the family together,' he said.

'Until push comes to shove, eh?' She smiled through the tears and blew her nose again.

'You're a mother. Even mothers are allowed to let go now and again. It shows they care.'

'And sisters, too,' said Rosie, sniffing back the tears and brightening. 'That was a turn-up for the books wasn't it? Alice I mean.'

'I'll say.'

'Lucky she found you.'

'In more ways than one. I seem to have got my other daughter back. She spoke to you about it then?'

'Yes. She called in on her way back to Oxford. I was as shocked as you were I expect.'

'Did she tell you . . .'

'About . . . Pippa? Yes.'

'Surprised?'

'No. Not at all. I think I've always known really.'

Timothy sat back in his chair and gazed into the middle distance. 'I suppose I should have done.'

'Why? Daughters don't tell fathers that sort of thing.'

'No; I suppose not.' He looked thoughtful for a moment, then asked, 'Do you think your mother knew?'

'No. Not at all. I think she might have had something to say about it.'

'Yes. I'm sure she would.'

Rosie said, 'I think that's why Alice took off like she did. Well, one of the reasons.'

Timothy rubbed his hands together, as if he were trying to wring from them some kind of truth. Then he said, 'She made me realise how I'd fallen short. As a father.'

'What?'

'How I'd let her down.'

'But you didn't . . . I mean . . . that's not fair . . .'

'No; she wasn't being unfair. She was being honest. She made me realise that passivity is every bit as influential on a child as intervention. I lived in a marriage . . . well, I suppose you've known for a long while . . . that was not . . . that was . . . uneventful, shall we say.'

Rosie said nothing, but listened attentively.

'You know how different your mum and I were. I can't claim to have enjoyed my married life much in later years. That'll come as no surprise. But I didn't feel I could just give up on it, even when you'd all grown up. When you were younger I thought it best to stay; there never seemed a good time to leave. First you were too young, then there were GCSE's, then A-levels, then you needed help through university . . . I didn't want to throw a spanner in the works by giving you even more to worry about. I had to consider your lives as well as my own.'

'And then we left home?'

'Yes. And if I'd gone then your mum would have been all alone. A woman in middle age, dumped by her husband. I've heard enough stories about the sort of anguish that can lead to. I simply couldn't do it to her.'

'So it was guilt that kept you together?'

'Mainly. But deep down I also loved her, you know. In spite of the way things had turned out. I could still see the girl I married, even if there wasn't much of her left. Sentiment I suppose. And . . . I didn't want to be unkind.' He stopped short. Aware that this delving into the past had opened up old wounds.

Rosie interrupted. 'Lots of men would have cut and run. Especially after we'd flown the nest.'

'Oh, it did occur to me.' He smiled. 'I wondered, sometimes, if your mum would even notice that I'd gone. But although I found it difficult to live with her, I think I'd have found it even more difficult to have lived with myself if I'd left.' He turned to face her. 'Pathetic isn't it?'

'No. It shows you're a kind person.'

'Oh; it's probably all to do with selfishness really. The fact that I would have felt bad about it – me, me, me, really, whichever way you look at it. I don't think Alice was altogether mistaken in her analysis of my life.' He sat up and took a deep breath. 'Anyway, it's you and this little mite we have to think about right now.'

Rosie was staring at Elsie lying in her cot. 'Yes. Fingers crossed.'

Timothy stood up, walked to the window and plunged his hands in his pockets. Then he said, 'Oh, goodness,' and turned to face his daughter.

'What?'

Timothy hesitated for a moment, then said, 'No. It's nothing. Nothing at all really.'

'Yes it is. Tell me.'

'You might think I'm being too intense.'

'You Dad? After what you've just been saying.'

'Or fanciful, then.'

Rosie looked at him with a confused expression.

'I met someone a few days ago,' he said.

The look on her face changed to one of foreboding.

'No; it's nothing like that. I was travelling to Rome. I met a nun on the train,' he said the words with half a laugh in his voice. 'She was on her way to the Vatican. She was Irish; Sister Mary Agnes her name was. A real chatterbox, but a lovely person. Her eyes sparkled and she had rather a wicked sense of humour. She made me think a bit. About things. I suppose I only met her for an hour or so. But she was very kind; very wise. How is it that someone who is supposedly detached from the world can have a clearer understanding of it? Perhaps it makes them more objective. When I got into the taxi after I'd said goodbye to her, I reached for my handkerchief and found this.' He pulled his hand out of his pocket. Dangling from his fingers was the rosary. 'Just slip it into *your* pocket will you?'

37

CHICHESTER

JUNE

'A relationship, I think, is like a shark, you know? It has
to constantly move forward or it dies.'

Woody Allen, *Annie Hall*, 1977

The relief that Rosie and Timothy and Ace felt when the tests on
Elsie proved that it was, indeed, viral rather than bacterial meningitis was palpable. Within a few days the child was home and
gradually things returned to normal. Except that true normality
had not yet been established. Timothy occupied the spare bedroom
in what was now Rosie and Ace's house – his and Isobel's former
marital home – and he would have to set about finding himself
a smaller home. That had been the plan all along. Until his Grand
Tour, of course. Now he was in a different situation.

The events of the past few days had put a different complexion
on things; had made him realise the importance of family and
that, even now, he could not just 'cut and run' as Rosie had put
it. He had responsibilities; pleasurable ones, and yet . . . and
yet.

He had rung Francine every day, but his calls remained resolutely unanswered. She knew his number. Why had she not called *him*? Was it that he had let her down by saying that he would be with her within the hour, and then had not turned up? But she must have seen that he had tried to call, surely? Why did she not have an answering machine? He assumed that was because of her divorce – not wanting to come home and find messages from Alain that were either upsetting or threatening. He had managed to put her home telephone into his mobile – the one she had written on the corner of his sketch pad – but in the euphoria of their relationship he had not asked for her mobile number. Why? How stupid was that? But then he thought that the number at her apartment would be enough, he supposed; trying to recall the moment when it was given to him.

On the fourth day after his return home, when things had begun to settle and Elsie had begun to smile again and eat heartily, he broached the subject over breakfast. Until then, conversations had revolved mainly around the child and his own need to visit estate agents and find accommodation. Rosie insisted there was no rush, but he himself knew that it would not be long before he was getting under their feet.

No one had mentioned the extravagant loan he had made and, thanks to the family preoccupation with Elsie's health, Oliver and Vita had stayed away.

He had shown Rosie and Ace his drawings and paintings, and shared with them the magic of his visits to Florence and Rome; regaled them with the story of his supposed heroics among the superyachts in Monaco and talked about Archie and Rosamund and Serena. When he was alone with Rosie he had gone into more depth about the delights of St Peters and Allegri's Miserere, of the cemetery at Montmartre and the doors of the baptistery in Florence and she sat entranced, sipping her coffee and marvelling at the gleam in his eyes as he remembered what he had seen and explained how these different places had affected him. It was a gleam she had not seen for many years.

'But you never got to Venice?'

'No; I never got to Venice.'

'Maybe one day we could do it together?'

'Yes. That would be nice,' he said.

But she saw that his eyes had a faraway look, and realised that his thoughts had turned elsewhere . . .

Over breakfast one morning, after Ace had left for work, he asked, 'Would you mind if I went away for a few days?'

'Of course not. Why do you ask?'

'I think they call it unfinished business.'

Rosie was reaching for a wet-wipe to clear Weetabix from Elsie's chin. She looked at him suspiciously. 'That sounds mysterious.'

'Yes. I suppose it does.'

'Is there anything I should know?' She asked the question levelly, without looking at him. Instead, concentrating on cleansing Elsie of her breakfast residue.

'I'm not sure. Not yet.'

Rosie lifted Elsie from her high chair and placed her on a mat on the floor where the scattering of toys would keep her occupied for a few minutes at least.

Then she came and sat next to him at the table. 'Alice said something. Not much. Just a sort of hint.'

'And?'

His daughter smiled. 'I'm not going to censure you, Dad. I leave that sort of thing to Oliver.'

'I met someone . . .'

'Good.'

Her reply took him by surprise.

'You don't know what I'm going to say.'

'I trust your judgement.'

'I wish I did,' he murmured.

'There you go, Dad; selling yourself short again.' She saw the look on his face; the look of a child chastised. 'Just be careful, that's all. But not so careful that you can't enjoy yourself. Don't feel that you have to be responsible for us to the detriment of your own life. Not now.'

'But you still . . .'

'Oh, we still need you – I think we've proved that over the last few days. But there has to be a happy medium, hasn't there?'

'I hope so.' He struggled for a few moments, trying to formulate the words. 'So you wouldn't mind . . . ?'

'If you found someone else? No. Not at all. I'd be glad for you.' Elsie gurgled from her play mat. 'We'd be glad for you.' Rosie smiled at him and added, 'You are a funny one, Dad. But you're rather lovely all the same.' She leaned forward and kissed him on the cheek.

'Yes. I suppose I am a funny one.' He thought for a moment or two and then said 'The money I lent—'

His daughter interrupted him. 'Dad, it's really none of our business what you do with your money.'

'That's not what Oliver thinks.'

'As I told you before you left, I don't care what Oliver thinks. It's really none of his business. You've seen us all through our lives so far, financially as well as everything else. When are you going to realise that you deserve a bit of self-indulgence? If you want to spend all your money on paintings or antiques or on the horses, why shouldn't you? Though I do think the horses would be a bit of a mistake.' She winked at him.

'The last person who winked at me was a nun,' he said.

'There you are then; confirmation from on high. Talking of which . . .' she reached into the pocket of her cardigan. 'I think you should take this with you.'

She dangled the rosary in front of him and let it fall into his outstretched hand. '*You* might be needing it now.'

38

PARIS

JUNE

'Most people die without ever having lived. Luckily for
them, they don't realise it.'

Henrik Ibsen (1828–1906)

He had no way of telling Francine that he was travelling to
Paris. Her phone remained steadfastly unanswered. His plans,
such as they were, were sketchy. He took with him an overnight
bag with the intention of going to the Galerie Bleu or the flat;
explaining to her what had happened; telling her why he had
not arrived when he said he would. Hoping that she would
understand and forgive him for standing her up.

He could not remember feeling so nervous since Alice had
appeared in Florence. As the taxi wended its way from the Gare
du Nord to the street where Francine lived and worked he felt
almost sick with anticipation. The sky was gunmetal grey. Why
could it not have been azure blue and lifted his mood. It was
not a good omen.

As the cab pulled up outside the gallery he noticed immediately that the blinds were pulled down. He paid the driver and the taxi pulled away, leaving him alone on the pavement with his bag. He felt the same as he had felt on his first day at school: alone and apprehensive.

He approached the door and saw the sign which hung in front of the blind:

Fermé jusqu'à nouvel ordre.

Fermé; closed. How he wished his French was better. What did the rest mean? He rang the bell at the side of the door; the bell that connected to the apartment above. He rang it several times. There was no reply. No one came to the door. What to do? There was only one thing *to* do. He picked up his bag and began to walk towards the Hôtel La Cocotte.

He hesitated on the pavement outside. The front door was closed, just as it was when he had arrived several weeks ago now, when the sky was blue and Paris was about to reveal her charms to him. He pressed the bell. The door buzzed and the lock snapped open. He made his way through it and down the narrow corridor into the small, light-filled lobby. There was no one at the desk. He waited a moment, nervously fingering the edge of the counter. Then, from within the room behind the desk he heard the squawk of a parrot. The door opened and Madame Lamont appeared. She took two steps forward, saw his face and stopped abruptly. 'Mr Grundy!'

'Gandy,' he corrected.

'Yes. Of course.' She looked uncomfortable; embarrassed.

'I'm sorry to bother you,' he offered. 'I was looking for Francine. I've tried her *appartement* but she's not there. I wondered if you knew where she was, only . . .'

'You haven't heard?' she asked.

He felt a sickening sensation in the pit of his stomach. For a moment he found himself unable to speak. Then he said, 'I haven't heard anything. I spoke to her briefly last week. I was on my way to see her but . . . something happened and I had to rush home. An emergency. I tried to contact her but there was no reply.'

'No,' said Madame Lamont coldly. She looked him up and down, then said, 'You'd better come in.'

In a kind of trance he followed the old woman into her room, the parrot singing one line of 'The Bridges of Paris' by way of a greeting before being told '*tais toi*' by Madame Lamont. 'You'd better sit down,' she said, motioning Timothy towards the overstuffed armchair to one side of the fireplace.

Timothy lowered himself into it and asked, 'Has anything happened to her? Is she all right?'

'Oh, yes. She's all right . . . I should imagine,' said Madame Lamont with an edge to her voice. 'I think before I say anything I should ask you for your version of events Mr Gandy.'

'What do you mean?'

'Oh, goodness! We're both grown up. But we're not so grown up that we can't make mistakes from time to time; mistakes in our judgement of people.'

'But I don't—'

'You've been led on, Mr Gandy, unless I'm very much mistaken. I know you were . . . probably *are* . . . in love with Francine. She has a way with her; she is very attractive to men.' She looked at him sympathetically. 'You wouldn't be the first, I'm afraid.'

He suddenly felt defensive. 'I didn't expect I was. Francine is a very attractive . . . beautiful . . . woman. I'm *sure* I'm not the first. And I knew she had been married, if that's what you mean.'

'*Had* been?'

'Yes.'

'She still *is* married, Mr Gandy. Very much so.'

Timothy sat silently for a few moments before saying, softly, 'Oh . . . I see.'

'Did she ask you for money?'

Timothy's hand came up to his mouth almost involuntarily. He did not speak; merely nodded.

'A lot of money?'

'Quite a lot, yes.'

'Oh dear. And you gave it to her?'

'Yes.'

'She would have given you some reason why it was necessary, I suppose?'

'Yes.' He hesitated, aware that what he would say was not complimentary towards his interlocutor. 'She said she owed you rent and that if she did not pay up you would turn her out of her apartment and the gallery.'

'Did she? And how much did you give her?'

'Twenty thousand euros.'

Now it was Madame Lamont's turn to be silent for a moment. Then she said evenly, 'Yes; it *was* a lot of money.'

'But she settled the rent presumably, which is why the gallery is still there?'

'Mr Gandy, the gallery has been closed since you left Paris. Francine has moved out of her *appartement* and I have not seen her for several days.'

'But I called her. I spoke to her on the phone less than a week ago.'

'You probably caught her on the day she came to take her things. Did she sound at all strange?'

'Well, she didn't say much. She did sound surprised, but I put that down to the fact that she wasn't expecting me to call.

And I was on a train which made conversation difficult at my end so I didn't think too much of it. Just that I'd caught her unawares.'

'Oh, you would have caught her unawares all right.'

'But I don't understand . . .'

'Do you remember what I said when you took Francine out to supper?'

Timothy looked at her vacantly; he was incapable of remembering anything much at that particular moment; his head was spinning with a myriad of thoughts.

'I said "be careful", and with very good reason.'

'But did she settle the rent?'

'There was no rent to settle. At least, not of that magnitude. She might have been a month in arrears but that was all. No; the money would be needed to fund her husband's gambling debts.'

Timothy slumped back in his chair.

'I'm sorry to be the one to tell you.'

'But I thought—'

'Yes, I know. She is very beautiful and very persuasive.'

'But if you knew . . . I mean, you told me to be careful . . . why didn't you tell me the full story?'

'And would you have listened? What would you have thought of me, that evening when you were taking her out to supper, your eyes all a-glow? You were as devoted as a spaniel. If I had said "Whatever you do don't give her any money" you'd have thought I was a jealous, vindictive interfering old woman.'

'But she told me she was divorced, and that Alain was your late husband's godson.'

'She was divorced from him geographically, that's true enough – he lives on the other side of Paris – and, yes, he was my husband's godson, but I'm afraid they are still married. He is a very manipulative man and for some strange reason that I can't fathom Francine is unbelievably loyal. Some women, Mr Gandy, are just bad pickers. I do have sympathy with Francine. Maybe that's another reason why I never interfered. She deserves some happiness after what she's been through with that ne'er-do-well godson of Patrice's. I'm surprised she hasn't done a bunk before. She's not an evil woman; not naturally wicked, just swayed by him. He threatens her – emotional blackmail it's called. I've done my best to intervene but I learned some time ago that it would get me nowhere.'

'So where has she gone?'

Madame Lamont shrugged. 'Who knows. The gallery has been emptied of pictures and the *appartement* emptied of furniture. She has *pffft!*; vanished. I just hope she has managed to give Alain the slip as well. It's about time.'

Timothy leaned forward and held his head in his hands. 'I feel so . . . stupid.'

Madame Lamont rose and opened a carved oak corner cupboard in her sitting room, taking out a bottle of cognac and two dumpy glasses. She poured a generous measure into each and handed one to Timothy. 'Here. Drink this. It'll bring you back to earth. I'll make some coffee in a minute but I think you need a bit of a stiffener.'

He looked up at her. 'You're the only other person I know who uses that word.'

'The other one being?'

'Me.' He took a gulp of the fiery liquid and felt it burning its way down through his chest. Then he said, almost to himself, 'I really thought she felt the same.'

Madame Lamont lowered herself carefully into her chair and said, 'If it's any consolation I think she probably did. I've not seen that look in her eyes for a long time; the real look of . . . love, I suppose. That was another reason I didn't say anything; I thought that this time things might be different.'

'But . . . I mean . . . have you seen this happen a lot? Don't you think you should have done something about it?'

'Like what? Call the gendarmes? You are a grown man – they were all grown men . . . Francine did nothing that was against the law; she just used her feminine wiles, that's all. No one was *forced* to do anything.'

She saw the look of alarm on Timothy's face and made to clarify. 'We're only talking about two or three – not entire battalions – and they were all willing captives. For a while at least. They enjoyed themselves . . .'

'I see. It just goes to show . . .'

'What?'

Timothy sighed. 'That there's no fool like an old fool.'

'Cheer up,' said Madame Lamont, taking a sip of her cognac. 'You'll get over it.'

'I'm not sure that I'll ever get over it.'

'Oh; you will. Time . . .'

'Just don't tell me that time is a great healer, OK?'

'Very well.' The old woman took another sip and asked, 'So what will you do now?'

'I've absolutely no idea. I have no plans at all. I came here with the intention of seeing Francine and hoping to persuade her to come to Venice with me but . . .'

'I see. Not a very likely scenario now.'

'No.'

'Can I make a suggestion?'

Timothy looked at her enquiringly.

'Why don't you stay here the night? Think about things.'

'I'm not sure that's a good idea.'

'It would let you . . . "get your head round it" is the modern expression I believe. Oh, and I wouldn't charge you, Mr Gandy. You could be my guest.'

'That's very kind but . . .'

'No buts. Your old room is empty; the bed is made up. Go out and get yourself some supper; have a few glasses of wine, numb the pain. You know where your key is. I'll see you in the morning. Perhaps then you'll have a clearer idea of what you want to do.'

39

PARIS TO ST JEAN CAP FERRAT

JUNE

'Reports that say something hasn't happened are always interesting to me, because, as we know, there are known knowns; there are things we know we know. We also know there are known unknowns; that is to say we know there are some things we do not know. But there are also unknown unknowns – the ones we don't know we don't know.'

Donald Rumsfeld, U.S. Department of Defense news briefing, 2002

It was a spur of the moment decision, but one that he took for the simple reason of needing somewhere to think, away from the hurly burly of family life: neutral territory where he could come to terms with what he must now regard as an embarrassing error of judgement. He was bruised, but more than that he was saddened that the one person in his life who had touched him so deeply was, it transpired, not all she appeared to be.

After a sleepless night he thanked Madame Lamont sheepishly, but she brushed aside his discomfiture with unexpected good grace and wished him *bon voyage*. He would travel to the South of France in the hope that Rosamund Hawksmoor might recommend somewhere close by that could offer accommodation for a few days. All he really wanted to do was sit in the sun and gaze at the sea, the better to 'get his head round' everything that had happened. It would take some doing, but he had felt comfortable on that stretch of coastline, if in no way up to its financial demands. But then, having lost the amount of money he had lost, what did a few more euros matter?

Rosamund's number was at the top of the letter he had kept in his wallet; the one she had written to him on his departure. He dialled it, and after explaining to the tipsy Jonathan who he was, he was connected with the mistress of the house herself who could not have been more welcoming.

'My dear man, don't even think about it!' she had said. 'You most certainly will *not* stay anywhere nearby, you will come here and stay as long as you want. How delightful! Company! You have no idea how pleased I'll be to see you.'

He had not said why he was visiting, only that his plans had changed and that before he returned home, finally, he would like to visit her again.

The taxi dropped him off at the top of her drive. He wanted to walk down towards the house alone, rather than being deposited at the front door; to hear the sounds of the Mediterranean countryside once more, to lose himself in that magical mixture of terrain and vegetation, of shimmering sea and azure sky, the better to salve his mind and his conscience. The sun had come out to welcome him, and as he approached the elaborate metal gates they opened as if by magic.

As he walked towards the house he heard the welcoming

tones of her voice: 'Hello, hello HELLO! How lovely to see you again.'

For a moment he could not see where she was, and then below the pastel façade of the house he glimpsed the vividly coloured flowing wrap that enveloped her as it emerged between the olive and citrus trees that surrounded the terrace. She stood there with her arms outstretched in welcome, and he moved forward, dropped his bag and gave her a grateful hug. Her perfume reminded him of that earlier, happier time – unlocking recent memories, but memories which now were tinged with wistfulness.

'Jonathan, take Timothy's bag will you – up to the Mimosa room – and we'll have two Martinis on the terrace when you come down.'

The tone of her voice, the warmth of her welcome and of the sun, the fragrance of her scent and the familiarity of his surroundings brought tears of happiness to his eyes. He brushed them away, hoping that she would not notice, and sat down opposite her on the terrace overlooking the sea, feeling a strange sense of coming home. The fact that he had spent just one day here only a few weeks ago made no difference at all.

'Tell me all about it! About Florence and wherever else you went but . . . oh, it's *so* lovely to see you!'

She seemed genuinely delighted that he had come, as if bursting with news that she needed to share. Her eyes sparkled – all the more when she had made inroads into the Martini that Jonathan had deposited in front of her. Timothy sipped his own, slipped off his jacket, and began to feel the merest hint of returning to the real world; a world which might not be quite so barren and bleak as it had appeared the day before. He put it down to the Martini, but was nevertheless grateful for its restorative properties.

He regaled Rosamund with stories of his travels, of the sights of Rome, of the two old ladies in Florence and the tragic outcome, and of the unexpected reunion with his long-estranged daughter. At this point even more of a twinkle came into Rosamund's eye.

'Talking of reunions,' she said, with the excitement of a child clearly audible in her voice, 'I've got a little surprise for you.' She turned her head towards the open French windows. 'All right, you two. You can come out now.'

At which point, through the open window stepped Archie and Serena, hand in hand.

'It wasn't arranged,' said Rosamund as if by way of apology. 'It just happened. Archie and Serena arrived yesterday, and then when you said you were coming; well, some things just slip nicely into place don't they? It's almost as if fate takes a hand.' The three of them greeted each other as though they had been estranged for years, and the evening was spent laughing over their combined reminiscences of the delights of Monaco as the sun went down and the cicadas began their evening song.

Timothy lay in bed that night with his French windows wide open and the mosquito blinds in place, the better to enjoy the Mediterranean night without paying for such pleasure in the morning. Though he took a while to drift off, he slept better than the night before, and as dawn broke he slipped out of bed, raised the blinds and walked out on to the small balcony which overlooked the sea. The air was clear and the warming rays of the sun were already releasing the fruity tang of the cypresses and the mixture of aromatic shrubs that studded the rocky slope that ran down to the sea. He breathed deeply, then heard a voice that came from somewhere below. 'You're up early. I hope you slept well.'

He looked down and across to the right and saw that Rosamund was already sitting on the terrace sipping her morning coffee. 'I did. Like a top. And you?'

'Oh, I sleep poorly nowadays. I seem to wake earlier and earlier. Come down. Have some coffee. Don't worry about changing. You'll find a robe in your bathroom.'

Timothy did as instructed and found himself sitting opposite Rosamund at the glass-topped dining table on the terrace, watching the colours of the coastline change as the sun rose higher in the sky.

After the customary pleasantries, and a wry remark about the unlikelihood of Archie and Serena appearing much before noon, she asked him gently, 'So things did not work out quite the way you wanted then?'

Timothy sipped his coffee before replying. 'How do you know?'

'Well, I should really write detective fiction rather than romances,' smiled Rosamund. 'You're wearing a different jacket – not that in itself it means anything; you could have brought several – but you only have hand baggage. I can't believe you packed such a small amount of clothing for a Grand Tour. I deduce that you went home afterwards, then came out again intending a shorter trip. Am I right?'

'Spot on,' confessed Timothy sheepishly.

'Want to talk about it?'

'Only to someone who's not going to judge.'

'Tea and sympathy?'

'I guess.'

'Coffee and sympathy I can offer,' she said, with a kindly smile.

Timothy told her in detail of his encounter with Francine at the start of his Grand Tour, of his feelings for her, of the unexpectedness of it all, of his loaning her the money and of subsequent developments and discoveries. Rosamund listened attentively and said nothing, confining her intervention to the occasional nod and shake of the head.

Reaching the end of his story Timothy said simply, 'So there you have it: The story of Mr Gandy and his folly; living proof that a fool and his money are soon parted.'

'You shouldn't be so hard on yourself,' offered Rosamund. 'Love is like that; it seldom asks the right questions. Come to think of it, it seldom asks any questions at all.'

'Which I know to my cost.'

'They do say, you know, that there are two kinds of people: those who love and those who are loved. I'd say you fell into the former camp, but life has taught me that the two need not be mutually exclusive. For the lucky ones.'

Jonathan appeared with a large tray laden with orange juice, croissants, jams and another cafetière of the rich, dark coffee that now seemed to be coursing through Timothy's veins and bringing his weary body and mind back to life. With a degree of stability seldom matched later in the day, the white-jacketed Jonathan put down the tray, distributed its contents with surprising celerity and disappeared into the house once more.

'Have a croissant. The apricot jam is delicious. Home-made. In someone's home at any rate,' said Rosamund. 'Anyway, stay as long as you want. Archie and Serena are leaving this evening, so I thought we'd have a lunch to celebrate their engagement. Does Archie know? About Francine I mean?'

'No; not at all.'

'There's no reason why he should. Let's keep it to ourselves, shall we?' She loaded a generous amount of apricot jam onto a broken-off corner of croissant and popped it into her mouth, clearly relishing the sensation. Then she took a sip of coffee to wash it down and said, 'It's a shame about the money, but I really wouldn't beat yourself up about it. You did it with the best possible intentions, even if you were blinded by love – or infatuation. Put it out of your mind, even if you can't put *her* out of your mind. Poor woman.'

'Why poor woman?'

'From what you say I think she probably *was* in love with you. But she suffers from what you suffer from.'

'What's that?'

'Misplaced loyalty. As your long-lost daughter perceptively informed you, it seldom leads to a happy outcome. You were loyal to your wife; Francine is loyal to her husband. Neither situation is a happy one. Or am I oversimplifying things?'

Timothy did not reply. Instead he followed Rosamund's lead and broke off a piece of croissant and loaded it with an extravagant amount of apricot jam before leaning back in his chair and sighing deeply. 'Perhaps I should give up on all that sort of thing. Just concentrate on my family.'

'Oh, I think you're just a bit raw at the moment. It will pass.' She drained her coffee cup and asked, 'Didn't you say you had a son? I don't suppose you've discussed it with him have you?'

Timothy choked on his jam-laden croissant. It was some moments before he could speak, his face red and his eyes watering. 'No; I haven't,' he croaked, after an interval of at least thirty seconds. 'Oliver and I have rather different views on life from one another.'

'Oh. I see.'

'No, you don't,' said Timothy. 'If I were rash enough to share my exploits with my son, then I would probably find myself being placed in care.'

'Oh dear!' said Rosamund. She smiled, then she chuckled, and finally collapsed in fits of laughter as the tears ran down her cheeks. 'Poor Timothy; you can choose your friends but not your relations, eh?'

'Just so.' He took several sips of coffee. 'Mind you, there are moments when I think he does have a point. And when it comes to choosing friends my judgement seems to have been a bit suspect of late.'

Rosamund stopped laughing and frowned.

Timothy made to correct himself. 'Present company excepted, of course. No offence?'

'None taken.' Then she laughed again and looked out to sea. 'You'll mend. You'll mend,' she said; adding as an afterthought, 'Life is full of surprises.' Then she rose from her chair, patted him gently on the shoulder and went inside to change.

'To Archie and Serena!' said Rosamund, raising her glass for the third toast in as many hours.

'Archie and Serena,' answered Timothy, as the happy couple looked at each other suitably abashed.

The four of them were sitting around the table in the noonday sun, their lunch of lobster and strawberries completed, the two fat bottles of champagne completely drained.

'You'd better let me drive back,' said Serena to Archie who, thanks to the unexpected reunion with his friend, had enjoyed rather too much Laurent-Perrier Grand Siècle to negotiate with safety the convolutions of the Grande Corniche. Archie turned to Timothy. 'No Bentley this time, alas; just a Volkswagen Golf.'

'With the lid off,' added Serena.

'Fancy a quick stretch?' asked Archie, nodding towards the path that led down the garden.

Timothy looked appealingly at Serena who smiled and said, 'Don't worry about me. I'm happy here.'

The two men rose and walked towards the winding rocky

path that led down to the sea. 'We won't be long,' said Archie over his shoulder, as they began their descent. Then, to Timothy, 'Are you sure you're OK? I sense there's something wrong.'

Timothy paused by a large rock. They were out of sight of the villa now and below them the waves were gently lapping at the shore. The cry of an angry seagull rent the air and then died away, leaving only the soft whisper of wavelets to break the silence.

'Oh, not really. I've been a bit of a fool, that's all.'

Archie looked alarmed. 'What do you mean?'

Timothy saw the look of fear and panic on Archie's face. 'Oh, nothing for you to worry about. Nothing to do with the law. Nothing like that. Just a bit of trouble emotionally, that's all.'

'Family?'

'No; thank God.'

'Oh. You mean . . . female?'

Timothy nodded.

'Dumped?'

'Yup.'

Archie put his arm around Timothy's shoulder. 'I'm so sorry.' Then, after pausing for a few moments he asked, 'Had you met her before Monaco?'

'Yes. It was all very sudden.'

'A *coup de foudre*?'

'Sorry?'

'That's what they call it out here: it's sort of "love at first sight" with bells on.'

'Oh, it was that all right. Bells and whistles.'

'And there's no chance of it being . . . rekindled?'

'None whatsoever. It turns out she was married. And she took me for some money, too.'

'A lot?'

'Twenty thousand euros.'

Archie whistled. 'God! You must have been smitten.'

'Oh, I was. Hook, line and sinker.'

During the conversation the two of them had been facing out to sea. Now Timothy turned to face Archie. 'Funny, isn't it?'

'It doesn't sound funny to me. Heartbreaking more like.'

'No; I mean, the last time we met I was listening to you talking about the sorry state of your love life. Now it's your turn to listen to me. Anyway, there we are.'

'Does Aunt Rosamund know?'

'Yes. We talked about it this morning. She didn't think you needed to know but . . . well . . . I just felt I should put you in the picture. I don't know why. Feeling sorry for myself I suppose.'

'I'm very flattered. That you told me. Thank you.'

Timothy brightened. 'But enough of my tale of woe. When's the wedding?'

'Next spring.'

'How's your father?' asked Timothy.

Archie laughed. 'Oh, he's delighted. I think for the first time in my life I've done something he approves of.'

'Well, I'm very happy for you both. She's a lovely girl. But just one word of warning . . .'

'What's that?'

'If she asks you to lend her money, run a mile.'

40

BLUE ANCHOR COTTAGE, BOSHAM, WEST SUSSEX

SEPTEMBER

'A contented mind is the greatest blessing a man can
enjoy in this world.'

Joseph Addison (1672–1720)

Timothy stayed with Rosamund for a week before returning
home. She sent him off with a firm instruction to make the
most of what he had and to avoid reproaching himself for his
actions which, she said, were not as selfish as he would have
himself believe. He was a kind man and should not slink back
into the shell from which he had begun to emerge on account
of one ill-fated liaison. There were, she assured him, other
fish out there in the sea, not all of them quite so dangerous
to man.

On his return he set about finding a bolthole; somewhere
small but with a studio where he could paint and sketch.
Somewhere by the sea. He settled on a tiny fisherman's cottage
in Bosham on the estuary, just five miles away from Rosie, Ace

and Elsie in Chichester; close enough to be able to see his grandchild grow up, but far enough away from Oliver and Vita to have the excuse of not dropping round more than a couple of times a year. Alice had promised to visit in between university term times and that pleased him more than he could say.

He moved in to the pale blue clap-boarded cottage during August, painted the whole of the inside white, lined the wall of the sitting room with a bookcase and made himself a minuscule studio overlooking the harbour. There he sketched the yachts and the landscape, taking himself off for days to West Wittering and the Isle of Wight, and making a passable living from local art galleries with his watercolours. It was not, he realised with some degree of relief, retirement. It was self-employment; something he now wished he had found the courage to embark upon years ago. But then the timing was not right, and neither were the circumstances. It was not something Isobel would ever have countenanced.

Isobel; it had hardly been a year since she had died and yet his life had changed out of all recognition. He could never bring himself to regret marrying her – not least on account of the children their union had produced. He would continue to struggle with Oliver, but Rosie – and now Alice – offered the prospect of great companionship, and he had the delight of watching his first grandchild growing every day. What would Isobel have made of it all? Of Alice's revelations and of being a grandmother? Time was beginning to dull the sense of futility that had become second nature to him in the latter years of his marriage; to convince him that he was not simply there to make up the numbers; to dare to be himself and, as Alice had put it so clearly when last he had seen her, to follow his bliss. He felt more confident in himself now, and the guilt associated with his unhappy marriage was beginning to fade. It was, he told himself, for the best. The past was the past, and if not quite another country it was on the other side of a border he had no intention of crossing.

In September a stiff invitation arrived to a spring wedding. He placed it proudly on the mantelpiece in his tiny front room. It read:

The Earl and Countess of Derwentwater
request the pleasure of
your company at the marriage
of their daughter
Serena
to
Mr Archie Bedlington
at The Church of St Enedoc, Trebetherick, Cornwall

The invitation would stay above the fireplace long after the union of the happy couple, as a reminder that friendships made later in life can sometimes be enriching and lasting, and that travel can teach you as much about yourself as about the places you visit.

There were two more written communications late that summer. The first was from Archie himself, with the sad news that Rosamund had died in her sleep on the first day of September. Jonathan had discovered her that morning after she had failed to rise at her usual early hour. She had not suffered long, said the doctor, the heart attack was swift, but it seemed she knew she was near the end, for at the bottom of her bed, neatly tied with a pink ribbon, lay the manuscript of her final novel. Its theme centred on the perils of finding love later in life; it's main protagonist, a man in his fifties intent on undertaking a Grand Tour of Europe. Apart from this, Archie reassured him, there were only a few similarities with Timothy's own experiences, and names had been changed to protect the innocent.

The second communication came with a French stamp. It was mailed to Rosie's address – Timothy's old house. He took it home and propped it on the mantelpiece next to the wedding invitation. It stayed there for the best part of a day before he steeled himself to open it. He sat down at the kitchen table and slit open the envelope with a knife. It contained a typed letter, which read:

Mon cherie Tom,

I have got a friend to type this as my written English is not very good and I wanted you to understand properly what I have to say and what I have felt over these past months. I am so sorry for what happened. You must think I am a dreadful person. When I met you in the gardens of Versailles I had no idea what would happen to us. At first, I admired your paintings, that is all, and I knew you had a great talent. You must think that I was making it up, but really I was not – you have a wonderful gift. What happened after this was unforgiveable. You should know that in spite of what I told you I am still married. For that deception I am so very sorry. What started out as a friendship with you developed into something much, much more. I felt myself falling in love with you, and although I knew I should stop I could not. When you love being with someone as much as I loved being with you it is not easy to let go. When we said goodbye on the station platform I thought my heart would break.

But I remember telling you that I was a one-man woman, and that is the truth. I wanted to stay with <u>you</u>, but I knew that I must be true to the man that I married. If I have not loyalty, what have I left? How could I be loyal to you while still being loyal to him, however hard it has been over these past years?

But the time has come where I can no longer carry on. Alain has gambled away all of our money and although I have tried very hard I have to admit to myself that I have failed in my marriage. When the man and the woman cannot find any happiness in each other it is best to make a clean break for both their sakes. I should have known this many years ago. I have moved away from Paris and I have not told Alain where I have gone. I have told no one; not even you. I am now living in a tiny apartment and selling my own paintings. In time I shall make enough money to pay you back. That is my one aim: to prove to you that I did not deceive you just for money.

I know that this is very complicated, and that I have let you down, but I hope that you can understand how difficult it has been for me. I know it must also have been very difficult for you if you loved me in the same way that I loved you. You should know that I will keep you in my heart always.

One day, when I have enough money to pay you back, perhaps we can meet again. Then I shall be able to see you and to love you in the way that I would like – completely and loyally.

Until then, *mon cherie*, do not think too unkindly of me.

With all my love,
Francine

He laid the letter on the table, walked to the window and gazed out on the tide as it ebbed slowly from the estuary. Dangling from the window catch was a chestnut-beaded rosary.

'Perhaps we can meet again,' she had said. Perhaps they could. One day. In Venice.